REDOUBT

Dispatch from Graves dated 12 June 698lc

For the attention of the Executive Assembly.

We have successfully held the border and Graves remains a sovereign territory. Having quickly captured the ringleaders of the insurgency, we were able to force the hand of their client state Shifter. A medium-sized force made of insurgent units and Shifter regulars made a push for the capital. We pushed back.

The civil unrest within Graves has quietened and our preferred candidate has been installed as the new Regent in the City port of Cauker. Whilst elements of the old Aristocratic Party remain, for the most part any organised local support has melted away and their military and financial backing has faded with Shifter pulling back its troops. Shifter seemed pretty shocked by how vigorously we pursued this campaign. I anticipate our forces will be able to withdraw within another month or so and I have ordered the fleet to prepare for the trip home. It is now highly unlikely that Graves will be subject to any further military incursions for the foreseeable future. During our final weeks here, I have established a chain of small border units to monitor any remaining mischief from insurgents who don't know when they are beaten.

However, on a personal note, I think it reprehensible that the Assembly felt the need to re-establish the Regent after the last one was assassinated. Having spent some time talking with key merchant families, they really couldn't give a rat's ass who was in power. The Aristocrats had (surprisingly) popular support and from what I can tell there was no plot by Shifter to create a client state. Seems to me we completely messed up the intelligence on this one. However I'm just a public servant and not party to the wider considerations of political expedience, commerce and the need to prop up failing allied states.

General McKracken
Commander Ashkent Expeditionary Force

Prologue

The clansman pulled back the leather curtain and entered the hut. It was dark inside and he allowed his eyes time to adjust to the gloom. He glanced around at the small room. It contained nothing special: just a sleeping mat and bedroll in one corner, a small chest in another. The floor was earthen but it was well kept for all of that. There were no windows; any daylight would have to come from the doorway behind him, but he did not recall a time that he had ever come here and found the curtain pulled back. The witch did not deliberately shun the daylight; it was rather that she shunned the outside world. He approved of that; better for her to know her place, to know that the boundaries of her life were controlled by him. It would not do for her to begin to question him; she had power, and rather than see it used against him, he would end her life quickly.

She sat before him now, on the far side of the small fire pit she used both for cooking and to perform her arts. Smoke curled up from the pit and he could see the soft glow of embers within it.

'What do you see, Lissa. Is the time right?' he asked.

'There is much death.'

'That is obvious,' he scoffed. 'There is always death. That is our life. Do not toy with me, witch. Not this day.'

He studied the slight form of the witch as she sat cross-legged on the ground. She was clothed in homespun rags and wore a black cloak, the hood pulled up. She raised her

1

head and looked at him. She had a hard face, though it was not aged, and she, like her small dwelling, was fastidiously clean. Her black eyes had a distant quality; she looked at him but she was watching a different scene playing out before her. She blinked and refocused on the clansman.

'I can see the future but it is not always clear, Vorgat. I can tell you nothing of the outcome of your plan. I can tell you only of what will happen in the pursuit of it.'

'And that would be?' he pressed. Often he would become annoyed and angry with her. It seemed to him that she was mocking him, believing that her knowledge was special, that it made her better than him. But to see her, huddled on the floor, dressed in rags, it was clear he was the master. Damn but this wench played games! He owned her. In the past he had taken her too, just to prove that everything of hers was his. He had become bored of her body, always cold, always without passion. Now he punished her in simpler ways. Bruises healed but inside the scars remained.

'That many lives will be lost, innocent and guilty alike,' she replied.

'And the bridge?'

'Yes, that will fall to you, Chieftain. As will the men defending it.'

The man called Vorgat smiled.

'Then that is a good start, witch. So I should go?'

The witch blinked and cocked her head.

'Oh yes, you should go, my Lord.'

'Then you shall come also. Perhaps as we go your vision will clear. I will have need of it.' Turning, he swept the curtain aside for a second time and returned to the light. The witch called Lissa watched him go. The embers from the pit flared brightly and her black eyes glittered in the dark.

Chapter One

A procession of the damned wending its way to one of the Nine Hells. At least that is what it looked like – a line of horsemen silhouetted on top of a sparse hill line, as the storm clouds parted long enough for the moon to shine briefly through. The clearing of the sky wasn't a regular occurrence in the weather of the region. Mostly it just pissed down.

Newly commissioned Lieutenant of the 1st Company, 7th Mounted Infantry Regiment, Ashkent Expeditionary Army, Ronin Locke gazed back at his very sorry looking command. Not that he could see much. There should have been some twenty-five men behind him. He could just about make out a dozen. The weather and the black army-issue storm ponchos conspired with the night to swallow his men whole. There was, however, no mistaking Sergeant Mac who was directly behind him. An old sweat soldier who had wed himself to the Army, not out of any real sense of duty or because he particularly enjoyed it; rather he couldn't really be bothered to look elsewhere for employment. He was good at his job; better that than working in a factory or on a farm, or in the Fleet. Of an indeterminate age and a stomach which had given up the fight against gravity a long time ago, what really marked out Sergeant Mac were his large fists. They came very handy when 'field discipline' was called for. That and his legendary nose. One hell of a big conk; round and pitted.

It emerged from his cowl like an enraged proboscis. Some of the lads claimed that he must have Dwarf blood in him. Others added that he could sniff out any bullshit the boys might try and pull. But at least you could see the nose coming; it gave you time to hide what you were doing. He was, however, the soul that the company built itself around. The nose moved left to right, trying to probe the night for hidden dangers. Lieutenant Locke rather doubted there would be any of those about. Not in this bloody weather.

Turning to look forward, he made out the form of Corporal Jonas some twenty yards ahead. Identifiable by the great ash bow he wore on his back over his poncho, this thin, quiet man was the company's best scout. He tended to talk in short sentences or handy catchphrases like 'bloody arsehole' or 'Porky Boy should cork it'. Wordy he was not, descriptive he was. Apparently the man was a half-Elf on his mother's side. Not that Locke could see it himself; Elvish blood was evident in the man's tracking skills alone.

They had been out on patrol for about three hours, searching for an 'elusive' enemy who were probably so described because they were all tucked up in bed. It had been raining all day and Locke felt sodden. Not just wet, beyond wet; the kind of wet that made your every movement a trial in clamminess. A wet that just said, 'This is really shit! What you want is to go home, sit in front of the fire and forget about going out until it stops bloody raining.' If he sat really still on his saddle then it wasn't so bad. Not that he could justifiably do that, what with him being in charge and all. Instead he reflected back on the events that had brought him to this sorry state.

A third son of a well-connected and well-established

merchant family, he had never wanted to join up. A top-rate education and an indulgent childhood had nurtured a natural laziness and arrogance that very firmly said no thanks to rough living. This was largely due to his mother's doting. His father had other ideas, however, and he informed Ronin in no uncertain terms that that there was no way in hell that the lad would gain anything in the way of inheritance until he'd done some real bloody work. 'I didn't get where I did today by living off the charity of others you know. I had to scrimp and save and earn my fortune,' his father would pronounce. A litany Ronin had heard before and felt was wearing thin. Especially as his father had also had the benefit of being the sole beneficiary of his uncle's shipping business. But the youngster had decided not to argue the point; his father could be somewhat 'physical' when crossed. Besides he figured that a three-year commission could be tolerated, especially if he wangled himself a nice garrison posting somewhere south, where the biggest threat would be some drunken Dwarf with a penchant for axe hurling.

There followed a short period at the Ashkent Military Academy where he was taught a great deal about being a good leader and strategy and tactics and political groupings. He also learnt how to switch off during lessons. He found himself surrounded by a mixed bunch of characters. The Ashkent military liked to draw its officer class from a range of backgrounds. It felt that there was room for people who were of lesser breeding but who possessed ability. It therefore opened its doors to the well-born and the well-trodden alike. Ronin tended not to mix with the latter, finding many like himself to ally with at the Academy. Of course, Ashkent also liked to promote other ranks who had earned success in the field. Like his

5

own officer commanding. That really grated on Locke. His captain always behaved as if Ronin was nothing more than a green recruit. Always bringing him up on decisions that he made. Always telling him to stop playing at soldiers as if he were a child. How dare he? At least Ronin had an education and a bright future. What did that old man have coming to him? A pitiful pension and a few meaningless words of thanks. For the time being he had to follow orders. But the way his commander treated him was seen and copied by the other men. Some were rather more open in their disdain; others you could just see it in their eyes. As if they couldn't trust him to make proper decisions. Well damn it, that was why he had been made an officer and they hadn't. And they would learn that true quality would always show through. Just let them wait and see.

Ahead of Locke, Corporal Jonas had stopped and was gazing forward. Locke moved up and reined in his horse next to Jonas's. He waited for a response but the Corporal remained silent, his bony face barely visible in the cowled blackness.

'Well?' he asked impatiently.

'Woods, ahead.'

'So?'

'So do we go round 'em or through 'em,' stated Sergeant Mac who had ridden up to join them.

'Well, it seems to me, Sergeant,' said Locke, not entirely able to disguise his annoyance, 'that if the enemy *is* in there, then we would be foolish to avoid them. Would we not?' Besides, he was rather keen to be able to get out of the rain for a small while.

'Yes, Sir.'

Locke waited for more and got nothing. 'Shall we?' He stared impatiently at his subordinate. Sergeant Mac

6

remained motionless for a second longer than was polite and turned his head to Corporal Jonas. Without a word the other man wheeled his horse and cantered towards the trees. The scout slowed his horse and stopped before the woods.

Locke guessed that the scout was riding ahead to check for signs. Fat chance in this weather. Muck and mud would be all that he would find. He waited a few more moments then started forward again and joined Jonas a few yards from where the treeline began. Jonas looked up and gave Locke his best neutral expression.

'Nothing come through here recently. 'Cept some deer two hours ago.'

'See, Sergeant?' Locke glanced with a small measure of triumph at Mac who had joined him. 'Nothing but wildlife.'

'Yes, Sir, as you say. But this is only one entrance in many.'

'I tell you, Sergeant, that this route is safe. No doubt we will find the enemy clustered round a pitiful fire. That is, if they are stupid enough to be abroad this night. Pass the word we are going in.'

Sergeant Mac gave no reply and turned his horse to the next man in line and bent in close to the man's hood.

'Smitty, tell the lads to buck up. Could be riding into shit.'

'Yes, boss.'

The trooper began to pass the word back and a quiet change happened in the line of riders. They sat up straighter and moved their weapons into a more accessible position. Most of the lads had been in the army for enough years now to know trouble when they saw it. You would not get to stay alive that long if you didn't.

7

Locke noticed none of this as he started to lead his procession of horses into the dark woods. Ahead of him he glimpsed Corporal Jonas notching an arrow to the bow, which he held lightly, resting the weight on his saddle. The darkness swallowed him up and moments later Locke found himself sucked into a world of shadows and endless motion. Although his night vision was now well adapted he still found it difficult to see much more than a few feet ahead of him. The rain was greatly reduced here and the wind spent much of its force on the outer wall of the woods. Due to the dank and claustrophobic atmosphere they were not accompanied by the usual sounds of the night, just the muffled sound of the footfall of hooves as they picked their way along a muddy but obvious trail through the trees. Locke found a small knot of panic forming in his stomach, which he fought to crush back down. It was the feeling of isolation and the absence of space that suggested he had entered some other place, somewhere he was alone, where the way out was hidden to him, where he was lost in the dark. He could just make out the black form of Jonas ahead of him and clung to that form as a lost mariner to a lifebuoy. He kept turning his head to check the progress of those behind him. He could sense, if not see, the presence of Sergeant Mac behind him. Of the others, he could not tell. Try as he might, that small nagging feeling of panic would not go.

Locke began to lose all sense of time. How long have we been in here for the Gods' sake? He knew logically that it couldn't have been more than a few minutes, yet the time stretched interminably. To quiet his mind he let his thoughts drift to their return to camp. Hopefully there would be a fire or two already lit and a pot of stew gently bubbling, awaiting their return. This was usually the case, as the men back at camp knew all too well what it was like to be on night patrol. Afterwards a flagon of ale would be passed around. He himself would indulge in a small tipple of his own personal wine supply. He absently registered another soft rumble of thunder as the storm grew in strength again. A few moments later a flash of lightning lit up his field of vision. About him were mossy branches slick with rainwater; the track was indeed a mess of mud and fallen leaves. Above him was a crisscross network of branches as trees vied for space. Some were very large indeed. One branch seemed grossly misshapen as if it had formed its very own humpback. Then he saw a glint of light reflected from a point halfway along the shape. In growing alarm Locke shook his head and stared at the shape. Light shouldn't reflect off wood. As he gazed left and right to better use his night vision he saw the shape move. Move in a very non-woodlike way. Before he had time to open his mouth to warn Corporal Jonas, the scout had released an arrow and had hit the waiting form. He heard a grunt followed by the crash of a falling body as it careened through the lower branches of the tree.

The next moment the woods became a cacophony of shouts and screams as hidden forms arose from the dirt and seemed to merge with the riders. The clash of metal could be heard and the cries of startled horses added to the general chaos. Locke looked about wildly and drew his sword to slash at momentary shadows. He could not make sense of anything.

'To me! Rally to me,' he cried, desperate to have some company, some allies against the dark. His shouts went unheard as men attended to the more pressing matter of survival. Suddenly a rider was by his shoulder and a voice shouted in his ear.

'Stop bloody sitting there and bloody move!'

The voice was Sergeant Mac and the body slapped the rump of Locke's already agitated steed. It bounded off into the dark and it was all Locke could do to hold on. The horse crashed through the trees, changing direction at random. Locke lost his sword as it was whipped from his hand by a passing branch. Head down he closed his eyes and could only place his trust in the horse under him. All semblance of composure was gone and he cried out in fear and pain as smaller branches licked and snapped upon his upper body. The sounds of battle were beginning to withdraw as his horse stretched the distance. Not that Locke noticed; he was too busy screaming. This was swiftly cut short as with a half-grunt, half-gasp he was forced forward in his saddle by the weight of a heavy object crashing into him from behind. He was vaguely aware of this weight having movement and purpose before he received a hard strike against his head. He momentarily blacked out and coming to realised that his assailant was preparing for another strike. It was all happening so fast that Locke felt powerless to intervene in his own death. He lifted his sword arm in a warding gesture, knowing as he did so that it was useless.

Sergeant Mac's horse was suddenly by him. The burly Sergeant leant over and swung his arm around and out. Though Locke could not see it, he certainly heard the scream of his attacker as Sergeant Mac's short sword slammed into the man's head. The body fell from the horse and Locke, feeling faint, collapsed forward. He felt a restraining arm upon him, keeping him in the saddle. As he began to pass out he heard the voice of the Sergeant.

'You're right in the shit when the Captain hears about this one, lad.'

10

Chapter Two

Captain Jon Forge, officer commanding of the 1st Company, 7th Mounted Infantry pushed aside the curtain that led into one of the smaller segregated areas that made up the Regimental Command Tent. Inside he found a small cluttered space that was filled mainly by a field table and two canvas chairs. He dumped himself heavily on one, put his feet up on the table and gazed an indifferent eye over the mess and piles of papers. Most were reports, demands, requisition orders and the occasional map; all the usual crap found on a staff officer's desk. He grunted approval at spying a half-drunk mug of coffee resting on a pile of now very soggy reports. He reached over and started to sip the lukewarm brew. After making a face he scratched his chin absent-mindedly.

Jon Forge was a well-built man of medium height. He wore the standard-issue uniform of black boots, black trousers and a padded leather jerkin. He liked black; you knew where you were with it, plus it left the locals in no doubt whom they were dealing with. He placed his leather gauntlets and a dented helmet on the floor. The helmet was a simple affair, a round bowl-like hat with a nosepiece and a skirting of chain mail around the back and sides. Years of wielding a weapon had given him a strong body and a fair few scars to boot. He had brown close-cropped hair and a full beard speckled here and there by the occasional grey hair. While he did not feel the need to impose dress or fashion codes on his men, his personal view was that short meant that you didn't have to wash it and a full beard meant you couldn't be mistaken for a young recruit or a foppish aristocrat. His brown eyes were capable of showing both anger and humour in equal measures. His crowfeet eyes were the result of too much time spent in harsh conditions. His smile was ready and benefited from having most of his own teeth. A rare feature in the Army and it was a blessing that he still had trouble believing. These days, however, his visage was usually given over to brooding annoyance. He had spent most of his adult life in the Army, having joined up at the age of sixteen. It wasn't as if he had much of an option; it was either that or spend the rest of his days living in the poor quarter of Ashkent City. The Army fed him (after a fashion), watered him (with something akin to water) and clothed him (but not in anything particularly comfortable). It had also recognised some quality in him suited to the job of war and had allowed him to make something of himself. Albeit this usually meant being responsible for a pile of corpses on some far-flung, fly-infested battlefield. For which, at the age of forty, he found himself as a company commander. Not too bad. Not too good either. His friends had often told him that if he just tried to toe the line once in a while, he might even get Major one day. Trouble was he wasn't very good at politics. He always felt there was no place for it in an organisation whose main job was the enforcement of politics by other means, when the politicians messed up and some executive action was required. Talking about things just got in the way of the fighting and usually meant his guys getting dead. Still he had a nice little nest egg saved up and he planned at some point, when he could find the time, to retire and make useful things. Like axes.

The flap was pulled open behind him and Major Dav Jenkins stepped through. Jenkins was a contemporary of Forge's. They had risen and fought through the ranks together. Dav was one of the few men who Forge could actually call his friend. Though physically similar, Dav had shoulder-length blond hair and a closely cropped goatee beard. He possessed a steady mind, a quick smile and a flair for organisation, which was why he had become the Regimental second-in-command. Rumour had it that he was in line for a Brigade job, an aide to McKracken himself. Forge wouldn't be surprised at all. But he wouldn't ask. It didn't matter to him what Jenkins was doing, he could still beat him in an arm-wrestle any time. Something that Dav had been eternally frustrated about.

Jenkins flopped into the other chair and stared at his friend. The years had treated them differently, mainly because Forge refused outright to be moved from his current job. The guy had always been too stubborn for his own good. But whereas Jenkins was more than happy to be out of the front line more often than not these days, he had to concede that that was probably where Forge belonged. He was very good at it. So Jenkins did what he could to keep the flak off his friend (and lifesaver on more than one occasion), who was not known for his skills in tact and diplomacy. He raised an eyebrow when he noticed his coffee in Forge's hands. Forge in turn raised his and proffered it back to Jenkins.

'No thanks, Jon. The Gods' know what shite is living in your mouth these days,' said Jenkins in mock disgust. Forge sniffed and had another sip. 'So what brings you to the rotten heart of the regiment then?' asked Jenkins.

Forge put the mug back and stared at his friend.

'When are we going home?'

Jenkins shrugged his shoulders and put his hands in the air.

'You know the McKracken. He doesn't like to outstay his welcome. Wants us out pretty soon, never likes the idea of becoming a police force. Too messy.'

Jenkins locked his hands behind his head and leaned back.

'But you know that already, Jon. What's going on?'

'You know bloody well what it is!' shouted Forge and tapped his finger on the desk. 'I'm stuck out there on a bloody limb. No other units supporting us and I have to curtsey to a bloody stuck-up bastard.'

'You mean Duke Burns?' asked Jenkins with a hint of a smile.

'Bloody right I do, you sarcastic shit.'

Jenkins couldn't help but bait his friend. The 1st Company had been sent to the northernmost border point between Shifter and Graves. As most of the action had been to the south it was considered a quiet area. The local lord, Duke Burns, a conniving arse of a man if ever there was one, had insisted that his own household troops and levies could contain the 'slight Shifter annoyances' without help. McKracken, astute in the ways of statecraft and bullshit, felt otherwise and had decided to send a small unit of troops north just to make sure a lid was kept on things. The Regimental Commander of the 7th felt that Forge and his boys could sort out any trouble. Sadly the Duke was a big player in Graves and so as not to insult him, the Ashkent forces were to be directly under the command of the Duke. This was a moot point for Forge. Jenkins, a more political animal, had a feeling the Captain and Duke might come to blows. But orders were orders.

14

'Well, I got your messages, Jon, but I didn't think it warranted a trip in person.'

'That's where you're wrong, mate,' said Forge angrily. 'That arsehole has been using us to do all of the patrolling. His guys just laze around the place looking pretty and telling jokes. My guys are the ones getting the crap. Shifter won't come out and play fair so we have to go play cat and mouse. The Duke won't give us back up so instead I lose men. And that...' Jon paused for effect, '... is going to bloody stop.'

'Look, Jon, I know you hate to lose guys but we are in a war you know. And some of the Shifter boys can be pretty handy. You just got to fight dirtier.'

'Like I don't? My hands are tied up there and you know it. Burns doesn't give me free rein. I can only go where and when he says. McKracken has got this one wrong. The Duke is an evil bastard. He knows what he's doing. He's grinding us down. We can't take much more.'

There was a note of exhaustion in his voice that made Jenkins sit up and listen. He had never heard this before from Forge. This was new and that worried him. Forge had always been the solid one. Did his job. Did it any way he pleased to get it done and the consequences be damned. Let the results speak for themselves. He guessed it was just the onset of middle age. They were both turning into cantankerous warhorses who would get set out to pasture in a couple of years. The Gods alone knew how Forge was able to keep producing the goods out in the field especially with his leg playing up more and more. He himself was finding life in Regimental Headquarters much less physically demanding. His spreading belly attested to that. He softened his tone.

'Jon, it's the political game. It gets in the way of

fighting. I know that given a free rein, within two days you could've cleaned out the northern borderlands and broken their will to fight. But we need Burns; he acts as a stabilising force in both the Merchants' Council and the aristocratic class. Got his fingers in too many pies. If we don't keep him happy, let him think he's the big-time commander, life gets stickier for the rest of us. Gods, half the population views us an army of occupation. You wouldn't think there had been a civil war or an invasion by Shifter at all. We just have to bear with it for a bit longer. It's ...'

'We lost Corporal Coates last week,' Forge interrupted.

'Oh, shit.'

'He was ordered by Burns to enter an old farmhouse near the border. I was still at camp. Hit in the face by a booby-trap crossbow. Burns and his men did nothing.' Forge spoke in a soft voice which barely concealed his anger. Corporal Coates had been a friend of theirs from the old days. Never possessed of an intellect or a sufficient capacity for tactical decisions, he was nevertheless a loyal soldier with whom they had shared bad times and good.

'Jon, I'm sorry.'

'That is why it has to stop, Dav. People like Coates shouldn't die like that. Not by a faceless assassin. He should have been in his bed at rest, dreaming of the good times, or with his sword in hand and spitting in the eye of the enemy. Not like that.'

'Look, Jon,' Jenkins said determinedly. 'I'm gonna have a word with the boss. Get you out of there. Hells, there isn't gonna be an invasion from up there anyway. We've pretty much finished off Shifter. They don't want to play anymore. I'll pull you and your boys back. Sod Burns, I'll make sure he's spun a line, make him think he's won

16

the bloody war single-handed. Just give me a couple of days. I promise.'

Forge sighed and nodded. 'Thank you. And you know how I hate saying that.'

'That's how I know you mean it,' said Jenkins grinning. 'Now, how's that young pup Locke doing?'

Forge grunted. 'He's arrogant, selfish and bloody stupid. Perfect staff officer.'

Jenkins laughed.

Chapter Three

Holis Lode was beginning to cramp up. His legs were tightening and the pain was insistent and sharp. With practised ease he slowly straightened his legs out and flexed the foot so that his calf muscles could be fully stretched out. He nonetheless had to grit his teeth and keep his body as still and silent as possible. This was nothing new; he had grown up learning the skills of the hunter and trapper. He had been born to it and lived it day and night. Besides he had damned well waited longer than this and in less comfort when waiting to catch an unwary deer or bear. He could normally wait a hell of a lot longer too, if it weren't for the fact he was so dog-tired. They had been laying in wait on either side of a well-travelled forest path, one of a number that made up the unofficial highways of these parts. And they had been waiting for three hours now. Lode finally felt the muscle contractions lessen and allowed himself a small inward sigh of relief. He gazed over to his right where, almost hidden amidst the brush, lay Old Hoarty. Hoarty had been watching him, assessing with shrewd yet playful eyes how Lode had dealt with his cramp. Hoarty gave his one-tooth grin and nodded his approval. Holis often wondered just how aged Hoarty was. The 'Old' in his name certainly suited his look. A wild frizz of grey hair and an equally unkempt beard disguised the man beneath. You'd still have to get through the dirt as well. Lode felt it was probably too ingrained anyway; it was his second skin. Old Hoarty was a legend amongst the trapping community. There weren't many who didn't remember Hoarty from their own childhoods – a half-crazy old man who knew more about hunting, trapping, surviving the wilds and understanding its inhabitants than most of the older hands would care to admit. And here he was still going strong. Some of the more superstitious village folk said he must have magic in him. On hearing this, Hoarty would cackle for a while and round it off with a spit of his foul-smelling chewing tobacco. Any trapper who knew his business also knew the truth. Hoarty was good, bloody good. That's why he stayed alive, pure and simple. Lode couldn't decide if he quite wanted to see himself in Hoarty's position in years to come. He was kind of hoping to retire and set himself up in a nice cottage that he had built himself. A wife and kids would be a quite welcome addition to the mix as well. In trapping terms Lode was still young; he thought he was in his late twenties and when he bothered to clean himself up, most reckoned he had quite a rugged and handsome face – blue-eyed and long blond hair tied at the back with a simple piece of leather. It certainly hadn't done him any harm with the local girls at any rate. Lithe and muscular he had learned to live off the land and how to read its signs. Older guys had been impressed with his cool head. He was patient and he was thoughtful. Lode wasn't into making rash decisions; he would rather bide his time and wait for the moment. A good hunting instinct is what he had. So he made a decent living and the others of his kind treated him with respect despite his youth. That was probably why he had been elected leader of this motley crew.

There were six of them, three on either side of the path: Old Hoarty, Sleeps, Juggs, Arald, Fuzz and Lode himself.

19

All that was left of their community, the town of Noel's Gap. Nothing special really, one tavern, a few tradesmen and some local farmers and goat herders. What it did mark was a nexus for all the fur traffic coming in from the northern mountains and the forest wilderness that spread east to west. The trapping fraternity used Noel's Gap as their home base and their marketplace. After weeks on end in the wilds, they would come into the town to sell their wares to the few local export businesses. In turn, once every four months they would ship out the furs and other ornaments of death on the backs of mules and packhorses. They would follow these very same trails that led to Shifter and to Graves. The goods would then find their way to every market stall, house and business. This trade would even cross the gulf and would adorn the wealthy classes of the coastal city states and beyond. Even Ashkent's army had fur cloaks from Noel's Gap, worn when the winter drew in and the men were mighty glad of them. So all in all it was a happy arrangement. The trappers got their cash and a place to drink, girls to play with and a soft bed, all courtesy of Jim's Tavern. Not the classiest of joints and not the loveliest of women, but it knew how to cater to its clientele.

Lode thought back to the evening, two days earlier. Back to Jim's where Lode and his companions were spending a few quality hours in the bar. Everyone knew everyone else and people would greet new arrivals warmly as they stamped through the front doors. Good-natured abuse was hurled, questions asked about good hunting grounds and much discussion given to migration patterns. The life of a trapper could be quite solitary and hunting trips could mean many weeks, if not months, away. Messages were passed to others encountered on the trail, an unusual mail system of sorts, so that friends could stay in touch over many miles and days. News of the outside world was provided by the export crews and much attention was given to the war between Graves and Shifter. Stuff like that was bad for business, as many a trapper was heard to mutter; others would nod sagely as they supped on their beer or pulled on their pipes. Lode was never too bothered. At the end of the day, people still needed fur, still needed the clothes on their back and the warm pile on their beds. It would blow over in the end. Someone would win or lose and then they could get back to business. It wasn't the most glamorous of lives they led, but none of them would ever care to give it up. Let the idiots in the big cities screw their own lives up. Hoarty always said, 'Simple don't always mean stupid. Too many make that mistake and pay for it the hard way.' Hoarty often came out with these little nuggets which left Lode under no illusions that the crafty old bugger had yet to lose his marbles.

So it was that many of the usual crowd were gathered in Jim's for one more night before they headed out for the last big hunt of the season ahead of the weather getting nasty. All wanted to get a good haul before the snows came in and game became scarce. Not that they couldn't still hunt, but what crazy bugger wanted to be out in the freezing cold? As always many of the guys were drunk to their eyeballs and carousing with the lasses that served the bar and serviced their other needs as well. Lode was staying off the strong stuff. He always did before heading out. He felt it was bad luck to start the trip on a low note of puking and stomach aches. He'd done enough of that when he was younger. He had left early and had traipsed up the stairs to his room. His was one of the attic beds on the fourth floor, furthest away from the noise, if not particularly large. He didn't mind; it wasn't as if he had much stuff and that was all packed ready for the off tomorrow. His mules were ready to go downstairs in the large stables and he could look forward to one more night of sleep on something other than hard, cold earth. As he started to undress he gazed absently out of the small window hatch. It looked out to the north and afforded him a clear view across the town, whose scattered buildings were mostly black as their occupants had long gone to sleep or were carousing in the tavern. He looked away and carried on undressing. But something stopped him. Something nagged and told him that things weren't right. He looked up again and studied the view before him. There it was, right on the edge of the forest where it made way for the cleared area of small fields and farmhouses. Movement. But not localised, not the solitary shape of another trapper coming in from the hunt. This was bigger. Much bigger. A whole great mass of movement as shapes began to detach from the darkness and edged towards the unsuspecting town. Instinctively Lode knew what this meant. Death had come to Noel's Gap and none would be spared. Noel's Gap was finished.

They weren't prepared, and why should they be? He didn't know who they were or why the town was coming under attack. There was nothing worth having. He grabbed his crossbow and his long hunting dagger. He dimly registered his luck at already having much of his gear stowed in his pack. Throwing it over his shoulders he charged down the stairs, imagining how, as he did, that the first of those dark forms would now be reaching the outlying homes. Those within wouldn't know what had hit them. Probably a mercy.

As he entered the bar few noticed his crashing entrance

and most were too interested in drinking to care. And he was damned if he knew what he was going to say. He leapt on to the bar and the owner, Jim, all hair and muscle shouted at him to get down. He ignored the irate barkeeper and gazed over the crowd. He suddenly felt very small and foolish, but nonetheless he roared, 'Shut the hell up!'

That gained everyone's attention.

'You have about two minutes left. There is a large bunch of men moving into the town. I saw them from my window. They are on the outskirts, and they definitely aren't friendly. I'm getting out. Now. What you do is up to you.'

He gazed around the room to gauge the reaction. There was a moment of silence and then a ripple of nervous laughter started. And there were lewd and crude comments made about his questionable sanity. He locked eyes with Old Hoarty. The older man made a thoughtful face and then nodded. Inwardly Lode was pleased. At least there was one old dog that wouldn't roll over and die. He leapt off the bar and ran out of the door. Behind him voices were suddenly raised; some in fear, some in anger. There wasn't time to get the mules. They would only slow him down. He heard the door open and the sound of the voices grow louder. He didn't look back. As he raced through the doomed town the dull tones of the church bell began to toll. So someone else had seen them. All too late, he thought. He swiftly covered the quarter-mile to the edge of the forest to the south of Noel's Gap. He swerved left off the main track out of town and cut across a field and into a depression that led straight into the trees. He wanted cover from view. There was no telling if those bastards had surrounded the village. As he neared the forest he forced himself to slow down. Now was not the time to start

23

acting like a startled boar. Softly and silent, that was his trade.

He climbed out of the depression and moved into the treeline. He could not make out anyone nearby and his senses, usually reliable, were not tingling. So Holis quietly merged into the undergrowth and watched the scene before him. He took the time to string and load his crossbow as he watched. The church bell had stopped at some point but he hadn't noticed. He expected the town to be put to flame but there was nothing. No sign of the undoubted carnage that was occurring in Noel's Gap. It was like some demonic pestilence had struck. Soon, though, he began to hear plaintive screams and wails and the occasional snapping sound of wood. Then all was quiet again. He began scanning the foreground, seeing if any had got away. Using his peripheral vision he spotted dark forms wending their way along the path at speed. One or two were moving across the field and seemed to be heading directly for the trees. They were the clever ones. As the larger group of fugitives on the path reached the entrance to the forest another mass of figures detached themselves from the shadows. This time the sounds of murder were much clearer; shouts and screams mingled as men, women and children were cut down. Lode hated himself for being right. He hated that he had just up and left. Of course the practical side of him said he had done exactly the right thing. It was now telling him that there was no point in hanging around. But Gods, did he want to make someone bleed. Even now, though, the dark assailants were moving back into the forest. No doubt to mop up those just like himself. Well, bugger them! He picked up his kit and moved off into the night. Ain't no way those bastards could out hunt him on his own turf. He knew exactly where to go.

Some two hours later and several miles further south he knelt beside the main trail and studied the old woodsman's shack set off in a small clearing on the far side. It was used only occasionally these days and certainly not at this time of year. It seemed quiet; no signs of life. Precisely what he was hoping for. He made a soft ululating whistle. A very passable impression of one of the local game birds, used to lure randy males of the species. A few moments later he heard a soft chirping sound. That was the cue. Bent low, he ran across the path and into the trees behind the shack. Gathered there were Sleeps and Juggs, the only female member of their fraternity. They were two of the older trappers and had been partners for years, though strangely not lovers. At least no one could ever remember a time when the two of them had ever displayed any behaviour to suggest it. Not in public at any rate. Lode always thought of them as brother and sister, though he knew that not to be the case. Juggs came from a long line of woodsmen and by an accident of birth had come out the wrong sex. Though she always claimed that nature had got it right in its selection for once. She certainly knew how to skin a rabbit. The pair both had their bows pointed at him as he moved into view. Satisfied they lowered their weapons.

'Thanks for the advice, Holis,' Juggs whispered.

'Yeah,' agreed Sleeps. A man of brevity that one.

'You're the first,' continued Juggs. 'No one else has come this way.'

'Reckon we're safe for a while yet. Those guys will want to do a proper clean-up,' said Lode.

'Looks like it,' said Sleeps.

Over the next thirty minutes they were joined by Fuzz, who sported a gash to his arm that he had hastily bound and who now settled down to stitch the wound himself. 'Not letting you butchers at it. Man's not a man if he can't perform basic surgery,' he commented. Soon after they were joined by Old Hoarty and Arald. Lode suddenly felt a lot better. He was with his own kind. Each one of these men were trappers and hunters. Tough and resourceful.

'Don't reckon there'll be anyone else,' said Old Hoarty as he spat into the undergrowth. 'Me 'n' Arald here took our time 'bout leavin'. Not like you bloody whippersnappers. Charging off into the wild like boars wantin' to rut. Everyone else is dead. Did a good job, them fellers. Smart.'

'But what the hell were they after?' asked Sleeps. 'Sweet load of nothin' in that town.'

'Me 'n' Arald were thinking 'bout that,' responded Old Hoarty as he scratched his beard. 'Now yer normal raidin' party would just burn the place down for the hell of it. Slay the men, rape the women. That sort of shite.'

'Not these guys though. Quiet as you like. Just did the killin' part,' added Arald.

'Northmen,' muttered Fuzz as he continued to stitch.

'What?' asked Lode.

Picking up on a tremor in Lode's voice, Old Hoarty looked at him and raised an eyebrow.

'I was the last to get away from the town I reckon,' continued Fuzz. 'Saw Jim just standing at his bar holding on to that bloody great club of his. He wasn't runnin'. Always liked Jim.'

'All right, what about the bloody northmen?' Lode pressed.

'Oh yeah. Well, that's how I got this. One of 'em took a swipe at me. So I left a knife in his belly. Good knife that. Anyway he was a Harradan all right. Seen enough of 'em huntin' north and east of the mountains, dressed up in their clan tartans. All blond-haired, bearded and full of bloody attitude. Not very hospitable, if you get my drift. Actually, always reckoned you were one of 'em, Holis.'

'You're not wrong, Fuzz,' said Juggs.

'But that lot are always at war with each other or the Goblin tribes,' said Arald. 'Makes no sense to go beatin' up the Gap like that.'

'It was planned, lads. These fellers were very definite 'bout their business,' said Old Hoarty.

Lode bit his lip. Something didn't seem right.

'They attacked in silence. They wanted complete surprise,' he whispered to himself. 'They didn't want anyone to know … They didn't want anyone to know,' he repeated to himself.

Old Hoarty stared hard at the younger man.

'Well, someone got pissed about something and it's time we found a new patch, lads,' announced Sleeps.

'No, wait!' said Lode as realisation dawned. 'They didn't want anyone to know. Nobody. That is why they surrounded the town. That was why they didn't burn anything. Too much attention. No one was supposed to know.'

'Go on, lad,' said Old Hoarty.

'They weren't there to nick stuff. They just wanted to make sure no one knows about them.'

'Hah! Didn't reckon on some folk being cleverer than them though, eh?' said Fuzz.

Old Hoarty took out a plug of tobacco, went to chew on it, stopped himself and put it back in the pouch. 'Which means, young Holis, that they aren't done with us, don't it?'

Lode nodded. 'They don't know if anyone got out but

they ain't gonna take a chance. They destroyed Noel's Gap for a reason. I reckon they ain't stopping.'

'So?' asked Juggs.

'So, they'll be comin' down this way pretty soon,' said Old Hoarty. 'And I lost a good packhorse back there.'

'What are we gonna do then?' asked Sleeps.

'Not as if we're the bloody militia,' agreed Arald.

As he listened to the others debate what to do, Lode found himself imagining the slaughter that had happened in the town. He had left many friends back there. It just wasn't right. He had never killed a man before but he had faced death many times. He felt he had a pretty good sense of his own mortality. He couldn't let it lie. Otherwise what was the point of anything?

'What we are is the only survivors of Noel's Gap,' said Lode. 'Survivors 'cos we just all happen to be bloody good woodsmen who can out-think any clever-arse northman. I just ran out on the only home I've known and left it to die. I ran because I couldn't do any good there. Well, I can out here. We know this land like the back of our hands. Between us we know every dirty trick and trap known to man and some that only the dirty mind of Juggs could dream up.' Juggs gave him a thumbs-up and a grin. 'I don't know if I can kill an army. But I'm gonna make them pay. Really painfully.'

'And how long do we keep that up for then? I'm not a young man, you know,' asked Sleeps.

'I don't know. Till they stop comin' and learn to fear these woods.' Lode looked over at Old Hoarty. 'What do you think, old-timer? Fancy hunting something different for a change, for Jim's sake?'

Old Hoarty stared hard at the young man. Lode felt as if he was having his soul examined. Old Hoarty broke out

28

into his best one-toothed grin. But there was fire in his eyes.

As they settled down to wait, Old Hoarty crawled up next to Lode, looked around and checked that they were a little way from the others.

'You got somethin' on your mind, Holis?' asked the old man.

'What apart from the fact all our friends just been killed?' Lode whispered back.

'Ain't that now, is it, youngster?' replied Old Hoarty. 'I was watching you when you heard about the Harradan. It shook you up.'

Lode did not respond immediately. He lay still and gazed out on to the trail.

'I'm one of them; Hoarty. I'm a Harradan,' he said quietly.

Grunting, Old Hoarty shook his head.

'Well, that ain't much of a surprise, Holis. As Fuzz said, we always had you pegged for one. Not that it bothers us. So what did you do? Kill someone you shouldn't have?'

'Something like that. Call it a difference of opinion. I was a young man and in love with a woman. A woman that our clan chief had claimed for himself. I could have fought him for her, but he was older and tougher than me and I wouldn't have lasted two seconds. When he found out he kicked my butt, but she begged me not to fight back. So instead he called me a coward, an outcast and hounded me out of my clan and the word went out to our neighbours. Any man made an outcast is shunned by the Harradan, a man not to be trusted. So I came south.'

'That was a good few years ago – never thought about going back?'

'Thought about going and killing that guy? Yeah. But I

29

got settled – what was the point in going back to a people I don't belong to? Noel's Gap was my home and the Harradan have taken that from me as well.'

'I can see why you're takin' this so personally,' observed Old Hoarty. 'Don't worry, I won't mention this to the others. We all got past history.'

Lode nodded his head in thanks.

A short time later a party of ten northmen moved quietly down the path. Moments later they were dead. It was hard to see an arrow in the dark of night. As the group recovered their arrows, Lode took a moment to examine the body of the man who had tried to run as the others had died. Lode himself had taken him in the back. He took out his hunting knife and prised out the embedded projectile. Years in the wilderness doing the same lent confidence to his hand. He just thought of the body as another animal carcass. Once this was done, he reached over, got both hands underneath the body and hauled it over. He took a moment to study the bearded, pockmarked face. His eyes wandered down to the garments and he traced the lines of the man's clan tartan. Yes, these were Harradan, his people. This one though was not his clan ... Broken Tooth, if his memory served him right. It was hard to tell in the limited light. A slight breeze touched him upon his neck and it made his skin prickle. Jerking his head up, he looked around him. It was a still night. Yet he had clearly felt it – cold, gentle but definitely a force. He felt spooked. A nagging fear bid him to linger no longer on the trail. He didn't know where that feeling had come from but he had learned to trust his senses. He stood and ran to the others, bidding them to follow him into the night.

Lode finished replaying those events and was pleased to

feel his cramps had gone away. Now he and the others were waiting to spring yet another ambush. They had taken to laying all sorts of surprises for their pursuers. Mantraps, spikes and stakes. They had led their hunters a merry dance through the forests and still the Harradan came. Slowly now, more cautious, but relentless. Somehow, they had kept one step ahead of the larger force, Lode always knowing when to strike and when to run. Lode had talked to Old Hoarty; he didn't quite know how he kept getting it right. Old Hoarty just smiled, clapped him on the back and suggested he keep up the good work. But something was bothering the old man, and when he shared his thoughts Lode quickly agreed. This wasn't just about catching the six of them. There was a large force of men out there. The woodsmen had to rely more on their ingenuity than firepower. The northerners were learning lessons and sent their scouts out in larger numbers. So they had a lot of swords and they had purpose. The trappers were being pushed south-west to the River Rooke; a long way off and with no point to cross the river for many miles north or south. He just didn't get it. But there was plenty of time for more Harradan to die. Like the scout party of eight, who were moving – oh so carefully – into view.

Chapter Four

Two days after his meeting with Jenkins, Forge rode back into the Company lines. He was dog-tired and piss wet through. He had travelled hard and had only caught a few hours sleep each night. It was now a couple of hours after dawn and that meant that he was officially having a bad day. The gate guard rose to attention and acknowledged his captain with the adopted greeting of 'Another glorious day in the corps, Sir.'

Forge nodded and replied, 'And a crappier one you won't find.' Whilst there were many who felt Forge's men were far too glib in the face of their officers, he wasn't bothered. Frankly he and his boys had been through enough to afford a fair degree of informality within the company. He noticed the guard's left arm had been bound with a bandage. He didn't ask. He wanted to sit down before the bad news came.

The camp itself was arranged in an orderly fashion. Rectangular in shape, oriented north–south, with an open area in the middle that doubled up as the parade and training ground. The longer sides were made up of accommodation tents for the men. The southerly line housed the commissary and stables. The north comprised the officers' and sergeants' tents and the planning tent. All to standard Ashkent doctrine. A ditch and earthworks bound the camp; a wooden palisade in turn topped this. The local troops had stood by laughing when the

Company had sweated their balls off to get it all built within a day. The lads themselves didn't rise to the bait. It was obvious which poor saps would get taken out first when a surprise attack ripped into their undefended, poorly sited encampment a hundred yards away from the Ashkent troops. And then guess which sorry bastards would be knocking at the gate to be let in before they got a spear up their collective arses?

Forge steered his horse to the stables, while around him the normal business of the camp continued. A mounted infantry company was trained to be self-sufficient in the field. Often it would operate as an independent force, be it on a roving border patrol or manning a remote fort. The men were taught to maintain their own equipment and keep their weapons sharp. Each man was also charged with caring for his own steed. It was pounded into them from the start of their careers that one day, more often than not, that big and smelly, bad-tempered lump of sweat and sinew would save their lives. Those that failed to take it in usually didn't last long or at least were missing a body part for their mistakes. This self-reliance led to a very capable and independent-minded soldier. Forge liked that; it meant you had men you could trust to get the job done by hook or by crook.

He reached the stables and slowly dismounted. He took the time to stretch out and relieve his cramped and, loath as he was to admit it, aging muscles. He winced involuntarily and bent down to rub his left knee. It was aching again.

'How's it holding up, boss?' asked Sergeant Mac as he walked over to Forge. In his hand he held a mug of steaming coffee. He passed it to Forge, who nodded his thanks.

'Same as usual. Bloody pain in the ass.' It had been three years ago when his old mount had been hit by a Goblin arrow during the Great Pacification campaigns in the west. He had been thrown from the horse and had landed badly. The result being that something had gone inside his knee which had left his leg permanently weakened. Whilst it functioned on a day-by-day basis, it had a habit of giving way under him. The doctor had said there was nothing he could do and that, unless Forge was willing to see a private medical mage, then he ought to think about echeloning himself into a less physically demanding military job. Forge had responded with his usual candour and had told the doctor he could 'get fucked' if he thought either choice had any merit. He couldn't decide if he hated magic users or paperwork more. They both baffled him equally. He sipped the coffee. It was bitter but hot. He wondered if they had any honey anywhere. He started the process of unsaddling his horse. Sergeant Mac leaned against a post and started to pick at some dirt under his nails. Forge dumped the saddle and began grooming. 'Go on then. What happened?'

'Ambush.'

'How so?' Forge asked, almost not believing what he was hearing. He stopped grooming and stared hard at the old soldier.

'Was the lad, Sir. Took us straight into a wood in the middle of the night. I couldn't talk him out of it. Did what I could to minimise the damage. The Lieutenant ended up getting the pommel of a knife to the back of his head, found him slumped over his horse a little ways out of the trees. He was lucky, could've been the business end that did for him.'

'Where is he now?'

34

Sergeant Mac tilted his head towards the officer's quarters. 'Resting up on his cot. Concussed. Feeling sorry for himself.'

Forge nodded. 'I'll make him feel sorry for himself in a while.' He turned back to his mount and carried on grooming. 'So that that means I almost lost both my subalterns in six months. That'll please Regiment. Don't mind Locke. Silly shite. Pity about young Hasam though; he might've been OK.'

'Tried to tell him, Sir.'

'I know. What about the men? Who did we lose?'

'Horst. Took an arrow through the face. Everyone else made it out.'

'Another one of the old hands.' Forge stopped. Sergeant Mac could see his captain's shoulders sag. 'Shouldn't happen. Not like this,' he said quietly so that Sergeant Mac felt he was intruding on Forge's private grief.

Changing the subject, Sergeant Mac asked, 'Good trip? Get the result you wanted?'

Forge straightened up and continued with his work. 'Major Jenkins said he would do what he could. Guess that is the best I can ask for. I know he'll try for us.'

'That'll do then, boss. We had some new arrivals over at the main camp last night. You might be interested in looking at them. Also Duke Burns sends his compliments.'

'I bet he does,' interrupted Forge.

'And he will see you at your earliest convenience,' said Sergeant Mac with a sour-faced grin.

Forge sighed and placed a feed bag over the horse's muzzle. 'Strictly speaking, my earliest convenience would be when the Hells freeze over. But that would probably upset our great leader. Know what he wants?'

Sergeant Mac shrugged his shoulders. 'All I know is we

35

have gained some new additions to our happy community.'

'Oh really?'

'Yeah, looks like slaves from the far south. The Gods know what they are doing here, or how he got them past our borders.' Although many states still practised forms of slavery, Ashkent had forbidden it many years ago. Anyone trying to move them through Ashkent territory, by land or sea, would find themselves stripped of their cargo, and, more often than not, their transport too. Traders would have to take long diversions around Ashkent and this proved to be a costly endeavour in itself.

'Burns is probably planning a new palace for himself or something.' Forge stretched once more. He gulped down the now lukewarm coffee and gave his beard a good, hard scratch. 'Right, let's go see the fat shit.'

Duke Burns winced as the corset he wore dug into the soft folds of flesh that threatened to spill over at any moment. It was even worse when he had to bend over. Forge regarded him with ill-disguised contempt. Not that the Duke seemed to notice such things. The man continued dressing by allowing his servant to strap him into his armour. A special set that had been tailored for comfort in certain areas. Forge had a few issues with the concept of the Duke ever being in a situation that required him to fight. Indeed, the whole effect was rather spoilt by his chubby, bewhiskered face.

Forge often thought of him as an aged cherub gone to seed. That was when he was in a charitable mood. Usually he just thought of him as an overweight, incompetent, conniving, greasy, untrustworthy, devious bastard. He was probably into little boys as well. Burns,

36

being aristocracy, had sided with the insurgency during the interregnum. When it looked like the wind was changing, he had re-established links, via his trading interests in Cauker, with the official government. When Shifter had invaded, he had denounced this move as a clear insult to the sovereignty of Graves's territory. Forge did wonder about that at times. The Aristos had made an agreement with Shifter to cede territory for aid. Burns might well have been concerned for his own holdings and didn't like how this plan was shaping up for his truly. The captain had surmised that whilst Burns was now nominally on the same side as Ashkent and the new administration, it was clear that he was a shifty bugger and McKracken had wanted to ensure his continued loyalty by the presence of the Ashkent mounted infantry. This was cold comfort considering the winnowing of that force on an almost constant basis.

Forge had been left to wait for ten minutes in the outer entrance to what could only be described as a mobile mansion in tent form. The Duke's home was a huge pavilion that had sleeping quarters, his own kitchens and a suite of offices, as well as a large reception area. When he was finally summoned, it was to the Duke's war room. Forge entered and stood to attention. That was the nearest he was prepared to go towards the usual formalities of rank. He felt he couldn't be responsible for his words if he opened his mouth or indeed his actions if he attempted a salute. He was very certain that his hand might just move automatically to his knife and place it right between Burns' eyes if he gave it half a chance.

The Duke was currently poring over a map that Forge did not immediately recognise as their area of operations. It took a few moments to register that he was looking at an area some four days' travel to the north-east. It was mostly forest country with the only notable feature being the River Rooke. In olden times this river had been the natural border between Graves and Shifter, but the latter, in the days before Graves had got its act together, had long held the land to the west of the flow. The Rooke served as a natural demarcation of the farthermost border of Graves and the wild lands beyond, before curving away into Shifter further to the south and east. He understood the north-eastern territory was home to no one other than hunters, fur traders and a couple of frontier settlements. Whilst Shifter claimed ownership, in reality it cared little for the few inhabitants of that region and was happy enough to let the fur trade govern itself.

'I have a new assignment for you and your men, Captain,' said Burns as he looked up. His goatee had acquired several more grey hairs, as had his rapidly retreating hair. He fixed the captain with a hard stare, expecting him to say something. Forge simply nodded his head.

'Four days to the north-east is an old fort. Don't know what its name is. Probably never had one. What it did use to do was provide protection to what was once a well-established trade route between Graves and the lands beyond. The fort itself is of no importance. What is, is the remains of the bridge that used to span that river. Soon this war will be over and it is high time that Graves was given the opportunity to rebuild and expand its shattered economy. I want you to rebuild that bridge.'

Forge was surprised. 'My men aren't engineers, Duke. Nor are they to be used for private ventures.'

'Perhaps not, Captain, but neither are they very effective at rooting out the few Shifter irregulars that plague this region.'

Right, thought Forge. Very soon, I am going to lose my temper. Damn you, Dav. Get me out of here or I swear I'll kill this man and anyone who tries to stop me.

'Anyway, I have made arrangements,' the Duke continued, seemingly not caring about the effect his last comment had made. 'Your men are to provide protection to the workforce that I am providing. Out of my own pocket I might add. Whilst the war continues you are soldiers serving Graves against the threat of Shifter. I do this for the greater good of my country, Captain.'

Yeah and I'll be shitting pineapples for my breakfast, mused Forge.

'You can take your whole command. Don't bother to leave anyone behind.'

'And what about these *irregulars* still at large?' asked Forge.

'Oh, I'm sure we can handle them. Besides I would have thought you would be jumping at the chance to head off for some peace and quiet. After all, that is what you went to ask your superiors for, wasn't it?' Burns smiled.

Forge hid his reaction. How the hell did he know that? It became obvious when a figure emerged from a side entrance into the war room and joined the two men. The new arrival was a tall willowy form wrapped in a thick robe of red, gold and black. A long red beard flowed in a haphazard fashion from a thin and pinched face. Dark eyes, a curious absence of eyelashes and a ponytail of yet more red hair combined to make an interesting, if disturbing image.

'Ah, right,' muttered Forge.

The new arrival was the Duke's personal mage, Portal. A magic-user whose talents, or so it seemed to Forge, lay more in political subterfuge and intelligence gathering than any arts of enchantment. The Captain had never actually seen him wield any sorcery as such. But then he expected it was all cauldrons and bats' shit and things like that with Portal. He, Forge, preferred the more in-your-face stuff that you might find with Ashkent's battle mages. Fireballs, plagues of killer frogs, that sort of thing. And what was it with all this one-name crap and looking sinister? He was pretty sure that the use of magic didn't require you to become a twat. Sometimes the stereotype got very boring. But hey, what did he know? – he mostly just hit things. Still it explained why Burns had rumbled him. He stared back at the Duke with his best 'don't give a shit face'.

'Portal will be going with you as my representative. Whilst you are responsible for all matters regarding security, he will be the final arbiter on the project and its conduct.'

And he'll be able to keep a nice beady eye on us as well, thought Forge. 'So who are the workforce?' he asked.

'You'll find them outside in a compound. Apparently they are quite skilled. They ought to be. I paid enough money for them. However, I expect them to be quite insolent. Feel free to apply the lash whenever necessary.'

Ah, so those slaves then, thought Forge

'Don't let them die till the job is done. That bridge must get built first.'

'When do we leave?' asked Forge.

'I expect you ready to move at dawn the day after tomorrow. That bridge must be ready in ten days.'

'Why the rush? It's not as if there's any trade traffic yet.'

'It is not for you to question Graves policy.' Forge noted that Burns had suddenly become a lot redder in the face. 'You will proceed to the site and you will see the bridge built. The war will soon be over and we must seize the opportunities that present themselves. Now prepare your men, Captain.'

Forge nodded and turned to leave. 'I'll meet you on the trail tomorrow, Captain,' said Portal. Forge could sense, if not see, the sarcastic smile Portal was wearing.

'I'm looking forward to it already,' he said and walked out.

Forge's next port of call was to see Locke. En route he mused over the forthcoming bridge build and did some sums. If Burns wanted this bridge built in ten days' time and they wouldn't reach it till the evening of day five maybe morning of the sixth, then that didn't leave them much time to construct the thing. He could hardly expect the workforce to be that keen and he'd be buggered if he would get his men to get involved. In fact, he could see no reason why the thing had to be done in ten days' time anyway. Sod it, the more time away from the Duke the better; Forge would see if he couldn't stretch this little trip away for a few days' extra. He reached Locke's tent, pulled back the flap and entered. Locke was lying on his cot with his eyes closed. A bandage was wrapped around his head and his complexion was pale, but he seemed to be breathing deeply and soundly. Forge took a moment to survey the tent. Untidy – in itself not a problem. The Gods knew he wasn't the most the domestic of individuals and the older he got the less he cared about it. What caused him concern were the details: armour left in a pile to one side of the cot, weapons tossed carelessly on to a canvas table. Locke's sword was not even sheathed. It lay balanced on top of its scabbard. And it looked like it hadn't been oiled in a while. He inspected the armour.

41

Spots of rust were starting to form on the mail. It showed a sloppy approach to soldiering. That pissed Forge off. These were the tools of the trade. If you were any kind of professional you took care of your kit. It kept you alive. He returned to the end of the cot, followed his arms and kicked Locke's left foot.

Locke's eyes flew open, he took a couple of moments to gather his wits and register who was standing in front of him. He levered himself up.

'Sir?'

'Did you come in here unconscious?' asked Forge.

'Sir?'

'I said did you walk in here or were you carried in? Because if you weren't, then I want a good reason why your kit is in such shit state,' replied Forge.

'Well, I ... uh ... I walked in, Sir, but I was pretty groggy. The doc patched me up and said I should get some rest,' stuttered Locke.

'You damn well get some rest after you have finished stowing your kit!' roared Forge, giving free rein to his anger. 'You ain't some piss-ant recruit who still ain't learned to wipe their own arse. You are an officer, lad. An officer in my company and you will set the standards that I demand. You hear me, Locke?'

If it were possible, Locke's face appeared to have grown paler.

'Yes, Sir!' he responded.

'I lost another good man because of you, Locke. And you almost got yerself killed in the process. Right now I would be a hell of a lot happier if the two of you could trade places ...' He jabbed his finger towards Locke. '... A crap officer I can live without. A good soldier I can't.'

Forge noted that a look of anger and affront passed

42

across Locke's face. He also noted that there was little resembling shame in Locke's demeanour.

'Now get your shit together, Lieutenant. Mistakes get made but I won't accept stupid ones. We are heading out the day after tomorrow and I am expecting you to start behaving like an officer of Ashkent. I need to know I can trust you to do the damn job. Do you hear me?'

Locke stiffened and snapped off a soldierly 'Yes, Sir!', though the effect was somewhat lessened by the fact Locke was still propping himself up.

Forge nodded.

'And sort your equipment out!' he ordered before turning and stalking out of the tent.

Locke watched the Captain go and let out a long breath. He noted his arms had begun to shake. Not because they were tired. They were shaking with rage. 'Bastard!' he said out loud. How dare he? That man had shouted so loudly that every soldier in the camp would have heard. He had deliberately humiliated him. How was he to command any respect with the men after that tirade? Ever since he had arrived he had been mocked and mistreated by Forge and his bloody cronies. Locke would remember this. He may only be a lieutenant now but he still had friends in high places back at home. He'd find a way to make Forge pay for the way he was treating him. He turned to look at the pile of armour. He ought to make a start cleaning it. Just to play Forge's game. The movement made his head spin. Perhaps he'd just give it another couple of hours. He gently lowered himself back on to the cot and groaned.

Chapter Five

Privates Smitty and Thom looked on with bemused interest at the occupants of the crudely fenced compound. Smitty rubbed at the bandage that was wrapped around his head. Underneath it he was sporting an ugly cut to his head that had ten stitches in it. And it hurt like buggery. Thom grinned back at him.

'Still hurting, eh?'

'*Yes*. Is that a bloody surprise?'

'Grouchy too.'

Smitty and Thom were both old hands in the company and were veterans of numerous engagements. Smitty was broad-shouldered and well muscled. Thom was smaller, shorter and wiry. The upshot being that Smitty always seemed to attract acts of violence about his person whilst Thom often received hardly a scratch. Something he took great delight in tormenting Smitty about.

'So what do you reckon to this lot then?' asked Smitty.

'Not your usual contractors, that's for sure,' replied Thom.

The workforce were manacled by their feet, one to another. Their hands were also bound. Thom figured there was about a score or so of them. Slaves, obviously. Lean and black-skinned. That immediately put them about eight hundred miles north of where they ought to be. They wore loincloths and had been given blankets to ward off the cold. Not that it did much against the rain. They all looked pretty fit; none of them seemed to be suffering from anything. That was pretty unusual.

'Special guests these fellers,' announced Sergeant Pike, the company quartermaster, as he joined them.

'How so?' asked Smitty.

Sergeant Pike, large, slick black hair and a larger-than-healthy belly, leaned forward conspiratorially. 'Speaking to one of the Graves non-coms, these guys have been specially shipped in. Big expense. Apparently these guys are expert builders. Like, very bloody quick.'

'What do they do? You can build only so fast. Besides I don't figure they are much bothered by anything more than dugouts and mud huts,' said Thom.

'Apparently they got something in them. Magic. They can shape wood.'

'Bollocks!' announced Smitty, who was ever the sceptic.

'Never were one for myth and magic, were you, Smitty?' laughed Thom.

'Well, believe what you want,' sniffed the Quartermaster. 'But you'll find out soon enough. You two can give me a hand. These guys are moving over to our camp tonight. The boss wants them fed, watered and clothed.'

'Righto,' said Smitty. He moved past the Graves sentries and stood before the seated prisoners. They regarded him with mild interest. 'OK, you lot. Up you getty. Nice grub. Thataway,' he indicated towards the Ashkent encampment.

There was a pregnant silence, then one of the prisoners at the back stood up. This was the cue for the others to do the same. They than began to shuffle forwards. Smitty joined the other two with a smug look on his face. Thom and Sergeant Pike laughed.

'You have a real way with words, Smitty. You're wasted here.'

'Indeed,' said the prisoner who had stood up first as he shuffled past. He had said it quite clearly in the common tongue of the Gulf states.

Smitty did a double-take and Thom scratched his head.

'Well, I'll be blowed,' said the Quartermaster.

A short time later the black men were seated in the square, each with a generous helping of Sergeant Pike's own special trail stew. Packed full of things that you couldn't tell what they might have been originally. But as the men remarked, it certainly filled a hole.

The Quartermaster joined Captain Forge and Sergeant Mac as they gazed over the scene. Others of the company would stop and glance over whilst they got on with business of moving off tomorrow morning. All that could be packed or prepared would be done so tonight. At dawn it would be a breakfast of bread and cold meat, then the tents would be taken down and packed, and finally the stakes that made up the camp wall would be pulled out of the ground and stacked on to wagons. The company knew that good sturdy walls were often hard to find and it was a damn sight easier than having to chop down fresh trees every time you made camp. Which, if you were on the move, was every night.

'Well, no one can say they'll be weak from hunger, Sir,' said Sergeant Pike.

'Aye, but maybe from the shits, Pikey,' observed Sergeant Mac.

'Piss off!'

'Did you manage to acquire those fresh blankets?' asked Forge.

'Well, it took a bit of persuadin', boss,' said Sergeant Pike. 'But you know me, ain't nothing can't be gotten when a few bottles of brandy are part of the bargain. Couldn't get any spare uniforms though. Just a bunch of hides and furs and the like.'

'That'll have to do. Hopefully they know how to stitch. Cheers, Sarge,' said Forge.

The Quartermaster nodded and headed off to oversee the stripping-out of the kitchens.

'So which one spoke?' asked Forge.

'That feller over there,' indicated Sergeant Mac. 'Distinguished lookin'.'

'Mmm, just means he's probably a right arrogant shite. Let's have a chat. Bring him over to the tent.'

Forge returned to his office and sat behind his canvas desk. On it was the map given to him by Burns. It was not particularly detailed and he had already had Corporal Jonas in to get what he could from it. Jonas was now moving amongst the Graves troops next door trying to eke out more information about the land they had to travel through. 'Might as well slit our throats and be done with it now boss,' the scout had observed as he played with his over-large, drooping moustache. 'The Big Smelly Cheese has probably got an ambush set up just for us.' 'Just try and make sure it doesn't happen then, Jonas,' Forge had replied.

Forge let out a long sigh and ran his fingers through his hair and then massaged his forehead. Got to get an early night tonight he promised himself. Sergeant Mac appeared at the entrance with his charge in tow. 'Boss.'

Forge looked up. 'Yeah, bring him in.'

He studied the man in front of him. And knew he was being equally measured up. The man was some six foot in height. Lithe and well toned. He had the short curly hair that was a feature of the many tribes from the southern savannah and jungle. Not that he had ever been that far himself. It was the face that drew Forge. It was certainly a noble visage. Not that that meant much. What was weird was the extra bits. On each cheek there were three slivers of wood, some two inches in length, that had been pushed through the skin then along the outside before being reinserted into the flesh. What was really weird was that the wood didn't look as if it was treated with any sort of preservative; it looked alive, like it had become a living part of the body it had entered. The dark eyes regarded him with a hint of amusement.

'They are part of our bonding with the earth and the gift of our shared lives,' said the man.

'I'll pretend that I understand what you just said and move on by asking what your name is,' said Forge.

'I am Juma. The Kai of my village. Of the tribe of Bantusai.'

'OK, Juma. Now we are cooking with dragon fire. I get the impression that you have a pretty good grasp of our language?'

'It took us some six months to reach this point. There was little else for us to do.'

'Can all of you do it?' asked Forge, sounding quite surprised.

Juma smiled. 'Some more, some less. Depending on how clever or stupid the man is.'

Forge grunted, feeling slightly foolish, and Sergeant Mac raised an eyebrow. 'OK, makes sense. Here is the deal. How much trouble are you gonna give me? Because I really could do without it.'

'I and my people are a long, long way from home. We

48

do not expect to see it again. But that doesn't mean we wish to live short and painful lives. Which is what we would have if we "gave you trouble".' Juma made a deadpan face.

Oh great, this guy is smarter than me, thought Forge. 'You got that right. You guys are apparently worth a lot of money. Well, I don't have much truck with the man trade. So for the purposes of this trip you lose the chains. They'll only slow us down. Besides, you'll probably drown wearing those things on the site. You do your job, keep your guys in line and I'll do mine. Plus it'll really piss off your master if he thinks I'm letting you move around like free men.'

'You have a cruel streak.'

'Oh yeah,' grinned Forge. 'Now I have stuff to do. You'll find some blankets and skins to make some clothes with. It sure ain't as warm as your home town.'

Juma's dark eyes studied him a moment longer, then seeming like he had come to a decision he nodded once and turned away. Sergeant Mac made a face at Forge and then followed Juma out.

'Oh, Mac?' he called after the Sergeant.

Sergeant Mac stopped. 'Yes, Sir?'

'After you have dropped off our guest, rustle up our two scouts. I want a confab.'

'About?'

'Just had a really good idea.'

Sergeant Mac made another face at Forge and left.

That's one problem sorted out, thought Forge. He knew there was more to Juma than met the eye. He hoped it wouldn't be the sort of thing that crept up in the night and shoved a wooden spike through his heart. Now he just had to look forward to the company of Portal on the trip. He

49

lay back and allowed himself the pleasure of devising some cruel and unusual methods of dispatching the wizardly shit that could be palmed off as 'an act of nature'.

It was some time later, in the early hours of the following morning, that a band of ten Shifter soldiers moved their way along a thin but well-used trail within a dense wood. Whilst it was still dark, the sky had begun to lighten and streaks of cloud had begun to stand out in the sky. The wood itself was some two hours' ride directly east of Duke Burns' encampment. That meant it was in territory claimed by Shifter. The group, hooded and dressed in the grey and blue garb of the infantry, walked casually through the trees in single file. Only occasionally did a head lift to scan the trees to the left and right of them. From a thicket ahead of the file of soldiers came a challenge. The lead figure raised his hand and waved at the thicket. From it emerged another cloaked figure, who raised his own hand in response whilst cradling a crossbow in the other.

'Quiet night?' asked the sentry.

'Boring,' replied the leading soldier. 'The Graves boys don't want to come out and play any more.'

The sentry laughed and moved to one side. The soldiers moved past him, worked their way round the thicket and entered a large clearing. Bizarrely, an old barn stood in the centre. Worn and crumbling in places, it was nonetheless a solid structure. Presumably, in ages past this barn must have been part of a homestead. Whoever they were, the inhabitants were long gone now and the wood had reclaimed the land around the building. Surrounding it was a hotchpotch, sleeping settlement of tents, lean-tos, carts, pickets and crudely built sheds. A couple of small fires continued to burn; the danger of being discovered within the clearing was very remote. Due to the fact they were officially in Shifter lands, the soldiers did not expect any attack from their neighbours. Ashkent and Graves had not shown any inclination to push the war across the original border line, seemingly content to re-assert the pre-conflict boundaries. The group made its way to an area of the clearing which was taken up by supplies and wagons. The camp was very quiet; no one else appeared to be up or about. The group hunkered down and the lead soldier pulled back his hood. Corporal Jonas glanced around once more and whispered to the nearest figure.

'Right, reckon we split. I'll go and 'ave a look at that bloody big shed over there. You go and take care of the sentry and any others out and about.'

'Sounds good,' replied Corporal Kyle. He nudged the man next to him and the two got up and headed back to the entry point.

'The rest of you,' said Corporal Jonas, 'get to it.'

Heads replied with a nod and the men got up and moved off into the quiet camp. Their orders were simple. Find isolated targets and slide a knife straight into the heart of their prey. The squad of Ashkent soldiers had been picked specifically for this task. They had become inured to death and did not entertain the demons of doubt over the killing they had to inflict. They were old hands who realised the value of not giving your enemy a chance to hit you back. Corporal Jonas pulled his hood back up and picked his way towards the barn. As he drew nearer he caught wind of the stench of horses. He skirted round the building till he came to a set of double doors. He could tell these were new; the wood had that fresh look about it. The doors were not barred in any way and it was a simple affair to pull one open and duck inside.

The interior stank of dung and horse sweat. Staring into the gloom Jonas guessed there were a fair few mounts in there. He moved to the back of the barn and knelt beside a vertical wooden beam which acted as a fixing support for the timbers of the building wall. As he had hoped, it was old, untreated and dry. He glanced around and gathered up a generous armful of straw, noting that at least the horses were being looked after. Corporal Jonas piled the straw at the bottom of the wooden beam then went and got another pile for good measure. From the depths of his cloak he pulled out a small glass flask which contained a rare and particularly unpleasant chemical. Its uses within the military had been kept to a minimum as it was very unstable. Contact with the air combined with a physical shock caused a violent, inflammatory reaction. Jonas stood, took a step back and threw the flask at the wood. The effect was instantaneous; the chemical flared into life and adhered thickly to the beam. Droplets of flame fell on to the straw, which immediately began to smoke. Corporal Jonas glanced round and in the flickering light studied the horses tethered around him. He was surprised; he figured at least thirty. Some had the look of draft horses but most were definitely used as mounts. His practical instinct was to leave them to the Shifter troops to save, but he sometimes had a streak of humanity in him, though not too often. As the fire built behind him, he moved swiftly and released the straps that held the beasts to posts throughout the barn. Those animals nearest the flames were starting to get jittery but did not start away as they were loosed.

Once he had freed all the horses he returned to the

entrance. He reckoned that it had only been a couple of minutes since he had entered. No one had appeared to hear anything. He stepped out into the night and gently closed the door, leaving it slightly ajar. The fire was beginning to spread and smoke from the scattered hay was making the atmosphere thick. He could hear the horses start to protest at the discomfort. He quickly headed back amongst the still silent encampment and stopped at a gently smouldering fire. He stooped, picked a branch that was glowing red at one end and stepped over to the nearest tent. Kneeling down he blew on the branch to feed the heat until a flame was rekindled. Then placing the burning wood against the edge of the coarse material of the tent, he began to blow gently on the brand. The flame played along the tent edge and then the tent itself began to burn.

Satisfied, Corporal Jonas stood and gazed around him. He waited for a few moments longer and watched as two figures copied his actions with other tents within the clearing. As both set light to their respective targets and then withdrew, Jonas turned his attention to the barn. Almost on cue, the barn doors burst open and out of a cloud of smoke came the first of the now highly agitated horses. As the creatures began to trample on those nearest the doorway, other sleepers roused themselves with shouts of anger and alarm. Corporal Jonas added his own voice. 'Attack, attack!' he shouted at the top of his voice. Others from the squad added their cries from others parts of the clearing. Now that things were nicely chaotic the Corporal raced for the entrance thicket. Twice he had to swerve out of the way of confused Shifter troops but, dressed as he was in their garb, none thought to stop him. Orders were being barked out, some calling for a stand to, others commanding men to fight the fire, and amid it all, a general stream of cursing and demands to catch the bloody horses. As he reached the thicket he spotted Corporal Kyle crouched in the bushes.

'All right, Jonas, you're the last.'

Jonas nodded and ran past. Corporal Kyle stood, smiled at the scene and then followed him into the trees.

Five minutes later he emerged from the wood and joined his fellow company scout and the other members of their squad. As they caught their breath they were joined by Sergeant Mac, still on horseback. He had stayed behind with four others to guard their escape route and hold the squad's mounts. He leaned over, spat, and then addressed the two corporals.

'All here?' he asked.

'Yes, boss, we all made it,' replied Corporal Kyle.

The Sergeant nodded. 'All right, mount up. We got a ride ahead of us if we want to get back before we're noticed.'

The men ran to their respective steeds, mounted and followed the Sergeant as he led them back towards Graves territory.

Chapter Six

An hour after dawn the following day, the 1st of the 7th was just about ready to move. The last of the palisade stakes were being withdrawn from the ground and loaded on the wagons. The men worked quickly but there was the inevitable grumbling. It was the normal human trait to set down roots, even in the roughest of environments. The men had gotten comfortable. They had forged some useful trading links with the local troops and some handy 'business' arrangements with some of the ladies that hung around camp. But such was life. A week from now they would have forgotten they were ever there.

Captain Forge was busying himself with stowing his own kit when Corporal Jonas ambled up on his horse.

'Morning, boss.'

'Corporal.'

'Found out what I could; spoke to a few of the locals. Lots of nothin'.'

'Uh-huh.'

'So I figure we head north then east 'til we hit the river. Mostly woodland and wilderness country up there. Oh, and Porky Boy must be genuinely mad.'

Forge smiled at Jonas's pet name for Duke Burns. 'Really? Again? How so?' he asked.

'Well, accordin' to his lads there ain't been any trading traffic since before any of them could remember. All the traffic goes south further to the west. That fort must be real old.'

'Thanks, Jonas. See if you can't get Sergeant Pike to get you some coffee.'

'Rather drink my own piss,' commented Corporal Jonas as he wheeled his horse around.

Forge stopped strapping his saddle and thought about Jonas's news. What was Burns playing at? Something didn't add up. Whatever it was, he was damned if he was going to be on the receiving end of it.

Forge reflected on the previous morning's results. Knowing that time was short he had deliberately hit upon a plan to at least hit back at Shifter. To try and redress the balance for the losses they had suffered. Burns was not told that fifteen of Forge's troops had been sent out on a hunt. Forge couldn't have hoped for a better result when the scouts had spotted the party of Shifter troops. A quick ambush and questioning had given them the location of the Shifter northern base. Hell, he would have been happy with taking out just those ten. Instead Sergeant Mac had led a raid into enemy territory. The result was another dozen enemy troops sorted by the blades of the infiltrators. Thanks to the stampede, there were probably a fair few nursing broken bones, sore heads and several bruises in uncomfortable places. The disruption in the camp would be sure to reduce the activity on the Shifter side of the border for a time, whilst they licked their wounds. What was interesting was the assessment by Jonas and Kyle that the base housed regular Shifter troops. There was nothing 'irregular' about them. And they had a cavalry troop, too. It helped to explain why operations against them had been such hard work. Someone on their side had an ounce of intelligence. Oh well, seems like they had sorted the problem for the time being. He adjusted his jerkin, waggled his scabbard into an easier walking position and tucked his helmet under his arm. 'Time to go stand in the shit storm I reckon,' he mused before ambling over to the command tent to see if the Duke had heard the bad news.

As Forge entered, he almost jumped at the speed of Burns rounding on him. Portal, who discreetly stood to one side, was smiling faintly.

'How dare you? What authority do you have to question my methods?' he screamed.

'Sir?' Forge responded, trying to sound as innocent as possible.

'Don't play the innocent with me, Captain,' said Burns. 'I know you sent out a patrol last night. A patrol that had not been authorised by me or any of my officers.'

'It was just a routine patrol, Sir. Turned out quite well actually,' said Forge brightly.

'What?' said Burns, a dangerous edge to his voice. Behind him Portal shifted uncomfortably and looked slightly confused.

'Yes, Sir,' replied Forge. 'As luck would have it, my guys stumbled on an enemy patrol. Tracked them, ambushed them and then paid a visit to their base.' He noted that Burns' face had lost its anger and had been replaced by a very odd look indeed. 'Snuck in, took out a few more Shifter troops and raised merry hell getting out,' continued Forge. He was starting to enjoy Burns' obvious discomfort. Clearly he was in a spot; he could hardly punish success could he? 'And these guys were regulars, too. Says a lot about our difficulties of late. We thought we were fighting *irregular* troops. Still, good thing we found them before we

57

headed off, saves you some unpleasantness. Oh and sorry for not telling you, I was going to report it but kind of forgot to in the preparations to move.'

Burns was standing quite still. Forge suddenly felt the desire to duck; the man looked like he was going to explode and that was a hell of a lot of body mass for such a small room.

'Are you telling me, Captain,' said Burns in a soft, quavering voice, 'that you, ignoring the chain of command, committed your troops to a possibly suicidal operation. And in so doing seriously damaged the enemy contingent ranged against us?'

'And that these troops were Shifter regular forces?' Portal chipped in.

'Yes to both,' replied Forge. 'Shifter regular troops with cavalry support. By our reckoning, some two hundred soldiers. In fact, if they had wanted to, they could have engaged us in a pretty even fight. What with my troops having been all used up in a questionable patrolling strategy.' Forge had wanted to bait Burns but all he got was more of the Duke's trembling face. 'I was going to forward my report to Regiment,' he continued. 'They ought to know what we are dealing with up here.'

'You will do no such thing!' screamed Burns, suddenly waking from his red-faced reverie. 'You have done enough damage, Captain. You have deliberately gone against my orders and have publicly humiliated me in front of the men. I will deal personally with the report. And rest assured I will be recommending the harshest possible punishment for your mutinous behaviour. In fact, if you were not already going north, I would have you in chains already.'

You could try, thought Forge.

'As it is, I do not have the manpower to change my plans. You will take your men to the Rooke and you will ensure that the job is done efficiently and speedily. Do this and on your return you might just come away with your life, if not your commission, intact. And don't doubt that my wizard will be telling me exactly what happens.'

Again, that self-satisfied sneer from Portal. 'Do I make myself clear, Captain?'

'As day, Duke,' replied Forge.

Forge gave a smart salute and left the command tent. Mutinous? Him? That was the first time he had ever been accused of that! He wasn't at all bothered by the Duke's threats. He had already dispatched a report to Head-quarters. Dav would get it and would recognise the value of Forge's actions over the Duke's remonstrations. Now all he had to do was take care of his men for the next couple of weeks. From what he'd been hearing, they then just might be on their way home.

He turned his attention to the task at hand. Until they returned to Ashkent he resolved to make sure the company wasn't caught with its arses out in the wind. He sighed, placed his helmet on his head and went to find his horse. Mounting, he rode along the all but empty shell of what had been their home for the past few months. Outside, the company column was forming up. It was a lot smaller then when it had first arrived. Forge could feel his bitterness well up again. He had sixty-seven men out of what had been a full strength company of a hundred. He had lost both of his original officers and some damned fine privates and non-coms. All because Burns couldn't organise a piss-up in a brewery. The Duke's operational strategy was haphazard at best; his own levy troops did not trust him and consequently were unmotivated. In the field they did not present any kind of military threat. So instead the Ashkent troops did all the fighting. Well, at least they were getting out of here. He could exert control over what happened to his men out there in the wild, away from the incompetence of the Duke.

The Captain rode down the column to the centre where the stores wagons were drawn up. Whilst each horse carried enough for a soldier to survive in the field, the wagons meant life could be more bearable. Food for men and horses, cooking equipment and all the other trappings of the company were the cargo. Two wagons had also been employed to carry the Bantusai. They sat quietly enough, watching with mild interest the hustle and bustle going on around them. He noted that they had wasted no time in fashioning some crude but passable attempts at clothing for themselves. Juma nodded his greeting from the rear of the foremost wagon.

'Thank you for the clothes. We are tough but we feel the cold like any other. It is not like our home here,' said Juma.

'Bet it ain't. I'll want your men pulling their weight on this trip. At the end of the day we stop and build camp. That means a ditch and then a wall on top of the spoil. The sooner it's up the sooner we rest. Standard procedure in unfriendly parts.'

'We do the same ... in a way,' replied Juma.

Forge tipped his head and then rode to the front of the column. Sergeant Mac and Lieutenant Locke were waiting for him. He noted how Locke was looking better and seemed to have made an attempt at getting his own mount fully prepared for the trip. The two men saluted the Captain.

'The men are mounted and ready to go. Flankers and rearguard are out and Jonas and Kyle you can just about see up ahead,' said Sergeant Mac.

'OK, thank you, Sergeant Mac. Let's get going.'

Sergeant Mac indicated back over his shoulder towards the Graves encampment. 'Oh, just one thing, Sir.'

Forge looked back at and spied Portal riding towards them.

'Oh yeah, thought the air smelt a bit fresh.'

They waited as the wizard reined in next to them. The gangly mage nodded haughtily to the two soldiers. 'Good morning, gentlemen. I trust all is well. Shall we?'

Arsehole, thought Forge. 'Good morning back,' he replied and then turned to his sergeant. 'Move them out, First Sergeant.'

Sergeant Mac spat to his left and signalled the column.

Forge took the lead and out of the corner of his eye he saw Portal take up station slightly to his rear. He didn't know if he actually approved of this act of deference to his command. He'd rather not have his back to this slimy individual. As they left the outer pickets of the encampment it began to rain. Ah, right on cue, thought Forge.

The next three days passed without incident for the company. The first day's travel took them through land they had already patrolled and the scouts knew the safest routes to avoid ambushes. Not that Shifter would engage a force this large. By nightfall the rain had stopped and the company had bivouacked in record time. Forge figured he might as well put his new builders to work and the Bantusai had attacked the construction of the palisade with gusto. Forge could not help but be impressed. For prisoners they seemed pretty damn motivated. It was not

61

as if he had actually threatened them or anything. That night he had doubled the guard. He couldn't help but feel uneasy. They were strictly speaking in disputed territory and therefore a higher level of security was needed, but that wasn't it. It was the foreboding he felt in the back of his mind for this entire venture.

That night he sat by the fire nursing a coffee; on the far side, the company sergeants were deep in conversation. He had also noted that Locke had taken to avoiding him other than to deal with professional matters. The lad was still smarting from his dressing down. Forge wondered if the lad would take it on the chin and sort himself out. Youngsters were bound to make mistakes; hopefully he would learn from them.

He felt a presence next to him. 'May I join you?' asked Portal.

Forge grunted his ascent as the wizard arranged himself next to him. He did so in a slow, precise method that left nothing to chance. That spooked Forge. Too damned in control, he thought. They spent the next few moments in an uncomfortable silence. At least the Captain did. Portal seemed more than content to watch the fire.

'I checked on the prisoners,' said Portal abruptly. 'They have a sleeping space in the centre of the camp but they are not guarded. That is not wise.'

'My prisoners, my rules.' Forge knew he was being deliberately obnoxious. Not that he gave a stuff. 'Besides, where are they going to go? We'd would find them again and give them a slap for their troubles. Unless Shifter finds them first.'

'They are not fools, Captain. You have at least surmised that. But neither are they helpless. You do not know them. They have talents you could not understand. Given a chance they might kill you in your sleep and slaughter every man here,' responded Portal hotly.

'I'm not a complete idiot, wizard,' snapped Forge. 'They are watched.'

'Aye, by men who grow tired as the night continues. You are fortunate that I am here. For I, too, watch them. By means far more reliable than your own. If they were to act unbidden, then I would know. And then I shall mete out more appropriate treatment.'

Forge wanted to make some sort of pithy comment but couldn't come up with anything. He settled for another question. 'So what is it that makes these guys so special?'

Portal glanced at him with that same sardonic smile. 'It is a magic I have no knowledge of. Suffice to say that they can bend wood to their will. It took much effort to bring them to this place...' he paused, as if thinking about whether to say more. 'You will see. Goodnight, Captain.' At that he got up and left the fire.

Forge watched him go. He was pretty sure that Portal had been about to let something slip and had stopped himself. They were building a bloody bridge, not a palace. Hell, his guys could probably knock something half decent up given the time. Time. That was it again. They were being pressured by time. But what for? The war wasn't going to end tomorrow. He knew this was really going to bug him.

Sometime later the next day they left the limits of the known terrain and entered the true wilderness. It was then down to Corporals Jonas and Kyle, the two company scouts, to guide them safely to their destination. Strictly speaking, the further north they went the less they should encounter any true resistance. They had very little intelligence about the land they were riding through. As the map had suggested, it was made up of lush meadows and rocky outcroppings with large tracts of forest. Oak, elm and birch trees competed for sunlight. There were trails of sorts, if you looked carefully. They hadn't been used for a long, long time. The scouts stuck to them, as they led in roughly the right direction. It meant the going was that bit easier for the wagons. Game, too, was abundant. It meant that they would be eating fresh meat each night and not the rations they had brought with them, although Sergeant Mac claimed he actually quite liked salt-beef jerky. The lads thought he was mad.

Sergeant Mac was not a worrier, at least not in the proper sense. He would just say he was being concerned. He was concerned about this mission and he was concerned about Portal. He was also concerned about their charges. Not that they had been any trouble but there were rumours floating around the lads. When he had asked Smitty about it, the big man had just tapped his nose and said, 'Magicians I heard, Sarge. Can turn you into a tree soon as look at you.' Sergeant Mac had quickly dismissed Smitty as being hardly the most reliable of sources. However, it didn't hurt to keep an eye on them like the Captain had said.

But it was the boss he was most concerned about. He had always been a bit of a cantankerous sort. Mac put it down to thinking too much about stuff. But Forge had been different of late. He looked more haunted. His eyes showed a strain that had never been there before. Sergeant Mac knew why of course. He himself had felt the deaths of the men as keenly as any other, but then he had the luxury of not having to carry the ultimate responsibility of the lads' lives. The Captain did that. You lost men in war, that came with the territory. But these months had been more like a slow leaching of the company lifeblood, not a straight fight like they were used to. Truth be known they were used to turning up and kicking butt in a rapid and rather fatal fashion. It had been a long time since they had had to face a really stubborn enemy in a slogging match. He hoped that at least now they might just get some respite. The men needed it and so did Forge. His brain was cooking and Mac wondered how much more the Captain could take.

That night, as the camp relaxed after supper, Forge made his usual tour of the perimeter. He would stop and speak briefly to each of the six men on the guard shift checking that they knew their orders and noting if they were alert enough for their four-hour shift. It also meant he had a chance to pick up on the mood of the men. Whilst they were interested in the Bantusai, they were not too bothered about the task itself. They were just happy to be away as a company again. Away from the Graves troops who they felt were nothing more than bad luck and bad soldiers.

As he made his way back into the centre he saw Corporals Jonas and Kyle skulk back into camp. It was the drill that each night the two scouts would venture back out and study the surrounding ground. Usually they would tour around on foot and then hunker down near any likely spots that an enemy might take to get a closer look or attack from. That way they might well intercept any surveillance and act as an early warning if anyone were to launch an assault. Whilst on the move, the two men were arguably the busiest and carried the safety of the company upon their shoulders. It did mean, however, that they escaped the required construction duties of the ditch and palisade and that they never had to do any commissary duties. So it wasn't all bad. Usually they would check into the First Sergeant, and true to form he saw Sergeant Mac ambling over to them. Stopping off to get a brew, Forge went and joined the three men who were hunkered down in conversation.

'... I'm not saying it is like, really unexpected,' Corporal Kyle was saying.

'What's up?' asked Forge as he passed the mug around.

'Boys were just saying about Shifter activity in the area, Captain,' said Sergeant Mac.

'Such as?'

'Just that there ain't none, boss,' said Corporal Kyle.

Forge raised an eyebrow.

'I mean, we know they do operate round here,' continued Kyle. 'Not in any great numbers but enough that we should find some trace. And we have found some older sites but...'

'We got jack shit,' added Jonas.

'Yeah, best as we could tell there hasn't been anything happening round these parts for at least two weeks.'

'So maybe they have gotten careful,' said Forge.

'And I'm shagging my horse,' replied Jonas.

Forge knew better than to push the point. If these guys said there were no Shifter troops out there, then he believed them. It would take a lot of magic to hide an enemy force and there were not enough mages left in Shifter to waste on this northern flank, let alone any that were powerful enough to do the job anyway.

'Reassigned maybe. Or just running out of manpower?' mused Sergeant Mac. 'After all, the camp that we hit was big. Perhaps they had pulled in all their troops?'

'Could be. Still makes our job a little easier.' Forge knew

he sounded unconvinced. 'So basically, as it stands we have free rein up here.'

'Not to say we aren't being watched though, boss,' said Kyle.

'Aye, true enough. Just keep your eyes open. It's one thing to know who you are fighting but it's what you don't know that worries me.' Forge stood up and moved away, leaving the other three to their discussions.

He now knew that there was a real problem with this whole venture. Too many things were happening at the same time. First they get packed off at high speed to rebuild an old bridge for a trade route that no longer existed, and then the enemy apparently gives up the ghost. 'Well, Shifter were beaten – they just didn't know it yet – but that was no reason for them to disappear up here. What he wanted to do was grab Portal round the neck and beat the truth out of him. However, he didn't really have enough to confront him with yet and he hardly expected the wizard just to volunteer the information. He picked his way through the camp to the central square where the Bantusai slept. He had to admit, they were surprisingly well behaved. They were clustered in groups, talking quietly to each other, except Juma who sat stoically staring into the fire. Forge hunkered down next to him. He proffered his coffee and Juma took it, nodding his thanks. The black man sipped at it and then passed it back. Somehow Forge had expected him to make a face at the bitter brew.

'So, you're a Kai. A headman, chief. Something like that right?' asked Forge.

Juma nodded. 'A Kai is the leader. A speaker of the truth.'

'What truth is that?'

'It is for me to decide.'

Forge started to prepare himself for lots of mystic bullshit but then realised what the other was saying. 'Ah, right. You make the laws, pass judgement. That sort of stuff.'

Juma smiled. 'Yes. You were thinking something else?'

'Huh, yeah, reckon I was. I hear you have some sort of gift. Good at singing to trees or some such.'

Juma chuckled at that one. 'Oh yes, we all sit round and sing at trees. How very useful.'

Forge felt his face begin to redden; he didn't like being the butt of jokes.

Juma put his hands up in placation. 'No, no. I do not wish to mock you. It has been said I have a playful manner about me. I am just shocked by the reaction I and my people get. In the time I have spent amongst your kind I have heard many things. That we are great magical creatures. Demons even. Yet to us we do nothing that is not sensible and right in our own land.'

'So what are you then? I reckon it might be a good idea to put the record straight.'

Juma shrugged. 'We are of the Bantusai. Our histories are held in our minds and told in song. Many years we have lived in our tribal lands. It is said it is a magical place. That perhaps in ages past something left its mark on the land. In the very roots of the earth. This may be truth. For as we lived and died and birthed anew we have learned or been given a gift. Where once we would work the wood to build our homes, much like you do now, we no longer do so.'

Forge cocked his eyebrow. Here comes the good stuff.

'Now we ... "sing"? That is perhaps one way of describing it. We work the wood with words. We bring it from the very depths of the trees and shape it to our will. In so doing we take of the earth but we do not destroy it.'

68

'So everyone is happy, eh?'

'Indeed, we respect the land and it treats us well.'

'OK. I get the picture. You can ... mould wood. What? Like arrows, spears, big clubs?'

'And more. We build our villages with it, use it for our tools. Everything. We have become known for our skills and have provided for others who have been our friends. It seems as if our fame has spread wider than we had thought.'

'You know what you are doing here? Why you have ended up travelling like this?' asked Forge.

'We are to build a bridge. We have done many before.'

'Just how fast could you build one? Given the right materials? Well, wood.'

'To make one such as I have seen coming here? That would allow for wagons and such? A day. Two.'

'You're shitting me!' scoffed Forge

'I do not shit on you, Captain. We are a clean-living people and very concerned about hygiene.'

'Just how in hell did you get caught?' Forge asked. 'You seem too smart for that.'

'Perhaps we have become too trusting. None have tried to harm us for many years. Our neighbours treat us with respect. And our wards and protections have lessened over time.'

'Easy to happen,' agreed Forge.

'We did not think that a powerful magic would be used to take us. A sleep spell. Though I understand that it is but a common thing in your world. But to us this was a new magic, one we could not ... did not think to counter. They entered my village and took all the men who were strong and fit. The others they slaughtered. They have no respect for life, these civilised men. I learnt the difference between civilised and civilisation early. The two words are not the same, are they?'

To Forge, the bitterness in the words of Juma was almost tangible.

'So your people have been destroyed.'

Juma looked up at him. 'Oh no, not my people, my village. My family. The tribe continues.'

'Then you could get back then. You could go home.'

'Yes, but how? We are far away. How could we escape notice? We do not blend in.'

'True, but if you were freed, you wouldn't be stopped. We have guys of your colour within the Army. Hell, you could join up, be part of the Engineering corps.'

'Captain, I would be content with one thing. That those who did this deed to my village be punished, that they be made to suffer. Then I would die with my vengeance complete.'

Forge decided again to change tack. 'Do you not think it is odd that you have been all this way to build this bridge? You said you could build it in a day or two. Why the rush?'

Juma shrugged. 'We were bought from the slavers and have come here. The one who bought us, he has spent much to get us. We were bound for other shores and work. Now we spend three months on the road to this place. It is much effort. I do not know the purpose. I am just a slave.'

'Hmm. I doubt that,' grunted Forge. He struggled up. 'I'll bid you goodnight.'

Juma grinned. 'You too, Captain. Do not let the bed insects feast upon you.'

Forge couldn't be sure if Juma was taking the piss. He had to admit, he liked the man.

70

As he made his way back to his tent he stared over at Portal's. Right, you shit, thought Forge. Just give me an excuse.

It was the afternoon of the fourth day that the 1st of the 7th finally arrived at the River Rooke.

Chapter Seven

Holis Lode was really starting to feel out of his depth. Things had taken a new turn and he didn't like the way they were going. As best as they could figure it he and his companions were about three days away from the Rooke. That meant they were moving in a roughly south-western direction. Not that it made any sense to Lode; there was nothing to attack in that direction. They had continued to shadow the force of northerners. What was interesting was that this force was clearly made up of a number of different war bands. No one Harradan chief could field as many men as this, a force that Juggs had estimated at around two thousand men.

He had only been able to do this calculation because the Harradan had decided to stop. The reason for this was certainly not attributable to the trappers' efforts at giving them a bloody nose. What had upset the apple cart was that yesterday the six of them had been so busy watching what was going on behind them that they almost ended up walking into an entire wagon train of armed men. They had quickly moved round them and pushed on to a safer position to the south-west. The Harradan had made contact with this wagon train and had bivouacked there.

Lode and the others had then scouted back to see what was going on. The armed men, who had met the northerners, were garbed in the colours of Shifter. There were three score of them. They had come up what appeared to be an ages-old trail, one that had no doubt taken a fair bit of clearing to make it passable again. The wagon train had then stopped in a sizeable clearing. Juggs and Sleeps had doubled back on themselves to take a closer look at the size of the force camped by the old trail. They also reported that it was indeed a resupply operation. There was a mass of food and drink held on the back of the wagons as well as extra weapons.

'A shed load of shitting arrows,' Juggs had remarked.

'That's what it looks like, Holis,' agreed Sleeps. 'Looks like these guys are getting ready to go to war.'

'And it ain't with us,' pointed out Fuzz.

'Well, it's obvious what's happenin',' said Old Hoarty. 'They're gonna invade Graves.'

'But that war is almost over,' said Lode.

'And how're they gonna invade from here?' asked Arald. 'It is not like they can cross the river without a bridge can they?'

'But they can swim across,' suggested Fuzz. 'Get some ropeways set up.'

'No, not here they can't,' said Lode. 'The river is running through a gorge and is impassable this far north. They'd have to go further south. But Arald is right. They still need a bridge.'

'Bloody right. Don't reckon they need to be buggering around building one,' said Sleeps.

'You know, there used to be one,' said Old Hoarty, scratching his chin. ''Bout three days from here. Not that you'd know about it. Long gone. But that trail back there? That used to lead right to it. And you could get across the river. All nice and flat country.'

'Hoarty, is there nowhere you ain't been?' asked Lode.

Old Hoarty grinned his best one-tooth grin.

'So what do we do now?' asked Arald.

'Not as if we can fight this whole bloody army,' said Fuzz.

'We can't,' said Lode. He agreed that there was little else they could reasonably achieve. They could only keep scratching at the Harradan until one night they made a mistake and one or more of them wound up getting caught. As it was they were all dog-tired. So maybe they could try a different way of snaring their prey. 'But if they are figuring on getting across the river, likely as not they plan to do some killing. Now I don't know much about the politics of it all, but Ashkent has an army over there and they have been doing some major butt kickin'. And you got to be thinking that these guys will be fixing to go up against Ashkent at some point. So ...'

'So we go', interrupted Sleeps, 'and tell the foreigners that the Harradan boys are coming and then they go and kill all the bastards.'

'That's about the size of it,' said Lode.

'Well, where do we find them?' asked Sleeps.

'We head down to this old bridge crossing. Get across it and head south. We are bound to find somebody eventually,' said Lode.

'And I bet there might be a nice reward or something,' said Juggs.

'You have all the best ideas, Juggs lass,' cackled Old Hoarty.

Lode felt pleased with the plan. The wagons would slow the Harradan down some, which meant they could get well away from them quickly and find the nearest Ashkent forces. Nice and easy and with the minimum amount of risk for them. He certainly hadn't expected to find himself being in the path of an invading army or indeed be in a position to stop them. Actually he didn't really care about who was fighting who. But it was the best chance to see the murderers of Noel's Gap punished. That was the important thing. That and to settle an old score. He hadn't paid it much thought beforehand but during the last ambush they had sprung Lode recognised the tartan of their targets. It was that of the Stone clan, his own blood kin. It had roused a multitude of feelings within him, old anger long buried and laid to rest. Or so he had thought. The chances were that the clan was still led by the same chief who had banished him. He was too tough a bastard to be gotten rid of. So if his clan were part of this army, then it followed that Vorgat Stoneson would be with them. And for the first time in many years, Lode could allow himself to think of a way to exact some measure of vengeance for what Vorgat had done. It was not the banishment that drove him, it was the girl; she had not deserved the attentions that old bastard would have given her. Lode had an opportunity to make up for hurts inflicted long ago. He wasn't going to let it pass him by.

The six companions gathered their meagre belongings and moved off west in the direction of the River Rooke. They could then follow it south until they reached the crossing point. They still had a couple of hours before sundown and there was no harm in putting some distance between themselves and the Harradan forces, who would be moving again soon enough.

Vorgat Stoneson spat into the fire. He gazed into the flames and watched where his missile had landed on to a log in the centre of the burning pile. The spit was beginning to boil and bubble. He continued to stare well past the time that all the fluid had evaporated. He was lost in his own thoughts. Brutal and hard-spoken as he was, he had the capacity for a degree of self-regard. This had given him an edge in his rise to his position as clan chief. Of course, it helped that he was a big man with an aggressive character. In his early forties, a good age for a Harradan, he possessed heavily muscled arms, covered in an over-generous amount of body hair. Corded muscles bulged from his neck, shoulders and legs. A brute of a man, he presented himself as an individual not to be messed with. His followers had learned the hard way not to disturb him when he was in this quiet sort of mood.

Dressed in animal furs he looked no different to a man from prehistory before civilisation had crept into the world. Whilst most of his men wore armour of various sorts and styles, he had always refused to wear such metal. He felt restricted by it and took the view that if a man couldn't take the pain of a few cuts then he was no man. Around him his men were relaxed, they told crude jokes and laughed at the suffering of others. Every now and then an argument would break out and the antagonists would come to blows. That was normal. These disagreements would always be settled by fists alone. Vorgat had forbidden the use of weapons. This ban had also extended to his clan's relations with the other clans that formed his loose alliance. This was no easy matter; the Gods knew that not to fight against your neighbour was as unnatural as not eating meat. He had threatened to kill any man who drew his sword against another Harradan, and had made good on his promise already. That lesson was learnt fast.

He cradled his sword in front of him. It paid to keep it close. He was in a foreign country surrounded by the loosest of alliances. There were men from six clans gathered here, of which his clan had the largest numbers.

It had been a huge feat for him to have persuaded so many of his countrymen to accompany his planned expedition to the south. The Shifter emissary had been wise to come to his clan first. By choosing the Stone the emissary had picked one of the most respected and feared clans in all of western Harradan. The words of Vorgat carried weight and others would listen. Once he had been bought by the offer of the riches to be had, he then undertook the task of persuading others to join him. Many clan chiefs were not interested in heading so far from their lands to engage in a war that did not concern them. Some felt, not wrongly, that by depleting their manpower, others might usurp their lands. Such was the level of distrust amongst the clans of the Harradan. But Vorgat had relied upon their greed, which was fundamental to all their natures. He had told them how the Shifter emissary had promised that all loot was theirs to keep and that a wagon of gold would be provided for each clan leader that brought his men south. He neglected to tell them that he himself had already taken ownership of a wagon of treasure as part payment and another two on completion of his tasks.

Six of the eight clan leaders of the western Harradan people had agreed to become mercenaries for the soft, southern state of Shifter. Each of the six clans had left fifty men to provide security against any human or non-human force that might enter their territory. He had also arranged for word to be sent out that any clan leader who moved in on his territory would have to face him on his return. Their success at the small town to the north had been a good start. The Harradan had done what they did best and enjoyed a virtually uncontested rape of the settlement. Their moods had soon soured when they had started taking losses after embarking on the journey south. The other clan leaders had voiced their anger at losing men to an unseen enemy and one or two had begun to question the whole expedition. Vorgat had swiftly reminded them of the riches to be gained and had then questioned their manhood. Kron Battlebane had taken offence and had begun to draw his sword. Vorgat had grinned at him and had positively encouraged him to continue. This had given Kron pause for thought. It helped Vorgat that he understood the nature of his own countrymen. Whilst he had the largest single body of men under his command, they could still be bested if the others chose to join against him. Vorgat did not believe this would happen as they would never agree to work together. Only Vorgat and the riches that were on offer had the power to keep them together. Hah, the fools! If only they knew the truth.

Vorgat was seriously considering a way of double crossing them completely. If he played this right, he might be able to return with his main force still intact, whilst the others were seriously weakened through conflict. He could make his clan the most powerful in all of Harradan, perhaps the *only* clan left in Harradan. But that was a thought for another day. As it stood he had other problems. Someone had obviously survived the assault on the town and had taken it personally. They were good, skilled in woodcraft, able to pick off small groups of them and disappear back into the forest. His main concern was that, whilst they did not present a serious problem at the moment, they were a constant thorn in his side. One that could fester and cause his loose alliance of war bands to split.

On the other side of the fire sat his witch. At his command she searched for the trappers – her spirit free from her body, she travelled through the forests looking for signs. The body itself sat cross-legged, the back slumped forward and the head resting on its chin. As always her cloak was held closely around her, almost like a shield, a means of hiding from the world. He had been waiting for her return for some time now and was becoming impatient. At that moment her bodied shuddered and he heard her take in a gasp of breath. Vorgat remained silent for a few moments longer; he knew that the witch would need to become used to her body again.

'You found them?' he asked.

The witch shook her head but did not look up.

'No, lord. I could not.'

Ignoring the heat of the fire, he leaned closer. 'You failed me?' he asked. His voice gained a dangerous growl.

This time she did raise her head and gazed calmly into his eyes.

'I have not, lord. I have searched and found nothing. They are no longer near.'

'Then they have fled? Are you certain?'

'I am certain they are no longer within my sight. That is all I can tell you.' She moved her eyes away from Vorgat. It would not do to look at him directly too much. It irked him and he would often lash out. Lissa had learned through many hard years how much she could risk. A more subtle man might have mistaken her actions for lies. But not Vorgat, his arrogance and her genuine fear of him worked in her favour.

Vorgat rocked back on his haunches. His witch was often short with her answers but she was never wrong. This was good news. It was an itch he might not have to scratch anymore.

The captain of the Shifter archers, Joran Lordswood, approached the fire. To Vorgat, he seemed a dandified fop of a man; very well spoken and arrogant with it. He sat still and fixed the man with a baleful stare.

'Well, how many of them are there?' the Captain asked.

'No more than a half-dozen,' replied Stoneson.

'So can you not just deal with them?'

'If we stop ... but you want us to move fast.'

'Well, we have a schedule to keep. Have they engaged you recently?'

'No, they have faded and not returned. Perhaps they have moved on.'

'I expect they have. We cannot afford to let them slow us down. We must push on to the river. '

'And what if I start losing men again?'

'Then you live with it, Chief. This was a problem of your own making. If you had been more thorough with the investing of Noel's Gap, none of your men would have been lost.'

'As you say,' responded Vorgat quietly, tilting his head in acknowledgement, his eyes appraising the Shifter captain.

Lordswood held his stare for a moment, then turned quickly and walked away.

'Leave me,' he ordered.

The witch stood silently and disappeared into the night.

It had taken every ounce of Vorgat's self-control not to gut the man there and then. But he was the means to the money. Vorgat could wait long enough to get the job done. After that, this fool would no longer have a reason to be alive. Aye, it would be a slow death. He would learn that he was no equal to the leader of the Stone clan. Instead, Vorgat cast his mind to what lay ahead. A bridge to cross, then into Graves and the slaughter could begin.

* * *

Lissa gathered her cloak about her and stared into the night. It was a quiet, pleasant night, though she shivered anyway. She knew she was walking a dangerous path. She had never in her life attempted such defiant actions. Vorgat was everything to her – past, present and future. She could only dimly remember a time when he wasn't present in some way. And it was the memory of that time, of a boy she had once cared for, which drove her now. If her lord and master ever found out she was keeping knowledge from him, oh how he would hurt her. Vorgat could do that – he knew how to frighten her, he would tell her how if it hadn't been for his continued favour she would have been given to his followers long ago. Even now, he told her, they waited to take her body and break it. And she believed him. She knew the animals that claimed to be men which circled him. Vorgat kept her safe as long as she did his bidding. What else could she do?

In the Shifter camp Joran Lordswood was starting to have his own doubts about the sense of employing the Harradan. A career soldier within the Shifter military, he did not agree with the use of mercenary troops. He was finding it hard to disguise his contempt and he also realised that Vorgat was well aware of it. That the clan chief did not seem to care was proof of the man's arrogance and ignorance. He did not realise how important this mission was to Shifter. If it failed then the war was over and a great many of the Shifter military hierarchy would find themselves out of a job, or worse. That was why he and his archers had been attached to the raiding force. His task was to ensure that the Harradan followed the plan that Shifter was implementing. To be honest, he would feel better once they had linked up with the infantry company and cavalry troop that were already in place in the northern borders of Graves. Then at least they could start conducting proper military operations and not the chaotic approach that the Harradan employed in warfare. Until then he would have to watch Vorgat. The man was devious and unpredicatable and that, to Lordswood's thinking, was a very dangerous thing.

The 1st of the 7th surveyed the scene as one man. They had been following the river and what appeared to be the faintest of trails, now little more than an animal run. The trail had suddenly widened and had opened up into a large clearing some three hundred yards north to south and two hundred yards east and west. At the northern end stood the skeleton of what appeared to be an old stone structure. There was a fair amount of vegetation in the clearing but nothing like the surrounding woodland. Dotted here and there were more piles of stones. Sometimes what looked like the remains of a wall, covered with moss and lichen, could be picked out.

Forge kept his men back from entering the clearing proper. He waited for the two scouts to come back in from a rapid inspection of the area. Corporals Jonas and Kyle took their time. Occasionally they would stop to inspect something on the ground before moving on. After a few minutes they trotted back.

'All clear, boss,' said Corporal Jonas. 'What we have here is an old, old settlement. Not more than a few families. Probably servicing that place.' He indicated the fort.

'Any signs of life?' asked Forge.

'Not recently,' replied Corporal Kyle. 'There is some spore. Hard to tell how old though. Old enough to say that there hasn't been anyone here for a long time.'

'OK. We'll move in. You guys go and do your thing.'

Both scouts nodded and rode off to conduct a more thorough search of the area. Forge looked at Mac.

'Sarge. Get the company in and get them building. I want the palisade up as quick as you can. Put it right here. That way we can use the extra vision afforded by the clearing. Don't incorporate the river though. I want a wall all the way round. Then get the boys to try and clear some of the easier foliage. Locke?'

'Sir?'

'You, me, the wizard and Juma will get our heads together. That all right with you?' he asked abruptly, staring at Portal, who had silently joined them. It was starting to really bug the shit out of Forge.

'Why do we need the slave leader at our meeting, Captain? Surely you and I can deal with the construction.' Portal waved his hand dismissively. 'The slave can be told of his work by your sergeant.'

Forge gave Portal his best 'well, aren't you an idiot' look. 'You are obviously the product of a well-bred family, aren't you, Portal. Well, what with me spending my formative years killing people and you no doubt buried in books about frog surgery, I didn't have much time to study the finer points of engineering. The Bantusai stays.' Forge hoped Portal would argue.

'Very well, Captain. Just remember that as the Duke's representative it is I that have overall control of this mission.' Portal's eyes were blazing. Forge kept himself cool and stared right back for a few moments before nodding his head.

'Absolutely,' he said.

As the camp began to take shape Forge decided to take a wander over to the old fortifications. As he crossed the short distance to the first walls he spied the two scouts, now dismounted, kicking about in the undergrowth to his left. They were intent on their work, but had not appeared to have discovered anything too startling.

He approached the ruins of the old fort and stood before its weathered stone walls. They were some ten feet in height at their highest point, though much of the perimeter had crumbled in upon itself. The old gateway, which faced south, was now just a larger gap within the wall. He measured the gap at about seven feet. The lack of stone or debris around the gap suggested that the gateway had been secured with thick wooden doors, which had rotted away through time. There had been no continuation of the wall and therefore no parapet above it.

He then made a clockwise circuit of the outside of the walls. There was no suggestion of a ditch surrounding the outside and he wondered why they had never considered using a moat, especially so close to the river. As far as he could tell, the stonework had suffered no serious assault. It was usually pretty easy to tell: smashed blocks, gouged walls, possibly fire-blackened. It appeared as if the fort had just died of old age. He paced out the distance and found that the structure had been rectangular. The northern and southern ends were the longer fronts of some forty yards whilst the east and west walls were thirty yards in length. At one time the northern wall would have faced a distance of perhaps fifty yards before hitting the treeline. Now, of course, that distance was a hell of a lot closer. The eastern wall was roughly fifteen yards from the river. It meant that the occupants would have had to travel to the water's edge to have a crap. Not exactly ideal, but then the river might have been closer in years past.

Forge returned to the gateway and entered the fort

proper. Standing inside the courtyard he saw that there was in fact a parapet running around the walls. At least, it used to. It was made out of wood and had collapsed around most of the circuit, although he could still see where the supporting beams had been fitted into recesses in the stone. On the north, east and west sides, stone outhouses had been constructed against the walls with the wooden walkway acting as a roof for them. Forge guessed they would have been stables, storehouses and barrack blocks. Enough to house a cavalry troop of about thirty men.

Directly in front of Forge was a low mound rising to about four foot, and upon it was a square tower, about twelve feet in breadth on each side of its walls. It was also in very poor condition, lacking a top and much of the higher walls. The perimeter walls had been incorporated into the north face of the tower and he could see an opening leading into the tower from the western side some three feet higher than the parapet level. Originally it looked to have had three floors and probably a walled, flat top for sentry and defensive purposes. Staring inside he saw the stairs leading up to the second floor; they were made of stone and reasonably solid. Gingerly he climbed up. He kept his helmet on just in case these walls decided to give up the ghost and come crashing down on him. The second level had lost its floor and much of the east-facing wall. The stairs continued to lead up to where the final level would have been. It looked like an open parapet, with evenly spaced embrasures much like the walls below, where one could have looked out over the surrounding land. It might even have had a wooden roof. At this height he was slightly above the outside walls but could not see much owing to the surrounding forest. He pushed his luck and continued up the stairs, mindful of the fact that he was being bloody stupid for his age.

Stopping at the second-from-highest step he gently balanced his hands on the supporting side wall. The view was better now and he estimated that he was approximately twenty-five feet up. Looking eastwards he could see across the river. At this point it was some thirty yards wide and quite fast-flowing. From what he had been led to believe, only a few miles north of here the ground became mountainous and that this river was pretty much impassable for at least two days' travel, even during the drier summer months. That would make sense with regard to the trade routes and placement of the bridge. On the far side there was a much smaller clearing, a little lower than the level of the fort. He could see that the treeline altered at one point, a place where the trees were fewer and of a younger age; this suggested a path that would have led down to the old bridge.

Whilst the place would have been solid enough in its prime, it had clearly grown up in a haphazard fashion. No doubt the bridge had come first. The tower was odd though. Maybe it had been the original protection for the bridge or a watchtower to signal against impending invasion. Normally a frontier fort would not have incorporated such a thing. Also, the walls were made of stone. That required money and effort. A troop of soldiers would usually make do with a wooden palisade not much more sophisticated than the one his men were building now, if perhaps more permanent. Then, of course, there was the evidence of dwellings outside. It was likely that a small village had grown around the fort and the thoroughfare of trade that the bridge had created. If that were so, then those inside would have been used to keep thieves and brigands from mounting raids on the civilians and the merchant traffic. If this bridge had become so important, maybe the tower was in fact the home of a local baron. That would explain the money that had been expended on building up the defences. Maybe there was a genuine military threat that they may have had to face. Forge, whilst being by necessity a practical man, enjoyed thinking on the hows, whys and wherefores of such mysteries as this fort presented. It helped pass the time and stimulated his mind. No doubt he, Sergeant Mac and the others would spend time arguing out the finer details of the defensive specs of the fort. No doubt over a flagon of ale or two. They would certainly have the time over the next few days.

He walked back down to his own encampment. On the way Corporal Jonas joined him briefly to confirm that an initial look at the surrounding area had produced no surprises. It looked like no humans or otherwise had been here in any numbers for a long time. It had occurred to Forge that maybe a Goblin war band or two might have been pushed this far south but that was only wild speculation. There had been no major conflicts with the races of the northern wastes for many years. Man had contented himself with picking fights with his neighbours instead. Indeed, many had forgotten that not so long ago, much of the north had been at war. People often had short memories about stuff that hadn't affected them. Ashkent had been too far south to get directly involved. It had sent troops to help but the civilian population had only whispered at the possibility of the war spreading. Thankfully it had never reached the southern shores of the Gulf. From what Forge had learned of those times, it was a terrible and bloody age.

*　*　*

Later that night Forge, Lieutenant Locke, Sergeant Mac, Portal and Juma, with Private Smitty in tow, gathered to thrash out the plan for the construction of the bridge. Portal started what was to be a very brief discussion with the announcement that he expected the bridge to be ready in no more than three days. Forge stared hard at Portal and then at Juma, who smiled back and nodded his head.

'It can be done. By the third day, the bridge will be ready. By the second day you may cross over safely, Captain,' said Juma.

'OK, I believe you. Don't know why,' replied Forge.

'You will, I'm sure, be pleased to hear that this time-frame is entirely achievable,' said the wizard. 'And that these … men will not have to be worked overhard. I am more than confident in their abilities.'

'Well, that is a relief. I don't suppose that you would care to enlighten me as to why we have been in such a rush?' asked Forge.

'No, Captain I would not care to,' replied Portal irritably. 'We both have our orders. That should be good enough for you.'

Forge sighed. 'I have never really understood the profit motive. It all seems a bit too mercenary.'

'Then perhaps you should look to your own masters, Captain. For are you nought but a mercenary, in this war as in many others your country has involved itself in – unbidden and unwanted?' asked Portal with an evil gleam in his eye.

The last thing Forge wanted was a political discussion at this time of night. He changed the subject quickly on to something he knew more about.

'As of tomorrow morning my men will provide the

guard and protection of the workforce. The bulk of my troops will be employed moving the camp into the old fort and seeing if we can't fix it up a bit. Locke?'

The younger man straightened his shoulders. 'Yes, Sir?'

'I'm putting you in charge of the camp itself; administration and routine. I'll be nabbing some guys for the fort but you'll ensure the infrastructure gets squared away.'

'Perhaps I could organise some fighting patrols?' ventured a disappointed Locke.

'I think we'll leave that for the First Sergeant,' replied Forge. 'For the time being at least.'

'I hardly think that all this is necessary, Captain,' said Portal quickly. Sergeant Mac, who had been playing idly with a stick looked up. That famous snout had obviously picked up on something. 'Your camp here is perfectly adequate,' Portal continued. 'Your scouts have confirmed there are no enemy forces in the area.'

'Absolutely,' replied Forge evenly. 'But it would be wrong of me not to provide the best protection for those under my care as I can. We are days away from any help in a land we do not know.'

'Surely your men would be better employed...'

'No, no,' Forge cut in. 'It will be good for them. They get too sloppy riding horses all day long. I am sure that a bit of labour will be good for them. Unless, of course, there is any other reason?'

He left the question hanging. Portal was silent a moment before nodding swiftly.

'Very well, Captain. If that is your wish. I am sure you will make us very comfortable.' The wizard stood and walked swiftly away.

'Tight arse,' muttered Sergeant Mac.

89

'Loose mouth,' added Juma as he, too, stood and followed Private Smitty back to the Bantusai fires.

Forge and Sergeant Mac exchanged a look and laughed. 'Can't help but like that guy, can you?' commented Sergeant Mac.

'Smart bloke all right. Look, Sarge, we need to watch this. I only wanted to bait Portal a little.'

'You did that,' observed Sergeant Mac. Locke made his excuses and also left the circle.

'But it got me thinking again,' continued Forge. 'Let's just stay extra-special sharp for our time here. There's no reason to worry but...'

'Don't worry, boss. I'll keep the lads frosty. Already got guard shifts organised; a bunch of our guys watching the Bantusai as well. Work starts bright and early tomorrow.'

Sergeant Mac rose and walked into the night. Forge sat and stared into the fire. Oh well, he thought. Let's see what tomorrow brings.

Returning to his tent, Locke fumed. He felt that he was being deliberately ignored in the discussion. OK, perhaps he didn't have much to contribute; he knew little about construction, but he was an officer and ought to have an input. It never struck him that by being invited to the meetings his commander was according him some respect. He still did not understand what on earth they were doing out here. They ought to be engaging in military operations not civil tasks. It just went to show how low in favour Forge must be to have been given this mission. Locke put his hand to his head as a dull wave of pain passed over him. His injury still ached from time to time. Damn, but he had to get out of this unit. He'd never get anywhere in the Army if he stayed here.

Chapter Eight

Forge was woken to the sounds of a camp that was well into its routine. He could hear a number of voices and the sounds of many people going about their business. He had trouble seeing straight due to the sleepy dust in his eye and one hell of a dry throat. He heaved himself out of his cot, scratched various parts of his anatomy, checked his balls were still in the right place and then ventured out, firstly sticking his head into the crisp morning air. For a moment he thought that it was still the night before but then saw the cooking fires of the Quartermaster and, looking up, observed the red sky on the horizon signifying dawn's approach. The First Sergeant always did like an early start. Forge himself was increasingly finding he preferred a slower start to the day. Just another sign of his impending old age. He pulled his boots on and half staggered his way out the gate and over to the river to relieve himself. His attention was drawn to where a number of flames moved amongst the trees. He could see a large number of shadowy forms moving in and out of the circles of light. Forge expected to hear the sounds of axes cutting down the first of the timber but none came.

'Morning, Sir!' said Sergeant Pike cheerfully.

Forge grunted his thanks to the Quartermaster who had arrived with the Captain's morning cup of coffee.

'Funny buggers, ain't they?' said Sergeant Pike.

'What, more than usual?' replied Forge in his usual acerbic morning tone.

'Well, you know, what with that humming and mumbling and shite. Quite distracting really.'

'Uh?' was all Forge could manage.

'The way they get the wood, boss,' explained Sergeant Pike, who was being far too talkative for this time of morning. 'You should listen. They seem to make a song and bosh!'

'Bosh?'

'Wood, boss. Shaped wood.'

'Uh-huh.' Forge wanted to go back to bed.

A couple of dark figures struggled by; they were carrying a long object between them and headed over to the riverbank, where a larger pile of the stuff was being stacked. Private Thom stood to one side with a torch, watching the work. Forge joined him and Private Thom stood to attention.

'Morning, Sir,' he said smartly.

'Apparently. So, what's all this then?' asked Forge.

'Planks, Sir. Got at least twenty of 'em. Not bad for an hour's work.'

'Planks?'

'Yup. Seems that this is just the supporting joists. They want to get some big stuff to drive into the river, so that means going deeper into the woods but they are waiting until it gets a bit lighter. That right, Kely?' Private Thom asked of a well-muscled Bantusai who had deposited another load.

Kely rubbed his hands to get rid of some dirt and nodded. He was much bulkier than Juma and the start of grey hair at his temples suggested he was in his mid-thirties, if not older. 'Yes, no need walking into tree. Hurts head,' he said, tapping his forehead.

92

Private Thom laughed. 'Aye, just plain stupid that.'

Kely grinned and rejoined his companion who was walking towards the forest.

Forge looked at Private Thom, who just shrugged. Since when did he feel so ill informed that even his men had a better grasp of the situation than himself?

He followed Kely into the woodline. He wanted to witness these guys in action. He could see that dawn was well on its way now and that he could pick his way quite easily. A short distance in he saw another of his men standing a few yards away from a Bantusai who appeared to be leaning against a tree. He joined the soldier, who put his finger to his lips and gestured towards the man by the tree. Forge looked over and could see where a Bantusai was standing as if he were trying to push the tree down. Now that he was still and quiet he could hear a faint murmuring coming from the black man. He leaned closer and could discern a definite musical lilt to the noise. The man was moving his hands slowly up and down the bark of the trunk as he sang.

The soldier leaned close to Forge. 'Watch this, Sir. It's amazin',' he whispered.

Forge gave him a quizzical look and stared back at the tree. He couldn't quite believe what was happening in front of him. As the man continued to softly sing, his hands pressed more firmly against the unyielding wood, then gently they seemed to melt or merge into the very bark itself. A few moments later he pulled back from the tree. As he did so, his hands appeared holding on to a piece of wood that seemed as if it had already been cut into shape. He had reached into the living tree and had just taken a part of it. How in the Nine Hells did that work? This was some crazy magic all right. He walked back out into the proper light of dawn and went in search of Sergeant Mac. He found him standing by the riverbank talking with Juma.

'Gentlemen,' said Forge.

'Morning, Sir,' saluted Sergeant Mac.

'I see you have not yet dressed,' commented Juma dryly.

Forge looked down at himself. Juma had a point. Boots, breeches and undershirt were not exactly fit for war. 'Got sidetracked.'

'Juma was just asking if he could send some guys over the river,' said Sergeant Mac.

'What for?' asked Forge.

'If I send some of my people across, we can begin work on the far end of the bridge. It will be quicker,' explained Juma.

'I said we would have to check with you. Don't want to let these blokes go wandering off by themselves. No offence, Juma,' added Sergeant Mac.

Juma tilted his head in acknowledgement.

'Wouldn't be a good idea you being over there unprotected. How you getting across?' asked Forge.

'I will move upstream a small distance. The river is fast. I will swim and will arrive there,' Juma indicated the far side. 'If you tie me with rope I will not be taken. Then I will tie it to a tree and others may use it to follow.'

Makes sense thought Forge. 'Still, my men would have to be lightly armed. Can't have them humping all their kit across.'

'Only for one day. We will have made a way across by the time the sun sleeps.'

'You think that you can have that much done in one day?' asked Sergeant Mac.

'You have seen what we do. It will be so.'

'Juma, you will have to explain how you do that stuff to me,' said Forge with a mixture of admiration and disbelief.

'I will try, Captain. But will you allow me to swim?' asked Juma.

'Yeah, reckon I can let you go across. But the first men over will be my guys. Just to check out the area.'

Juma nodded. 'Very well, I shall prepare.'

As Juma walked off, Sergeant Mac folded his arms. 'Just to check out the area and to make sure we stop any of 'em making a breakout,' he observed.

'Damn right. Having seen these guys in action I think we might have to double the guard. Better send Jonas across first,' said Forge.

Sergeant Mac laughed. 'Oh he's gonna love you.'

Forge shrugged. There wasn't anything that he hadn't been called or that he had heard said about him that could shock anymore. Still, Corporal Jonas did have a way with words.

'I'm off to get dressed and have breakfast,' said Forge. 'Let me know when they are set on the other side.'

The crossing went smoothly enough. As predicted, Corporal Jonas had responded to the task with a suitably pithy response. He nevertheless shed himself of armour and his jerkin, wrapped his bow in a waterproof oilskin which he tied to his back and then wrapped the rope around his waist. He made his entry into the water some fifty yards further upstream and then allowed the fast-moving current to take him. He struck out for the far side strongly and covered the distance quickly. He still ended up going past the agreed point by about another fifty yards. This was greeted by catcalls and abuse from the other soldiers who were watching. He climbed out of the

95

water, gave them a crude gesture and then moved swiftly into the treeline, unwrapping his bow as he went.

A few minutes later he emerged and gave the all-clear. He tied the rope around a sturdy oak and then called for the slack to be taken up. Once the line had been made taut and tied off on the home bank, a further six soldiers, clad similarly to Corporal Jonas, struggled their way across. As they waded in, it only took a few yards before it became impossible to stand on the bottom. They were then reduced to the slow and laborious hand-over-hand method, using the rope suspended above them. It became difficult at the centre of the flow, as the men were caught up in the strong current. A moment of panic ensued as one hapless individual lost his grip and was whisked away. Fortunately he had the presence of mind to continue swimming to the far side. He arrived back at the site ten minutes later looking bedraggled and suitably chastened. It wasn't so much his near-death experience that bothered him, more the constant steam of abuse he would no doubt get from his mates that evening. Next came a party of eight Bantusai led by Kely. The big man had given a thumbs-up to Sergeant Mac and informed him that they would 'be back for scoff tonight'. He then plunged into the water and made it across with his companions without any mishap.

Later that morning Forge took a party of twenty soldiers and set about clearing the new site for the camp. He had a plan in mind to incorporate the old fort into their own usual camp structure. He would house the Bantusai within the walls, which would make guarding them easier. The first step was to remove the flora that had grown around the clearing. He split the men into two parties. The first group he had doing the digging and dragging away of the undergrowth, whilst the other group he tasked to commence the removing of the rubble and useless, rotten wood from within the walls themselves. This humping and dumping work continued until they broke for lunch. As they wandered back, Forge noted that the men were laughing and joking. They were clearly in good spirits and morale was on the up. It was heartening to see his men in such a mood. Just putting some distance between themselves and the Duke had been the best thing to happen to the company for a while.

Forge felt a renewed confidence that the company would never shatter in combat; they would always give the utmost commitment to the fight. Its spirit could not be broken in battle, even if it could be severely damaged by misuse and lack of care. Morale had been affected by poor leadership and poor decisions. Neither Forge nor his men were blind patriots without a proper sense of right and wrong, but all the same you had to believe in something. For them it was the brotherhood of the 7th Mounted Infantry. A lot of the guys had nothing else to call home. Forge, if he admitted it to himself, was the same. He still maintained quarters within the barracks back in Ashkent, even though officers and sergeants didn't have to live in if they didn't want to. Not for the first time he began to wonder how much longer it would be before he gave up life in the field for a more sedate existence.

As Forge ruminated on his future he glanced over at the worksite. There was already the semblance of the beginnings of a pier being constructed. Two large and thick, vertical posts had been placed in deep holes. In fact, they looked more like complete tree trunks. They had been placed some ten feet apart and would act as the major load bearers for much of the bridge weight. On the far side one post was already in and the other hole was being dug. Usually a surveyor would have laid out guide strings to ensure the two sides were level. Not these guys. Forge did a rough guestimate and figured that they were close enough. He put it down to another example of their strange talents. On the far side he could see a similar number of wooden posts and planks being stacked by the water's edge. He could see only two of his men, standing by the planks in conversation. The professional in him said that meant the Bantusai had the guards at a disadvantage in numbers within the wood. However, he trusted his men to be keeping an eye on things. He also didn't feel that these guys would take off without their leader.

As he wandered over to the commissary tent to grab some stew he noticed that Sergeant Pike was busy directing operations down by the ropeway. He had got one of the Bantusai to fashion him a crude, bowl-shaped vessel, which was now being attached to the main rope. Within it he had put lunch for the men working on the far side. The Quartermaster had secured cloth over the top to offer some protection against the elements. The safety rope that the men had been using earlier was also attached to the bowl. It would be used to pull the bowl across. There was much shouting and banter coming from men on both sides of the river and he even heard bets being taken on whether the bowl would make it across.

Taking a piece of bread and a bowl of stew, Forge hunkered down to watch the performance. One of his men took up the strain of the rope and began to slowly pull the food towards the far bank. The bowl itself was caught in the swift current and had a tilt to it that meant the water was only inches way from the lip. As the pulley rope dragged it forwards this only helped to take the tilt to the edge of the lip. Hoots and cheers came from the home bank whilst on the far side the men waited quietly. Sergeant Grippa stood by the soldier whispering choice words of encouragement. Forge dunked his bread into his stew without taking his eyes from the scene. Slowly the package made its way across the river until it was only a few feet away from the bank. Private Thom rushed into the water, grabbed the bowl and dragged it on to dry land. Behind him the big shape of Kely ran up, untied the rope and lifted the bowl (which was none too light) above his head in a display of triumph. The far bank erupted into cheers whilst those near Forge hurled abuse and catcalls. Forge grunted and smiled. Sergeant Pike trotted back up to his kitchen looking pleased with himself.

A few moments later Corporal Kyle joined Forge.

'Back, Sir!' said Kyle brightly.

'No shit,' smiled Forge. 'So what did you find?'

'Well, headed out just after daybreak, just like you said. Followed the line of the river north for about three hours. Something of a game trail running alongside it. About a quarter-mile from here the river gets narrower. Deeper and stronger, too. Ten minutes' walk further on the land starts to climb. Pretty rapidly as it goes. What we get into is some real hilly and wild country up there. Before you know it that river is flanked by one hell of a gorge. I carried on for another couple of hours and I guess we're talking fifty-foot drops over a span of about the same width. Rapids too, here and there.'

'So what do you reckon?' asked Forge.

'My guess is that the gorge cracks on right up to the mountains. And I sure didn't see anyone rushing to build any rope bridges up there. Guess our intel was right.'

'Jonas back from the south yet?'

'Not yet, boss. Knowing him he's probably gone into Shifter again.'

'Cheers, Kyle. Tomorrow I want you and Jonas to go and scout round the eastern side of the Rooke. Go get yourself some scoff,' suggested Forge. 'That's if you didn't stuff yourself with nuts and berries like you normally do,' he added.

Kyle grinned and went off to get some stew. Forge mulled over that information. He had wanted to check if this exercise truly was a necessity. By the sounds of it, this area was indeed the first practicable site for a crossing south of the mountains. The country to the north of them had probably never had any real habitation and had remained only a source of game for those who lived on the northernmost borders of Graves. Hence the remains of the earlier settlement and watchtower. Still, it didn't sit easy, him and his boys being used as building contractors. Some ten minutes later he saw Corporal Kyle heading back out into the woods. On questioning he said that he had been nabbed by Sergeant Pike to go get some meat for the evening meal. Forge suggested he take a break first but Corporal Kyle just shrugged, saying he would get some rest whilst waiting for supper to show up.

Corporal Jonas soon arrived back from his recce from the south. Stopping to grab a brew, he joined Forge.

'Not much, boss. River bends away to the east about a mile away. I carried on following it. There was a game trail a bit like the one Kyle used. After a while it turns south-east again.'

'Life?' asked Forge.

'Jack shit.'

'No crossings then?' Forge prompted. Sometimes it was like getting blood from a bloody stone from Jonas.

The wiry corporal shrugged. 'River gets a bit wider, still deeper than a man though.'

Forge decided to leave it there. Jonas would have done a thorough job.

'All right, Corporal. Tomorrow you are across the river. Kyle's just headed out to catch supper. You joining him?'

'Bugger that. His own fault for getting back early.'

As Corporal Jonas strode off, Forge marvelled at how the half-Elf scout displayed absolutely none of the poise and grace one expected of his woodland kin. Still, he was glad really; he found Elves incredibly boring.

For the rest of the day he took only an occasional interest in the bridge build and put his efforts into overseeing the fort reconstruction. He rather enjoyed seeing everyone busying themselves with the tasks at hand. As the sun began its final descent into dusk he was pleased with the results. Around the fort there was now a clear field of vision all the way to where the woods started proper. To the north, the encroaching forest had been pushed back to a fifty-yard open run. The detritus from inside the fort had been cleared away and all the stone that had looked like it could be reused had been placed in a pile by the gateway. The next stage had been to place a wall of palisade stakes running parallel to the eastern wall, starting from just inside the gate wall's eastern arm and moving straight across the floor of the fort until it met the far northern wall. In so doing they had created a rectangular cage for the Bantusai with three stone walls and one wooden one. There had been only one area of the eastern wall that had needed to be augmented by the placing of more palisade stakes. As long as it was well lit, a guard in the tower and another by the gateway should suffice. That way, anyone attempting to scale the walls

101

would be seen and an arrow in the back would be the reward.

He had grand plans for repairing the walls themselves, getting a new rampart built and maybe constructing some new gates. It would be good if they could actually move into the fort itself. It may be a tight squeeze but the horses could be corralled outside and a separate area built for Sergeant Pike's set-up. They could build a new ditch and palisade as an outer ring. He felt that reconstructing the tower may be too great a task given the timeframe and the resources needed. But he looked forward to outlining his plans to Sergeant Mac and the others. He felt sure they would have their own input regarding the venture.

Forge wandered out of the fort and back to the encampment. A couple of hours earlier he had seen Corporal Kyle return with a couple of deer and some rabbits. Not bad for an afternoon's work. He could see the cook fires burning and had been sniffing the savoury scent of meat in the air for some fifteen minutes now; his stomach had been rumbling for about the same period of time. He diverted his path towards the bridge to see how it was looking. It suddenly occurred to him that he hadn't really considered how the men on the opposite side were going to get back across. Forge figured they would have to use the rope again; an option he was sure at least one individual he knew would not be best pleased about. As he joined a knot of men on the near side he was somewhat surprised to see the solution.

As the Bantusai were rounded up to be escorted back, he watched as one by one figures trod warily over the river. It turned out that on both sides of the Rooke piers had been constructed, with the home side's being more advanced out into the water. Whilst they were simple affairs, lacking any railings either side, they appeared sturdy enough. Underneath he could see the large wooden supporting beams had been driven through the water and deep into the ground. The pier ended with two further supports standing alone in the water. The gap between them and the nearest supports on the far side was about six yards and a long plank had been manoeuvred out and rested on the left-hand side. It was here that the last of their slaves were picking their way across. The guards followed them at a rather slower and less sure pace. Last across was Corporal Jonas. He then chivvied the whole party back towards the camp. Forge joined the scout as the men walked slowly back.

'I'm impressed. Any problems?' he asked.

Corporal Jonas shook his head. 'Nope. The guys say they didn't cause any trouble and just seemed happy to be getting on with the work. They were even quite happy to piss about in the water. Bloody weirdos. It's icy cold that stuff.'

'Imagine they're used to water a bit warmer,' mused Forge.

'They can keep it,' Jonas replied.

'I guess you went for a look around before heading off tomorrow?'

'A quick one. The track is still pretty obvious. Heads east for a bit then turns north. If there has been anyone around it hasn't been recent.'

'Well, I guess they are hoping for more business when this thing opens up,' surmised Forge. 'But we'll be long gone.'

The two men were the last back into the Ashkent camp. Only the two sentries on picket duty in the entrance were outside the perimeter. Corporal Kyle was waiting there for

103

Jonas. The scout took his leave of the Captain and the two men moved out for their silent patrol.

Over supper Captain Forge wandered across the camp to join Juma and his men. The Bantusai were sitting in a group with two guards watching over them. The atmosphere was light-hearted, however. There had been good-natured banter amongst Forge's men and the slaves all day. It seemed that the soldiers had gained a respect for the skills and attitude of their charges. Like them, the Bantusai had accepted their lot and got on with the job at hand. Juma was in conversation with Kely when the Captain approached. He glanced up, smiled and indicated that Forge should sit. Kely withdrew to let the two men talk.

'So, do you like our work?' Juma asked.

'Well, I'll wait till you're finished. But you don't mess about, do you?'

Juma looked shocked. 'No, Captain. We don't mess about.'

Forge put his hands up in a placating gesture. 'No, I meant you aren't slow in your work.'

Juma looked pleased and had a devious look in his eye. 'I am sorry, Captain. I know what you meant. I am making fun.'

Forge gave him a hard stare. Juma laughed.

'In answer to your question, yes, we have been quick today. Tomorrow I think we will have a bridge that can be crossed by many men.'

'Finished in two days then?' asked Forge.

'It will be finished properly in three, but it will work in two.'

'Good job!' He looked down at the mug of ale he was

104

carrying and offered some to Juma. He looked at the mug, cocked an eyebrow at Forge and then accepted the mug and took a sip. 'Gah, it is a bitter drink. Not like ours. We sweeten with honey.' He then smiled and offered it back. 'But a man can get used to many things and a drink shared freely is not to be dishonoured.'

Forge took the mug back, sipped and thought for a moment.

'When we are done here, what will happen to you?'

Juma shrugged. 'Then our new master will have more work for us. We are useful.'

'Guess so,' said Forge. 'Nice to be wanted.' He got up and bid Juma goodnight.

Juma inclined his head in return. As he went Kely rejoined his chief and the two began to talk softly to each other. A group of his men then burst into a song. It was a tune and a manner of singing that none present, except perhaps one or two of the older heads, had ever heard before. One of the Bantusai sang in a strong, warbling tone for a line or two before being joined in a chorus by the other men. Then another would sing, followed by a chorus and so it went. Those of Ashkent were silent and found the music gentle and soothing. Even hypnotic, thought Forge to himself as he stood there, in the darkness between fires. He felt a strange kind of peace and found himself imaging a life that was empty of war, politics and the cold hand of chance. Where a man could live a life without fear of dying by the arrow of an unseen archer. Where those that deserved life would not lose it at a whim in a place where justice did not exist. He found, for a moment, a calm and a peace he had not felt since ... well since he couldn't remember. Certainly not for the last few years of his war-torn life.

As the singing finished, the spell was broken and the men of the company clapped and cheered. For the most part, the Bantusai smiled and grinned with pleasure. As he went to make his leave Forge caught Juma staring at him with a thoughtful look in his eye. Then it was gone and replaced with a smile. Forge nodded and moved away. He felt disarmed but wasn't sure why. Behind him Smitty and Thom had decided to treat the Bantusai to a rendition of their favourite drinking songs. Forge shook his head with a wry smile, feeling sorry for the strangers and walked away from the group.

Forge walked over to another fire where Portal sat waiting with Sergeant Mac.

The wizard looked up with eager eyes.

'So, Captain. It appears that all is going well. I understand that the day after tomorrow we will be finished here.'

'Seems so,' agreed Forge, switching into defensive mode.

'And we can travel back to inform the Duke that our task has been successful. Believe me, the Duke will be pleased that everything has gone without a hitch.'

'I'm very happy for him.'

Portal fixed him with a stare.

'You should be. The Duke has been displeased with your attitude and performance of late.'

'Well, he can carry on being so. And tell him from me he can shove this bridge up his arse for all I care. You can go back now if you want. I have no intention of hurrying back just yet. I'm getting used to my men not being sent off and getting killed under your boss's orders.'

Portal bristled. 'You have specific instructions, Captain. Do not think you can get rid of me that easily. I will stay and ensure you do as *our* commander wishes.'

He got up and stormed off.

'Does that a lot these days,' observed Sergeant Mac.

'Yeah, was it something I said?' asked Forge dryly.

'Probably. You know, I have actually talked to him a couple of times. Found out a few things, too.'

'What, other than that his preferred sexual implement is a vegetable?'

'No,' Sergeant Mac continued with the practised air of a man well used to ignoring his boss's less savoury comments. 'More like his family are Shifter stock.'

Forge raised his eyebrows at that. 'Well, well, well. Sounds like some divided loyalties there.'

'Not sure about that.' Sergeant Mac paused and drank some coffee from his mug. 'They *were* Shifter until they were killed for planning sedition. As Portal puts it, they backed the wrong side in a local power dispute. He was still a teenager, sent to study magic under some second-rate hedge wizard further south. After he learnt about his ma, pa and little brothers being taken out he figured that he wasn't safe in Shifter. Took off for the border before anyone could nobble him.'

'So he sought refuge with Burns?' asked Forge.

'Nope. Not right away. Did some government work in the capital for a while. Pissed people off there and then came up north.'

'So he didn't continue with his magic?'

'From what he says, it doesn't sound like it,' agreed Sergeant Mac.

'So basically he's a bloody civil servant,' said Forge in an annoyed voice, throwing his hands up in the air. 'He might've been able to turn frogs into toads once. Now the only thing he's good at is over-inflating his opinion of himself.'

107

Sergeant Mac shrugged.

'Maybe, boss. But he ain't no fool. He plays political games. And you and I know; never trust a politician.'

'I'll drink to that.' Forge took a long draught of the ale he had been nursing. 'Anyway, I want to talk over my grand plans for our new fortress.'

Sergeant Mac grunted in mirth. 'I wondered when you might let forth on that one.' He turned his head and cupped his hand to his mouth. 'Hey, Jonas, Sergeant Grippa, Pikey. The boss is gonna tell us what a master of engineering he is again.' Men turned round and laughed as those called gathered round to talk shop.

Later, the Bantusai were ordered up and taken back under guard to their new home. It was a strange sight as they laughed and joked with the Ashkent men; they seemed like friends of old walking back home together. Forge noticed that some of the slaves were carrying blankets and others piles of wood and kindling. He walked up to Sergeant Pike and gave him a half-accusing, half-quizzical look. Sergeant Pike looked suitably embarrassed and shrugged his shoulders.

'Well, you know, it's still chilly of a night and they ain't got tents or warm bedrolls like our guys. So I thought to myself a nice little fire might do the trick. Just to take the edge off, so to speak.'

Captain Forge shook his head in astonishment. 'There was a time, Sergeant, when it was easier to get an egg from a rooster than to get anything free, and not signed for first, from you.'

'I know that, Sir. Can't help liking 'em, can you? I must be getting soft in me old age.'

'Don't remind me,' said Forge ruefully.

With that he went to find his own bed. Damn, but his joints were starting to ache. Why did Pikey have to start talking about old age?

Chapter Nine

Early the following morning Corporal Jonas led the guard shift over the half-built bridge to the far side of the river. Following closely behind were a bunch of Bantusai with Juma leading the way. The scout noted that they were in good spirits; they laughed and talked in their fast-paced tongue. Juma had a wide smile on his face.

'You guys seem a lot happier these days,' stated Corporal Jonas.

Juma nodded. 'It is good to be working like this again. Good because we remember what it was like to be at home. Singing to the wood is special to us.'

'Singing is special to me. 'Cept I don't think you'd like the lyrics of my songs,' called one of the soldiers.

'Perhaps we might trade song stories. We have many to do with mating you might like,' offered Juma.

'Great. More songs about shagging,' muttered Corporal Jonas to the amusement of the guard shift.

'For a devious bastard you are a right prude, Jonas,' laughed the musical soldier.

'Piss off and get to work,' suggested Corporal Jonas. This caused more amusement.

For all that the scout was colourful in his brevity and opinions on life, he was strangely respectful of womankind. Most figured it was because they were the one species he could never figure out and therefore could never predict, hunt or track. His nemesis. A lot of the guys could at least appreciate that sentiment.

Corporal Jonas stared around the clearing and sniffed the air. He walked towards the treeline and stared into the pre-dawn gloom.

'You worry?' asked Juma, who had joined him by the clearing edge.

'Not sure,' admitted Corporal Jonas. He continued to stare into the trees, his eyes moving left and right so that his peripheral vision, which was better adapted to darkness, might pick up something. He cocked his head, trying to pick out the one sound that might be alien to the forest.

Juma also studied the darkness. 'I too feel something is wrong.'

'Wrong but hidden,' said Jonas. He pulled his bow from off his back and notched an arrow. He moved slowly to where the overgrown path opened into the clearing. He then pushed on to the path itself and took a few tentative steps along it into the darker confines of the forest. He then knelt and allowed his senses to open up to his surroundings. He did not strain himself to see what was there; rather he remained passive, breathing slow and evenly. He tried to siphon out the noise of the work going on behind him by the riverbank. Corporal Jonas trusted his instincts. He was seldom spooked for no reason. There was, or had been, a presence nearby. He was sure of it. And he was pretty damn sure that whatever it was, it was doing a bloody good job of not being tracked. He hoped it wasn't some sort of supernatural beastie. He bloody hated them and they never wanted to die easy.

Behind him he sensed Juma come up. These Bantusai were good at woodcraft as well. Jonas reckoned that Juma had wanted him to know he was there and could quite happily fade away if he so wished. The fact that Juma thought the same as he was more than enough proof for Corporal Jonas. He still wanted something physical though. A trace was all he needed and then straight back to the Captain. He glanced back briefly and locked eyes with Juma. The other man had a thoughtful, intent expression. Corporal Jonas pointed towards the path and inclined his head. Juma nodded his understanding. The two slowly stood and began to make their way along the path. They had penetrated some ten yards along it when Juma stopped and took a deep smell of the air. Corporal Jonas did the same. There. An odour. Something that was out of place. Corporal Jonas crouched and glanced around him. He scanned the undergrowth, searching through the detritus that littered the floor of the forest path. It was beginning to get lighter and he could pick out individual objects but nothing that shouldn't be there. Then he stopped. Just ahead he saw what he had been looking for. The soil had been disturbed; twigs broken and earth and leaf compacted by weight. Something had been on this path but had ventured no further on it towards the water's edge. Could it be a deer or boar? No, too much disturbance. Maybe a litter then? No, something bigger. He felt a tap on his shoulder. He glanced up at Juma, who was bent over him. Juma pointed at his own nose and then at a point on the ground. The soldier followed the finger and saw, at the edge of the path proper, a black shape. No, not a shape, a mark. A mark with a particular smell. He touched the shape and brought his finger to his nose. It was tobacco. That was all the proof he needed. He stood up and motioned to Juma to head back.

'Morning,' said a voice from behind him. He spun round, raising his bow.

'I wouldn't,' suggested the voice.

Corporal Jonas could not make out the face but he could see a figure standing on the side of the path a few yards away from where he had crouched. The figure held a crossbow pointed right at him.

'And before you think about having a go 'cos there are two of you, there are another five of these aimed right at you.'

'I got the dark feller, Hollis,' piped up a rasping voice from the undergrowth.

'Yeah, cheers, Hoarty,' said the figure.

'I think we have found our visitors,' said Juma sardonically.

'No shit,' muttered Jonas as he lowered his bow.

Forge was making his way back from having a very satisfying bowel movement when he noticed that the camp seemed to be in a state of mild excitement. There seemed to be a buzz in the air at any rate. He had already noted that there had been an outbreak of good morale. Have to stamp that out, he thought, smiling to himself. As he entered the outer gates he glanced over at the commissary tent. Ah, that'll be why then. He counted four men and probably one woman who were dressed in a mixture of furs and animal skins. They also looked as if they hadn't had a wash in a while; in fact one of them, who looked particularly ancient, seemed to be held together by dirt. They were hunkered down by the fire, greedily consuming some bread and broth that Sergeant Pike had provided. Corporal Jonas and two others stood to one side, keeping a watch. By his feet was a pile of weapons: four crossbows, a couple of short bows and hunting knives. Forge guessed these guys were probably

113

trappers or some such. He also saw that Corporal Jonas had one hell of a sour expression. At least, a lot worse than usual.

'We have guests, Corporal?' asked Forge.

'The Sarge is in your tent, Sir,' was Corporal Jonas's curt reply.

Forge's eyebrow raised in surprise. Curious indeed. He wandered over to his tent and entered. Crowded inside were Locke, Sergeant Mac, Portal and another one of the new arrivals. The man looked tired and travel-weary. He was sporting several days' growth of beard, which added to the general grime of his appearance. Despite these factors, Forge guessed him to be around thirty, noting the ponytail of blond hair and the piercing blue eyes.

'Gentlemen,' said Forge, gazing at each man in turn.

'Sir, this man has some news he thinks might be of interest,' said Lieutenant Locke.

'Although thoroughly doubtful, from what I have heard so far,' added Portal airily.

'Yes, well. Corporal Jonas found these guys on the far bank and brought them in,' said Sergeant Mac.

'OK,' sighed Forge. He sank heavily into his chair and stared up at the young man. He guessed this wasn't going to be good. 'My name is Captain Jon Forge. Officer Commanding the 1st Company of the 7th Mounted Infantry Regiment. Ashkent Expeditionary Force under General McKracken.' He spread his arms wide. 'Let's have it.'

The man folded his arms and stared hard at Forge, who had to admit that, whatever else, those blue eyes were both intelligent and hard.

'My name is Holis Lode. From what was the town of Noel's Gap. About a week away from here to the north and east.'

114

'*Was* the town?'

'Aye. Right until a whole bunch of Harradan fell upon it. We are all that is left of it. And those bastards are right on our tails.'

'You see, Captain?' said Portal. 'These men are fugitives and are being hunted down. We should send them on their way. It is of no concern to us.'

Lode's eyes fell upon Portal and the man visibly flinched.

'You don't get it, do you? We were just in the way. They're coming here.'

Forge knew it. Just as he was starting to have a good time. 'Are you telling me that there is a force of men making their way here, right now? To this place?'

'Yes.'

'OK, how many?'

'We reckon about two thousand or so. Minus the few we've already killed.'

Sergeant Mac whistled in surprise. Locke looked shocked and Portal looked outraged. Forge just felt depressed. He hated being right all the time. This job had always stank of shit and double-cross. And guess what? Here comes the sucker punch.

'I think you had better start at the beginning,' he said to Lode. He could feel that sinking sensation creeping up on him again.

Over the next few minutes Holis retold the tale of the fall of Noel's Gap, the subsequent flight of the survivors through the forest and the appearance of Shifter troops with the Harradan. Before he had stopped speaking, Forge had already put a few pieces of a puzzle together and didn't like what he was hearing. He glanced over at Sergeant Mac, who was clearly thinking along the same

115

lines, and then at Portal who was looking decidedly uncomfortable.

'All right, Mr Lode. I am going to assume that what you have told me is not a pile of steaming bullshit. So what I then want to know is what the fuck is going on, Portal?' He shifted his gaze suddenly towards the wizard. Portal put his hands up in a placatory gesture.

'I assure you, Captain. I do not know anything about this. Surely I would not be so foolish as to accompany you on this trip if I knew of the fate awaiting you.'

'Come on, Portal. I'm not a completely stupid bastard. Your boss suddenly wants a bridge built in the middle of fucking nowhere, sends us off with some cock-and-bollocks story about trade routes and says it has to be built bloody yesterday. Oh, and here's some really clever bloody jungle boys who can knock it up for you.'

'I know how it looks but I have no part in this. The Duke never ...'

'The Duke is a fucking traitorous bastard! That's what the Duke is,' shouted Forge. 'Give me one good reason why I shouldn't arrest you where you stand. Or are you going to magic your way out of this?'

Portal shook his head. 'I have no excuses but to protest my innocence. Besides I do not have the skill to dispatch all of you before I too was killed.'

'Damn right,' said Sergeant Mac.

'You might not have that sort of combat magic, but I bet you have a few tricks up your sleeve, don't you? From here on in you are confined to your quarters.' He glanced towards his tent flap. 'Corporal Colls?' he called out.

A passing soldier stuck his head in.

'Yes, Sir?'

'Take this individual to his tent and then mount a two-

116

man guard on it. Then mount another guard to watch them from a safe distance. No one goes in and he does not come out without my permission.'

'Yes, Sir!'

Without another word Portal stalked out of the tent. Forge turned his attention back to Holis Lode. 'I think you should go get some food.'

'What are you going to do?' Lode asked.

'That is what I am going to figure out now. Lieutenant, find a spot for our guests and let Sergeant Pike know they will be staying with us.

'Yes, Sir,' replied the young officer and strode out of the tent. Lode nodded at Forge and followed him out.

Forge indicated to Sergeant Mac to take the other chair and the grizzled soldier took it thankfully.

'We have been thrown into a bloody set-up,' said Forge. 'Burns has ground us down. Weakened us. What's left he sent here to do his dirty work. Build a bridge and then these Harradan cross, wipe us out and move down to join forces with him. Bloody clever. As the only people who could have reacted, he has tried to remove us from the frame.'

'Except he didn't expect us to find out that they were coming,' added Sergeant Mac.

'Right,' agreed Forge. 'We were supposed to have been surprised while we slept. Probably that bastard out there would have cast a sleep spell on us or something. Gods alive. He wanted to open up the northern flank take McKracken by surprise. Roll up our forces; get behind the supply lines. What a damn shitstorm that would be.'

'So we're taking this Lode feller's word for it then? We don't know him, so it's hard to trust him,' proffered Sergeant Mac.

117

'S'pose we shouldn't do really. But it all makes too much sense. We've always known Burns was a devious bastard. He has already shown he'll turn to whoever will give him power or money. No doubt he has been maintaining good relations with Shifter during the whole conflict. Perhaps even earlier; we know he has financial links there.'

'So the plan is ...?'

This gave Forge pause for thought. What if Lode was selling a load of bullshit? Forge had never heard of Noel's Gap, but he had heard of the Harradan. Disjointed clans mostly. But vicious buggers. Burns must have promised a lot to get a force of that size on his side. Hell, he probably expected to run Graves himself as a province of Shifter and could therefore afford the costs. Whatever, none of this helped with his immediate problems. He believed Lode all right, though by rights he should check his story out. But if he were telling the truth, then they didn't have much time. Time for what, though?

'Looks like we have two choices,' he said to Sergeant Mac.

The other man scratched his bulbous nose. 'The usual, huh? Stay and fight. Or run.'

'I think the term is "tactical withdrawal" but yes,' said Forge. 'I would like some proof though. Just to satisfy my own curiosity. Get some idea of the type of troops we are facing. That way we can work out how to play this. By the sounds of it they are walkers, not cavalry.'

'Except for some of the Shifter guys they have with them,' added Sergeant Mac.

'So we could make a run for it. Get back to Burns' gaff in a day and a half. Give him a surprise.'

'There's about a hundred and fifty levied troops

stationed with him. I doubt they would know what their lord had in mind, let alone be inclined to fight for him if they knew. So we can neutralise that force with a bit of savvy. Then it's still another day's hard ride south to our boys in the 7th,' said Sergeant Mac.

'So by then the Harradan get across. Best forces we could muster would be what? Three hundred in the regiment, plus another couple of hundred more locals within a day.'

'For what they're worth. Only good at making up the numbers,' added Sergeant Mac.

'Well, we need numbers. We could expect elements of the 5th Regiment to arrive the following day. If we destroy the bridge immediately the Harradan would still have gotten across by then, though slower than they would have wanted. That would have lost them surprise and any prep time they might have wanted. In that scenario I reckon we could handle them. Hells, they might even give up and go home if they find that Burns has been taken out. But we don't know whether by reacting to this invasion, by pulling back and then calling the 5th to join us, we are just opening gaps in the border for other incursions.' Forge chewed his lip. 'Shifter is expecting the 7th to be hit and destroyed. Once that has happened they would be working on our response to be one of two things. Either the 5th moves to the north in response to the 7th's plight and Shifter moves into Graves. Or the 5th stays put in a defensive posture because it is waiting for McKracken to move up with reserve troops from the south. In that scenario Shifter will only attack once the Harradan engage us from the north, and then they'll cross the border taking our forces in the rear or flank. Either way, we end up facing them piecemeal or keep pulling back, allowing

119

them to gain ground and consolidate. We just don't know how quickly McKracken can mount an effective response.'

Sergeant Mac listened intently. The Captain was always at his best at times like this. His mind became clear and he was able to quickly grasp the roots of a problem before Mac had time even to begin to worry about the whys and wherefores. It was good to see him at work again.

'Well, why don't we just pull all the way back south to the 5th's location?' asked Sergeant Mac. 'That way we have a combined force of two regiments facing the Harradan and any Shifter troops that have crossed the border to join them.'

'You're right, but it means letting Shifter take a huge chunk of land off Graves, a third of the country. We suddenly find ourselves right back where we started. I have no problems trading ground for time but it'll be a hard slog fighting our way back north again.' Forge nodded to himself. He had reached a decision.

'We are the one thing they weren't expecting. And it's that unexpected thing that always buggers up the best-laid plans. We are going to nip it in the bud. Contain it and rob it of its momentum.'

Sergeant Mac nodded. He wasn't surprised by the conclusion he was hearing. It was just like the boss to be bloody-minded like this.

'So we're staying then, boss.'

'Yup,' said Forge, nodding his head. 'We stay, hold out for as long as we can and kill as many of the bastards as we can. And, if we are lucky and we get a message back to Regiment, then there won't be enough of them left to mount a proper assault by the time relief gets here. Or if we fall before they arrive, wherever they meet the Harradan on their way south.'

'Pardon me, boss, but I'm just doing some maths. There are sixty-seven of us at last count. So that's odds of twenty-two to one roughly. And at best effort, we are looking at five and a half days before we get any help.'

Forge nodded in agreement.

'But on the plus side,' continued Sergeant Mac, 'we do hold the bridge and we have got the makings of a defensive position. So they'd have to do all the work.'

'How far behind did Lode say the Harradan were?' Forge asked.

'Two days roughly.'

'OK, so two days to prepare. We send a rider off soonest and then we have to hold them for three and a half days.' Forge looked at Sergeant Mac with a grim expression. 'Here we go again, Mac.' Then he smiled. 'But this time at least we get to choose the ground.'

Sergeant Mac stood up and stretched. 'Makes a change. Want me to get the boys in?'

'Yeah, council of war I think. Invite Lode, too. And Juma.'

That stopped the Sergeant in his tracks. 'Really?'

Forge glanced up. 'Hell, yes. We just happen to have some of the finest labourers and woodworkers within a thousand miles or so. I want to know exactly what he can do for us.'

'Got a point,' admitted Sergeant Mac as he left to gather the management.

'Oh and, Sarge, get me Corporal Kyle. He'll be heading south.' Sergeant Mac nodded and disappeared.

Forge sat back and rubbed his hands through his closely cropped hair and scratched his beard. They didn't have a chance. Sergeant Mac probably guessed the same but he would never utter it. Less than seventy men could not

121

hope to hold off a force of two thousand, not for as long as they planned to. Give them a day and they would get across the river. Another day perhaps and then an assault. It was a simple numbers game at that point. But he had to try. They all had to try. This was his job and it was his responsibility to make the hard choices. And then live by them, even whilst his men fell around him. They had to buy the time needed for Dav and the rest of the boys of the 7th. Better they lose a company than the whole regiment.

A few minutes later and Corporal Kyle appeared at his tent flap. Forge briefed Kyle to ride as hard as he could to get to the rest of the 7th, find Dav Jenkins and then ride even harder to get back. Corporal Kyle pretty much knew the story anyway. The men had been pressing their new arrivals for information and worked out something was up, something which would probably involve them having to get bloody. Corporal Kyle then took his leave and went to ready his things. Before he left Forge counselled him to be wary and to steer clear of Burns and his troops. He had no doubt that even now they were preparing to join the Harradan when they came south. If the Duke had any sense he would not trust to the complete success of the company's demise. He would have watchers out, looking for any soldiers who might escape the trap and flee southwards. Corporal Kyle nodded. 'Don't worry Sir, they won't sniff me until I ride back with three hundreds swords aimed at their yellow arses.'

Forge smiled and wished him good luck. Once the scout had left he was joined by the brains trust of the outfit. Along with Sergeant Mac came Sergeants Pike and Grippa. They were joined by Locke, Lode and Juma. Also came Corporal Jonas who, whilst not strictly in the hierarchy, gained entry due to his role as lead scout and

122

troublemaker. Over the next twenty minutes Forge outlined the situation, inviting Lode to repeat the pertinent points of his tale and then summarising what he felt to be the courses of action open to them. He intended to deny the bridge to the enemy, then the river and then hold out in the fort for as long as possible. When that went, they would fall back to the tower.

'That will be our redoubt, gentlemen. We make them fight for every bit of ground and we don't make them stop until we are all dead,' he told them. He then looked at Holis. 'Thank you for coming to us. Your actions may have saved the lives of many.'

'But not the lives of my town,' said Lode.

'True, but rest assured we'll make them bleed for that. What about you and your friends? What will you do now? I'd advise you to make plans to move on pretty soon. I think you have done your fair share of killing already.'

'Always room for more,' said Lode simply.

'True. So for your part, I would ask if you would go with Corporal Jonas and show him what our approaching guests look like. I believe what you are saying. Hell, this meeting is counsel to that. But the Corporal is a military man. He might pick up things you missed.'

'Well, me and the boys talked about it already. We'll stay and fight, but don't expect us to hang around when they get across. We aren't soldiers and revenge is no good if you are dead. But we can cast arrows from a safe distance whilst we have them. Yeah, I'll go back across the river.'

'Good,' said Forge. 'And you ...' He turned his gaze to Juma. 'You are still officially slaves but if you stay you'll most likely die.'

Juma shrugged but said nothing.

123

'So, for the next couple of days I'll be using you as my workforce to strengthen the defences of this place. Then, after that, you are free to go. Make your way back to your own lands or whatever. I doubt I'll be in a position to worry about it.'

Juma looked surprised. 'You give what I did not think you would. We will work. We are still slaves.'

Forge nodded. 'Well, we'll keep you in the compound just to make sure. No offence.'

Juma inclined his head graciously. 'I never took any.'

'Captain?'

'Yes, Mr Lode?'

'Holis will do, Captain. One other thing about the Harradan. They aren't just one bunch you know. They're clansmen. If they ain't fighting Goblins and such, hells ...' Lode barked a short laugh. '... They're quite content to fight each other.'

Forge thought for a moment. 'Well, I did figure that it had to be a combined force. Three clans?'

Lode nodded. 'I'd say more like a half-dozen or so. Judging from the different patterns of cloth they are wearing. I tell you, it ain't often that you see that many clans fighting along side each other. Must have been offered a real stack of cash.'

'So they don't like each other much then?' asked Forge.

'From what Old Hoarty says, and he would know, he's never heard of such a large band. The clan leaders don't trust each other. Expect their neighbour to stick a knife in their back given half a chance. And they're probably right,' replied Lode.

'So what can we figure from this?' mused Forge.

'It means they probably aren't a tight, disciplined force,' said Sergeant Mac. 'Too busy watching each other's backs.

I guess they are being held together by a strong personality. Persuasive; keeping the others in line.'

'Could be we might be able to get some of the buggers upset. Lose interest,' added Corporal Jonas.

'Just what I was thinking,' agreed Lode.

'OK. Useful stuff. It may be that these guys might cut and run if they think there is nothing in it for them. Make 'em believe the cost is too high. Sow a bit of discord.' Forge nodded. 'Good. OK, gentlemen. Let's talk about how we organise the welcome party.'

Forge and his men then got down to the nitty-gritty of the tactics they would employ. He took his men outside to better appreciate the ground they would fight on.

'We could just bust the bridge now. But I'd like them to get slowed up before they get to it. Hit 'em, see if they bite, then draw 'em out.' He indicated the skeleton framework of the bridge. No further work had been done on it since the arrival of the trappers. 'We pull back across the Rooke, destroy what we can and then retreat to the fort. Whatever happens, they would not be expecting an attack from a large force. That will slow them down. Make them have to think a bit. When they have sorted that mess out they then have to deal with not having a bridge. It's all about time; if we don't engage them, they walk right on up to where the bridge was then sit down and work out a plan.' Forge stopped to look at his men. 'Every hour we delay them, the nearer our own troops will be to us.'

'How do you figure they'll get across then?' asked Sergeant Grippa.

'They can't come from the north. Corporal Kyle has already checked that out for me. The land rises further up and the Rooke issues from a deep, fast-flowing gorge. They could risk it but it is too near to the fort. The river is stronger and if they lose someone then we might get wind of their crossing. My guess is they would just go south. More places to cross and less chance of resistance. So we plan that they will have to cross further south. That'll take them a while to get across in force.'

'Won't they just pass us by?' asked Sergeant Pike.

'Not if they have a commander with any sense. You don't leave an enemy behind your back. No, they'll want to take us out and that is just what we want them to do.'

'So are we just going to let them get across and surround us?' asked Locke.

'We could put a blocking force further downriver,' suggested Sergeant Mac. 'Try and shadow their movements, identify where they might cross. When they do, hit 'em with missile fire. Then pull back to the fort.'

'Good idea. We can try and match their bet,' agreed Forge. 'But we don't want them to know we're waiting. As soon as we pull back over the bridge they are going to have eyes on us from their side.'

'So we send some guys down to the far side of the clearing and keep watch,' said Sergeant Mac. 'Soon as they see the fort they'll be looking to the south.'

'Yeah, we'll do that,' agreed Forge.

'Got a problem if they have archers,' observed Corporal Jonas, who had been staring over the water. 'They can get a bunch of guys in the wood line opposite the fort. Those trees go right up to the bank, shooting one hundred yards.'

Forge nodded quietly.

'Damn,' said Sergeant Pike. 'They just need to keep lobbing them over our walls. Keep us pinned down nice and tight.'

'Lode, did you see any archers?' asked Forge.

'Not on the Harradan. But the wagon train was full of

126

arrows and bows. But then it isn't their style. They like to get up close.'

'Don't matter how badly aimed the arrows are if you got a hundred coming at yer,' announced Old Hoarty, who had snuck up behind the group uninvited.

Forge glared at him but agreed with the point. 'What about the Shifter men, do you know what type of troops they were?'

Lode shrugged. 'Don't know about that. Military stuff isn't my area.'

'In which case, something for Corporal Jonas and yourself to find out.'

'Sir,' put in Sergeant Mac, 'we seem to be relying heavily on missile fire to keep these guys at bay. But we are infantry. Apart from about half a dozen men with hunting bows, there is only Corporal Jonas with that bloody great longbow of his that knows how to shoot straight.'

'And us too. Most likely worth three men apiece when it comes to hitting a target first time,' piped up Old Hoarty.

'Don't doubt it, old-timer,' said Forge. 'So that's a dozen bowmen. But more would be good. Nothing fancy. I guess our construction crew might be able to help?' He glanced at Juma.

'Yes, we can make bows and use them. But only the wood. We do not have ...' he struggled for the word and mimed the action of pulling back a bowstring.

Sergeant Pike nodded. 'Ah, gut or sinew or some such. Bowstring. That's what you're after.' He spoke slowly and enunciated his words as he would to a simpleton or a child.

Juma smiled and inclined his head. 'Indeed. Bowstring.' He repeated the words like Sergeant Pike had spoken them but laced with sarcasm.

127

It caused a moment of laughter from the others.

'All right, all right,' said Sergeant Pike, clearly embarrassed. 'I'll see what I can rustle up.'

'Good,' said Forge. 'Right, you two.' He indicated Corporal Jonas and Lode. 'I want you leaving in ten minutes. Get to their camp. Have a look-see then get back here soon as. And try not to get caught.' He eyed Jonas, who raised an eyebrow at that unlikely scenario. 'Now let's look at the defences.'

They spent the next hour running through how the defences might be bolstered. Forge was secretly pleased at his own foresight in ordering the clean-up of the fort. It would make the work ahead much easier. It was decided that the first job would be to rebuild the parapet around the walls. They already had a stock of timber that had been collected for use on the bridge the following day. Whilst the Bantusai worked on that, the Ashkent troops could be split. Some would aid the captives they should be guarding, whilst others were sent out into the woods to fell trees. These would then be used to replace the smaller palisade stakes in the walls as a much larger and stronger barrier. A further party of twenty men under Lieutenant Locke would commence the digging of a fire trench that would run around the fort at a distance of twenty yards from the walls, shortening to ten on the river side.

Sergeant Pike and his small quartermaster section went about dismantling the original camp in anticipation of moving into the fort. While this work was going on, and quite forgotten by everyone, the men of Noel's Gap had bivouacked in the trees to the north of the fort. They had rested for a time, lit a fire and had talked amongst themselves. Sleeps and Juggs then disappeared into the forest to check some game snares. The remaining three watched them go with interest.

'Aha, bloody knew it,' said Arald triumphantly.

'Don't take two to check,' sniffed Fuzz.

'I knew them two were at it!' Arald was grinning with self-satisfaction.

'Course they are,' observed Old Hoarty nonchalantly. 'Been rutting since they were kids.'

Arald looked over open-mouthed. 'You bloody knew?'

''Course. Most other people would 'ave figured it if'n Juggs had ever got with child. They never did though. Not much point a marryin' if there ain't a child.'

Fuzz leaned back and scratched his head thoughtfully whilst Arald muttered to himself and poked at the fire.

'Anyway,' continued Old Hoarty, 'I got an idea.'

Another discussed ensued. Then Arald and Fuzz casually wandered down to the bridge site. Most of the work at that time was happening on the western side of the fort; the fire trench would be dug along this side last. So whilst a few noticed the two shabby men pointing and nodding at aspects of the construction, they quickly dismissed them as ignorant civilians and got back to their own ball-breaking tasks. In this way they didn't notice when, with a quick glance around, Fuzz stooped down and collected one of the ropes that had been used the day before and which had been coiled and left for possible future use. Both he and Arald turned and strolled back to their spot in the forest, glancing about with polite interest at the activity around them. Old Hoarty grinned and gave them a discreet thumbs-up as they drew near.

By the end of the day the fort was looking far more respectable. However, there was still much work to be done and it continued for many hours into the night. Forge had torches lit and Sergeant Pike built a large cook fire in the centre of the courtyard. He had cooked up another of his stews using the rest of the meat caught the previous day and was feeding the workers on a rotational basis. In a large pile near the fire was a collection of brush and smaller branches. These were being dried by the heat of the fire deliberately. It would act as the tinder for the fire trench. As they had no pure alcohol, it was critical that the trench could be lit and brought to an adequate flame as quickly as possible. Corporal Jonas still had some of his flammable liquid but Forge was reluctant to use it unless absolutely necessary.

Men were still working on the fire trench and had been joined by those that had been felling trees earlier. The gap in the eastern wall had been replaced with three thick tree trunks that had been cut to fifteen feet in height and then the bottom third lowered into the ground. The work was gruelling and there had been a great deal of cursing, swearing and sexual insults bandied around. The parapet was two-thirds complete and the Bantusai were erecting the final sections. There was very little banging and hammering going on; the Bantusai were using a system of joint and tongue-and-groove fittings to put the wood into position. They also used crude pegs that they moulded into the wood itself. As they worked, instead of the usual banter of construction, gentle murmurings and lilting voices were heard as they sang to the wood. Soldiers followed on behind and tried to make good those parts of the rampart that had crumbled. Crude ladders had been put up to allow access to the upper level, and stone was scavenged from what had been piled outside the fort and from the surrounding ruins. They humped the heavy material to the walls and then heaved them up and into place. Whilst not as solid as the rest of the walls, they would at least afford protection and a shield from missile fire.

Around midnight the men began to retire, exhausted from their day's labour. The Captain insisted that they get sufficient rest as they would need their strength soon enough. The Bantusai returned to their corral and men set to watch them. Though all were tired and the shifts for the guards would be short. The woodworkers did not seem as weary as the soldiers but were soon as sound asleep as the others. Most of the men were now rolled up in their blankets on the floor of the courtyard, up against the walls and partly sheltered by the new walkway above them. Forge slept in the tower by himself. He wanted to see how much of it could be restored tomorrow. This would be their last bastion if the walls were breached. Though if that happened he couldn't see whoever was left lasting long. And of course they still had to build a new gate. And how long did they have left? And how were his two spies getting on? Despite his troubled thoughts, fatigue aided in sending him swiftly to sleep.

Outside the walls Lieutenant Locke prowled restlessly. He had left the fort to check on the sentries placed on the far side of the river. At least that was his official reason. In reality he had had to get out of the suffocating confines of their new home. Hah! It was a tomb. He worried at his nails as his mind made sense of the day's activities. He had listened with disbelief to the plans that the rest of them had been laying. He couldn't believe that Forge wanted them to stay and fight. The man had lost his mind. And to include the slave leader in his planning! It went

131

against all manner of military and social protocols as far as he was concerned. His captain was making a dreadful mistake, Locke was sure of it. He was quite prepared to throw all their lives away on the word of a bunch of uneducated mountain men! And all this because Forge had lost control, had lost so many of his troops that he wanted to reassert control over his men. He clearly wanted to prove his military prowess, be the hero. Well, Locke saw through him, but he had learnt better than to voice his views in front of his commander. No doubt the man would shout him down, clap him in irons or some other humiliation. It made simple sense to Locke; all they need do is dismantle the bridge and pull back to rejoin the regiment. It was obvious to anyone with a shred of military sense. The Captain even had his sergeants fooled. As Locke had supervised the building of the fire trench he had listened to Sergeant Grippa who was digging nearby. The man had seemed positively cheerful; the prospect of going into battle in a hopeless cause appeared to excite the man and the soldiers around him had all caught this infectious insanity.

Locke knew the truth: they would all die here. As the day had progressed so the knot of unease in his stomach had began to grow. The enemy would cross the river, surround the fort and slaughter them all. He didn't want to die here, but what could he do? Well he, at least, could still behave like a proper officer. He stalked off into the darkness towards the river.

Chapter Ten

With a start Forge sat up. It took him a few moments to realise that it was still night. He glanced around and scratched his head.

'Not like me,' he said to himself. 'Wonder what time it is.'

'It is an hour before dawn,' said a voice from the shadows.

Forge whipped his head around towards the direction of the voice. Leaning against a dark corner was a large human form, the shadows hiding its face and true shape. It leaned forward and the light from the stars illuminated a Bantusai face. It was Juma.

'What the hell ...?' began Forge.

'Please be quiet, Captain. Be in no ... doubt that I could kill you quickly and all your men would follow.' Juma's expression was hard and his eyes glittered. He leaned down next to him. Forge fell silent.

'You have questions. I will answer them. My people live in the *Barra*, the wood,' he whispered. 'We know how to move silently. Your cage was never strong. Your guards have been taken and my men only wait for my signal. Your men are tired and sleeping. Their deaths will be quick and painless. You want to know why?'

Forge did not respond. He felt a cold anger welling up inside him. He felt rage and betrayal like never before. He also felt like a fool for having been so easily duped.

'We were sent to kill you when our work was done. Now we must kill you before it is done. The Duke promised that when we returned he would give us passage back to our home. I am sorry, for what it is worth.' He put his hand up as a warning. 'Do not shout Captain, It will only wake up those who are sleeping. They need their rest.'

Forge was now very confused. Juma had changed his manner, becoming less menacing. He now moved to stand up. He turned and walked to the exit of the tower. He then stopped and spoke again. 'I am not a fool. I am a speaker of the truth. The Duke is fat and lazy, and is a man of lies. We would not live to see our land. If we killed you and ran, what then would we do? We are in a strange place with no friends and we do not know the way. But, perhaps a new trust? Would you see us home? Would you provide a ship to take us across the sea and allow us to walk without fear in your country?'

'I might think about it.'

'You are a man of better trust. So, tonight I will let you live.' He turned and grinned at Forge. 'Besides, I like you. It would have been a pity to cut your throat.' With that he moved back out into the silent night. He stopped and whispered back, 'Oh, Portal. He knew nothing of this.'

Forge, sat there for a few more seconds and then blew out his breath. He lay back down and stared up into the night. About thirty seconds later Sergeant Mac burst into the tower.

'Boss, it's the Bantusai'

'Let me guess, the sentries just told you that they had been grabbed and held by our guests. Then a few minutes later they were released and the Bantusai all went back into their pen?'

'Well, yeah but...'

'Go back to bed, Sarge, there won't be any more trouble tonight.'

'What about ...?'

'I'm knackered. I'll tell you in the morning.'

With that he turned over and closed his eyes.

The following morning, as dawn was breaking, Forge emerged from the tower scratching at his beard and looking forward to taking a leak. The courtyard was strangely silent. Whilst men were moving out in the open beyond the gates, things were somewhat different inside. The Bantusai were all still sitting in their pen and looking nonchalantly at the ten guards who were stationed on the opposite side of the open space, their backs almost to the walls and staring intently back. Above them on the parapet were five men with bows, arrows notched but resting by their sides. In the middle of the men on the ground Sergeant Mac stood glowering. It might have looked like a real stand-off if not for the absurd sight of Sergeant Pike attending to his cook pot. It was bubbling away nicely over the fire and the Sergeant was clutching his ladle as if he would batter the first man to come near him. Gathered around the fire, munching happily on porridge and bread, were the five trappers who kept looking around interestedly in between mouthfuls, keen to see what might happen next. Old Hoarty spotted the Captain and waved a half-gnawed chunk of bread at him in greeting.

Right, thought Forge. Let's get this sorted.

He marched down to the pen and raised the bar to the entrance. He pulled back the small gate and stood there eyeing Juma.

'So are you going to hang around then?'

Juma smiled.

135

'OK, get back to work.' He stood to one side and bowed, holding his hand out to indicate the way. As the Bantusai filed past he looked up and saw Kely grinning at him. Forge gave him a cold, perfunctory smile and walked over to the First Sergeant, who looked suitably nonplussed.

'OK Sergeant Mac. Our prisoners are now free men and for the duration of this exercise will be joining us as … levies.'

Sergeant Mac chewed this over. 'Right you are, Sir. Can always use the extra help.' He looked up at the men on the parapet. 'Well, don't just stand there. Put those bloody things away and get grafting. *And* you lot!' He indicated to the men around him. The soldiers looked at each other, shrugged and headed off. The First Sergeant scratched at his nose and looked at Forge. 'Go on then.'

'Well,' said Forge. 'These blokes were all set to bump us off. Orders from the Duke. Luckily they seemed to take a liking to us and never trusted the Duke in the first place.'

'And they could have bloody done it, too,' said Sergeant Mac. 'Still, they are crafty buggers. Don't doubt they might be good in a fight. Specially in the trees.'

'Just what I was thinking.'

Sergeant Mac looked over at the five men still happily eating their breakfast and raised his voice. 'And what about this lot. Can't we put them to work as well?'

'Sorry, we ain't conscripted,' said Arald.

'And I got a really poorly arm,' added Fuzz, freely waving his bandaged limb in the air.

Forge looked at Sergeant Mac and smiled. 'Guess not. I think we should be grateful they are willing to lend us their arrows for a while.'

'That's right,' piped up Old Hoarty. 'We're specialists. Not bloody labourers.'

136

'All right, all right,' muttered Sergeant Mac. He stalked off mumbling something about 'bloody civvies'.

Despite it all Captain Forge couldn't help but smile. He then ordered that Portal be collected from his incarceration. He grabbed a couple of mugs of coffee and waited by the fire. A few minutes later Portal strode into the fort. He was flanked by two grim-faced guards who were keeping a close eye on their charge. Portal himself had a face like a thunder cloud and had the dishevelled look of a man who had slept little. He was marched to stand a few feet in front of Forge. The Captain didn't stand but regarded the taller man silently.

'Well, Captain? Have you brought me here to gloat, to enjoy belittling me? Well, I'll tell you. You are not the first. I have many who have tried to put me down. To *presume* that they have the right to judge themselves my betters. Well, I have more intelligence in my little finger than you and your men have together. And I tell you now, when certain people in the capital hear about this, your career will be over. Do you hear?'

Forge continued to study him impassively, which caused Portal's face to glow an even darker shade of crimson. 'Finished?' he asked. It was Portal's turn to stay quiet. 'We were all to be killed. You know that much. But not by the Harradan. By the Bantusai.' He paused to let that sink in. He could see the confusion in Portal's face; the red colour slowly draining from his face as realisation began to dawn. 'According to Juma you didn't know this. From what I hear of your Shifter history, that makes sense. And if you apply a little intelligence, which I apparently lack, then the following fact is obvious. That you weren't due to be going back either.'

The blood had drained from Portal's face completely at

this point. He opened his mouth, closed it and then looked at Forge in disbelief.

'N ... no!' he stuttered. 'I have been a loyal servant. The Duke would not do such a thing.'

'Yes, he bloody would. You of all people know what he's like. The man would betray anyone, use anyone to get what he wants. Your name is mud in Shifter. I seriously doubt he would have included you in any future power play involving your home country. Hell, he probably agreed to have you taken out deliberately. I'm sure that would have bought him some negotiating currency.'

Actually, Forge doubted that anyone cared about Portal in Shifter. But Portal's own inflated opinion of himself might just make him believe so.

'Damn him!' cried Portal, coming round to Forge's way of thinking. 'So this is how he repays my loyal service!'

'There you go then. So here we are, all dropped in the shit. But we got lucky. Seems Juma and his boys have decided that they don't trust the Duke much and want to give us a shot. So ...' Forge levered himself up slowly, grunting in displeasure. 'I might as well do the same for you.'

He bent down, picked up a coffee mug and offered it to Portal. As a token of peace it wasn't up to much, but it was the best that Forge had and the most he was prepared to offer. He waited for Portal's response. The wizard's face was a tapestry of emotions: anger, disbelief and downright confusion. Forge could imagine how Portal was feeling. To be betrayed by the man he had given his loyalty to and then to be cast aside was hard enough. Forge had been feeling something similar himself. To cap it all, he had to endure the galling fact that now the man he had been sparring against was suddenly offering a truce. Hell, mused Forge, on an off day I would probably tell me to piss off and be damned.

A few more moments passed. Portal stared at Forge. His eyes turned hard and he made to give a scathing response. Instead he stopped, shut his mouth and shook his head. He looked again at the Captain with a resigned expression and sighed. He raised his hand and took the mug from Forge's hand. Inwardly Forge was relieved; he really wasn't in the mood to have to guard a surly prisoner, least of all one with magic at his disposal. 'It seems, Captain, that we find ourselves in a somewhat difficult position.'

'How so?'

'Now that it transpires my employer no longer wishes my services, I find myself without work or a master. You could say that I am now a non-combatant; a civilian if you will.'

'Ah,' said Forge, knowing what was coming next.

'So, if there is to be a battle ...'

'Then you want to be a hundred miles from this place.'

Portal inclined his head. 'Precisely, Captain.'

'OK, Portal, I can't hold you here. If you want to go, you go. I'll give you provisions. Enough to get you back to civilisation.'

'You are most gracious.'

'That's me. A fucking angel.'

'So I will make my preparations.' Portal bowed low, with a tight smile on his face and then turned to go.

'Just one thing,' said Forge. Portal turned round with and irritated look on his face.

'Yes?'

'You planning on getting even with Burns?'

'That particular thought is at the forefront of my mind, yes.'

139

'Going to try and get to him? Take him out perhaps? Or maybe his business interests?'

'Something like that.'

'You know that if we don't hold this army, if they get across, things could be pretty screwed up for our side. Think about it. If Burns' plan works, ain't no way you'll get to him. If we do hold them off, unlikely but hey, do you think Burns will be hanging around? He has staked everything on this. If he fails here, then he is finished. Certainly as far as Graves is concerned.' Forge stopped and took a sip of his coffee. 'If you want to hurt Burns, really screw him up, here's the place to do it.'

Portal looked incredulous. 'You are suggesting that I stay here?'

'Why not? Besides, I'm not suggesting. I'm asking. We could use your help. You're clever.'

'That must have hurt,' said Portal drily.

'It did. And you do have some magic about you. According to my First Sergeant at any rate. Something like that could give us an edge.'

Portal was quiet for a moment.

'Captain, I am no hero and I am no soldier. I have little liking for you or your people. And I have no desire to stay and be slaughtered in a hopeless fight.' He shook his head. 'I will not stay.'

Forge nodded. 'Very well. Then go and good luck to you.'

Portal turned and continued on. Forge sipped his coffee as he watched him walk away. Well, nothing ventured, he mused. It was not as if he had actually expected him to stay anyway.

The rest of the morning passed without incident. The trappers had once more headed off across the bridge and into the woods. No one was that bothered with what they were up to. The majority of the Ashkent manpower went towards finishing the fire trench. The final result was a ditch six foot wide and three foot deep. The spoil was placed in a high bund on the inner side. Wood was now being piled up into the trench and the kindling placed at intervals along it. Even so, it would take a while for it to catch and therefore it was critical to get the timing right. Lighting it as the enemy were charging on your heels would not be a good thing. Meanwhile, the Bantusai had been busy constructing a new gate. They had effectively copied the concept of the tree trunks in the eastern wall. Large, thick planks of wood had been forced into the ground at spaces and planks ran along them horizontally to make the wall. They had been heavily reinforced with buttressing. To one side of this a hatchway had been left open. About five feet in height, this was the only access into and out of the fort. A free-standing door was leant against the wall and would be used to seal the fort once it was surrounded and engaged. They had now moved on to working on the tower within.

Sergeants Mac and Pike approached the Captain whilst the gate was under construction.

'Sir, I imagine it hasn't escaped your notice that what with the gate being blocked like that ...' said Sergeant Mac.

'Where are the horses going to go?' interjected Sergeant Pike.

Actually Forge had to admit that was a bloody good point.

'Buggered if I know. But I think they were right to make that hatchway. There wouldn't have been enough space for all of us and the horses in there.'

'They would just get in the way and panic when the

arrows come flying in. Probably kill a couple of us in the process,' agreed Sergeant Mac.

'Well, that's all well and good. And it's obvious to all we are staying put,' said Sergeant Pike. 'But I still want to know what you are going to do with 'em. The lads, and myself I might add, are fond of our horses. It's what we are. Mounted infantry.'

Forge thought about it for a few moments.

'Reckon we could let them go?' he suggested speculatively.

'Mmm, best not. The silly buggers would only hang around. Get caught in the crossfire,' said Sergeant Mac.

'How about tying them?' offered Sergeant Pike. 'Take them into the trees aways. Deep in so that the northerners won't find 'em if they try and flank us.'

'Which they no doubt will if they get the chance,' said Sergeant Mac.

'True,' said Forge. He didn't want the horses to get killed but tying them up would leave them defenceless as well.

'Tell, you what, Sergeant Pike. You round up a gang of guys and start shipping those nags out of here. Lead 'em south for an hour and let them go. Leastways they'll be out of trouble.'

Sergeant Pike nodded. 'Right you are, boss. And after we've finished our little set-to, we should be able to round most of them up afterwards.' He turned and went off to get his party organised.

Sergeant Mac shook his head and smiled. 'Got to admire the optimism of the man. Somehow I don't think we'll be needing all the horses back by the end of this.'

Forge looked at his sergeant. 'No, if any at all.'

With that he stalked off. Sergeant Mac watched him

go. So the boss didn't hold out much hope. Well, he guessed *he* didn't either. They were a delaying action, nothing more. He wondered if this was the final cast of the dice for Forge. A chance to carve out a little dignity. To let his men die for something that had meaning for a change. If die they must. At least the boys in the regiment would remember what they did. A cold comfort to know that someone cared what happened to a bunch of hairy-arsed squaddies fighting in a minor war miles from home.

A little later Corporal Jonas and Holis Lode came loping across the bridge that had now been largely dismantled. The far side pier had been removed and only the sunken support pillars remained. On one side of this was laid a plank crossing. When the time came, the last man would cast the planks into the river. Then only the upright verticals would be left standing in the river; the nearside pier, too, would remain intact. The two men look tired and had been moving fast.

Forge met them at the gate.

'OK. What's the news?'

'As Lode said. They're comin' all right. We snuck up to their camp last night. All strung out along the path they were. Then we watched them as they got ready to move this morning,' said Jonas.

'We had to head north before turning west again. They had a whole bunch of scouts out. Looking for me and my friends,' said Lode.

Forge nodded and looked at Jonas. 'Strength?'

'I guess a couple of thousand. Those Shifter soldiers ... they're archers.'

'Shit.'

143

'Yeah, the Harradan look like a rough crew. They'll want to get in close, take a swing.'

'Guess that's why Shifter deliberately sent their bowmen for some extra flexibility.'

'Flexible my arse,' said Corporal Jonas. 'The Harradan will charge and bugger the rest.'

'Even so. It might have made life easier without those archers. What about time? How long have we got?'

'Six hours. Should get here just before nightfall,' said Hollis.

'Good, that'll give us time. Hit them and then they'll have to spend the night working out what happened. You two get some rest and some grub if you can. I think the pot's still hot.'

The two men nodded. Behind them Forge spotted Lode's five companions returning over the bridge. 'What have they been doing?'

'They spent the afternoon putting some surprises out for the guests,' said Holis.

'Oh really? What sort?'

'Well, you reckoned they could get up to the bank and take potshots at the river. So we just made it a bit less inviting. Rope traps, pits, sharp pointy stakes, that sort of thing. If you want to set an ambush for 'em, I recommend you stick to the road for the first fifty yards from the bank. Never know what you might find.'

Jonas gave an evil smile. 'I like the way these blokes think.'

'That's because they're almost as nasty as you, Corporal Jonas. Good work, Lode. Now you guys go and get your heads down whilst I brief the troops.'

The Corporal accompanied Forge up to the fort whilst Lode waited for his friends.

'Mornin', Holis,' said Juggs.

'Afternoon,' corrected Fuzz.

'Yeah, whatever. Saw our friends again?'

'Yep. And they will definitely be wantin' words with us,' replied Lode.

'Well, we got a few words for them,' laughed Arald.

''Cept ours are a bit spikier and more painful than what they might be used to,' said Juggs.

'Well, we got six hours or so till they get here,' said Lode. 'I'm off for a kip.'

'Before you do that, lad. We got another little scheme if you will,' replied Old Hoarty.

He put an arm round the younger man and they strolled off to their little camp in the trees.

'Well, that does it then,' announced Sergeant Pike. 'Off you go, darlin's. Don't stray too far.'

He took one last look at the crowd of horses that had been brought further south down the river trail. Most now stood idly by, grazing amongst the trees or drinking from the water.

'Let's go, lads. The Captain'll want us back pretty sharpish. Got work to do.'

The men accompanying him started the hour's walk back to the fort.

Private Smitty still stood by a horse, gently stroking its muzzle.

'Sorry, feller, it's for your own good.'

Private Thom walked up to him.

'Come on, you sentimental old sod. Your nag has got the easy end of the deal. She gets a chance to stay alive.'

'I know, but me and her have been buddies for a long time now. Five years she's carried my weight.'

145

'Yeah and bloody glad she'll be to get a break from you.'

Private Smitty turned to look at his old friend. 'Do you reckon we can get out of this?'

'Well, I intend to. I'm expecting you to keep my backside covered like you normally do.'

'Isn't it more like me keeping all of you covered as I take another beating on your behalf?' he said, laughing.

'Exactly. Stick to what you're good at. Come on. Let's get it over with and we can come back and fetch your girlfriend in a couple of days. I doubt she'll get far. Probably got arthritis from carting you around.'

'All right, I'm coming.' Private Smitty gave his horse a final pat. 'You heard the man. Don't go running off and I'll come get you soon.' The horse turned its head and nuzzled his face. Smitty laughed. 'That's my girl.'

'See I knew it,' came Private Thom's voice a small distance away. 'You and she are lovers!'

Smitty shook his head then turned and ran to catch up with his friend.

Forge had quickly passed his orders to the troops. With fours hours left to go, most of the building work had now stopped. Men were readying their own kit. Making sure blades were sharp and that armour was in good condition. It was a drill they had conducted a hundred times and each man had his own way of getting ready for battle. There was little banter as minds focused inward. Not a few were actually getting some extra shut-eye in; the sign of an experienced old hand. He had never been able to do that himself, always got too keyed up before a fight. As he had risen through the ranks, his extra responsibility towards his men made it even harder. How could he sleep at a time like this? Forge knew they would all do their jobs and it was all he could ever ask of them. He also knew it wasn't too late. They could still pull out and head south. Practise some hit-and-run tactics. But that wouldn't work, he had to fix the enemy here. That was his duty. Sergeant Mac ambled over with a hunk of cheese. He split it in two and offered half to Forge.

'No bread?'

'You want it, get it yourself. Sergeant Pike'll kill you before you get three paces.'

'How'd you get that then?'

'Bribery.'

'With what?'

'Said I'd kick his ass if he didn't give it to me.'

'Well, I could try that too.'

'No you can't. You're an officer. It'd be bad form.'

'Whatever.'

As they ate in companionable silence Forge gazed at the old campsite. A thought struck him.

'Portal get away OK?'

Pike looked at him in mild surprise.

'Get away? He's still here. See,' he pointed, 'there's his tent, still pitched. And Pike took his horse with the others.'

'Now that is interesting. Come on.'

They two men wandered over to Portal's tent and ducked inside. As their eyes adjusted to the gloom they saw the wizard seated on a canvas chair. The man appeared distracted, head resting on a balled fist, gazing at the floor. A few moments later he glanced up at the soldiers.

'Do you think you can hold them here?' he asked.

Forge shrugged.

'I am tired of being used, Forge,' continued Portal. 'I

147

care little for this war or for you. But I want to hurt Burns. Your little command seems the most obvious way.'

'We aren't just here to help you get revenge. We ain't doing this for our health, Portal,' advised Sergeant Mac.

'Indeed. I am not sure that you are doing it out of any sane reason I can see. No matter, I will stay and lend you the benefit of my modest powers.' He turned his eyes back to the floor.

The two soldiers exchanged a surprised look.

'OK, wizard. Plans meeting in one hour for the heads of sheds,' said Forge. His first words to Portal in the exchange.

Portal nodded his head. Forge looked at Sergeant Mac and shrugged his shoulders. He tilted his head towards the door and made to leave.

'Oh and Captain?'

Forge stopped and looked at Portal.

'Whilst I doubt you will listen to my counsel, I would suggest you keep a close eye on your young lieutenant.'

'Really? Why?' responded Forge with genuine interest.

'I am a student of human nature; in the current light of things perhaps not as good as I thought but...' He stopped and shrugged. 'I often know when a man is masking agitation or fear. I would suggest that the man may be hiding both. Often a very bad combination, wouldn't you say?'

Forge tilted his head and sucked in his lips and chewed them. 'Indeed they are, wizard.'

Portal gave another tight smile and departed.

Forge and Sergeant Mac left the tent and walked back to the fort.

'That's a turn-up for the books,' Sergeant Mac observed.

'Just goes to show I guess,' agreed Forge. 'Reckon he'll be any use?'

'Could be. Interesting he said that about Locke; just what we were thinking.'

'Yeah, maybe a warning in the shape of an olive branch,' surmised Forge.

'Still, even if he is wrong, Portal must know a few tricks and such,' added Sergeant Mac brightly.

'Well, let's see if he can't do something with our fire trench, give it some extra ...' he paused as he searched for words. '... Oomph or something. Flames, fire demons, big explosions. Whatever.'

'Right, boss. Oomph.'

Juma joined them.

'Captain, my men have gone back into the woods to fashion weapons.'

'Oh right, the bows and stuff.'

'Yes, but not for your men. I am sorry. We make weapons for ourselves; that is all the time we have. But we can use them, too.'

'Pity. But I guess you have been working your balls off.'

'I do not have any balls, but I think I understand,' said Juma. 'Would you like to see your new tower?'

Forge had hardly noticed the construction work that had taken place in the last few hours. Juma led him through the gate hatch into the courtyard. He had been loitering outside all day, constantly looking across the water; just in case the Harradan arrived early. Not that he distrusted the estimates of his two scouts. He was just antsy. So he was pleasantly surprised to see the fruits of the Bantusai's labours.

The tower now looked like some crazy fusion of wood and stone. The missing walls of the eastern side had been rebuilt in wood, similar in construction to that of the gateway. They had been extended to the height of the third, open storey of the tower and a little over to mimic the protection of the battlements at the top. They now had a working tower again. Indeed, he had his redoubt. What particularly pleased him was that the Bantusai had not stopped there. They had constructed a further small lookout tower on top of the third storey. It was a simple, hasty affair but it gave them a greater view and another place to attack from. He looked over at Juma. 'I'm impressed.'

'Please.' Juma indicated that he go inside.

To do this Forge had to get past another obstacle. The three wagons that the company used to transport its stores were drawn up in a box formation around the entrance. There was only one gap between the end of the western-facing wagon and the tower wall. It was wide enough for one man to get through if he went side first. Inside, benches had been set up so that men could stand upon them and reach down upon any attackers on the other side. Good, that would slow down the enemy and give them a chance to get safe within the main tower. Anyone wanting to break the door down would have to heave the wagons out of the way, and catch hell from above in the process! He walked through the doorway into the base of the redoubt. Another hatchway, similar to that used on the gate, was resting against the wall. Above him he saw a sturdy-looking wooden floor.

At the side of the tower, where the stairs started, another crude barrier had been erected. The once-open stairway was now covered by a wooden wall as it led up into the next level. Forge was mindful that in a siege the enemy might try and burn them out. Fortunately, Juma had had the same idea and the wood was fresh and green, having come from the hearts of the trees. They would not burn easily. This all meant men could defend against a successful penetration into the building. He could see how this would pan out for real. Whoever was left would be able to make them fight for every square inch of territory. Just as it should be.

Forg walked up the stairs. Once more he found another enclosed space. A trapdoor was now laid to one side to cover the stairway. As he had seen from outside, the eastern wall was now made of wood and a small opening led out on to the eastern parapet of the north wall. This mirrored the stone-framed exit in the west wall. That way if the fort was breached, men could retreat along the parapet and get inside. Further barriers were set to seal these holes when necessary. Above him was another wooden floor and running at a steep angle were the steps to the third storey. He climbed these and emerged into the daylight. Around him set in piles on each side of the parapet were large rocks and blocks of stone from the ruins. They would break the heads of those trying to enter the tower. He glanced around him nodding approval.

'Hey, Juma. Damn good work. Sure you still don't want a job with the engineers?'

'No, Captain,' said Juma with a grin. 'It sounds like hard work.'

Forge laughed and then walked up to the watchtower set in the middle of the roof. Climbing up it he went through a crude hole cut in the bottom of the floor and emerged on to the top of the platform, some ten foot above its base. It did have a guard rail that went up to about waist height and even a roof above it. One man could stand relatively comfortably up there. Not that he wanted to. He wasn't very fond of heights. In this position looking out he could see the fort below him and all his men. In fact, being a very clear and bright day, he could see for miles, if you liked looking at trees that is. Northwards he could see how the land rose sharply, climbing up into the mountains. He could trace the line of the river, a jagged cut in the treeline for quite some way. He could do the same southwards for a couple of hundred yards, before it went out of sight. In the far distance he could actually see where the forest ended and the more open country began. The very way they had travelled only days past. It felt like a long time ago. Sadly, his view to the east was not very useful. They weren't going to get much of an early warning of people making for the crossing. He turned away feeling that he had seen enough. At this height, the effect was such that unless you bent over the side to look, you couldn't actually see the tower below you. It gave him the unsettling feeling of being on top of a very thin, very precarious pinnacle. He climbed down and got his feet back on the solid floor.

'Juma, you guys have excelled yourselves. If we get out of this I will personally pay for you and your boys to go home in luxury. Comfortable beds, a nice big boat and nice fancy coaches.'

'Really? You would do this?' said Juma in surprise.

'Didn't you hear? Officers get paid a fortune,' stated Sergeant Mac as he joined them from below.

Juma raised his eyebrows and again looked at Forge, who shifted in embarrassment.

'Well, no. Not personally. But I would make sure the bloody Army did.'

Chapter Eleven

In the west the sun had begun to sink beneath the line of the trees and dusk was swiftly upon them. The Ashkent ambush party, who were strung out in the woods on either side of the trail, had been in position for an hour. They were along the trail that led from the eastern side of the river about two hundred yards from where it entered the clearing and the bridge site. Captain Forge lay in the dense foliage about midway down the line. By his reckoning it was about time for the Harradan to make an appearance. He glanced up and down the track but there was now little but gloomy shadow; only memory could tell him where the men had been positioned. What made it harder was that half of the ambush party was made up of the Bantusai contingent, though, it had to be said, they were particularly well equipped for hiding in the dark.

Earlier they had emerged from the woods about the fort like some tribal hunting party. Well, when he came to think of it, that was exactly what they were. They carried simple wooden bows and clutched wooden staffs that had been shaped into spears. Over their shoulders were slung crude packs of arrows that, because they were featherless, looked more like miniature versions of their spears. Forge guessed that they were only good for short distances, but they would be fine for the environment they were fighting in. The Bantusai had also brought a couple of extra bundles of shorter spears, which, they explained, were

153

better for throwing like javelins. These they stacked around the walls of the fort for later use.

To take part in the ambush, Forge had taken Lieutenant Locke and twenty of his own men, as well as the Bantusai. The younger officer was about midway down the line of troops. Forge had been tempted to allow Locke to command the ambush by himself but had thought better of it. The young man had become sullen and introspective, especially in the last day or so. In all honesty, Forge had started to lose his remaining confidence in the man. He clearly wasn't happy with the way things were going and, whilst he had not voiced his opposition, Forge could see in Locke's eyes that he didn't agree with his decision to stay and delay the enemy. Portal's words also hounded him. Whilst he still didn't like the man, let alone trust him, Forge couldn't help but be swayed by them and the evidence of his own eyes. But, ultimately, there wasn't much Forge could do about it right now, except watch him. Hopefully the chance to see some action and fight alongside the men would help to spark some fire in Locke.

In anticipation of the night fight ahead, the Ashkent soldiers had taken off their armour and had blackened their weapons and exposed skin with a paste made from the burnt wood of their fires. That way there was less chance of being caught out by reflected moonlight. Their light attire was also necessary because the plan required them to be able to make a swift exit back up the track and over the bridge. Sergeant Mac had pointed out to Forge that perhaps he was not in the best condition to be part of this endeavour. Whilst privately he acknowledged that his sergeant was probably right, he politely told him to piss off. He wanted to be here just to get a look at the Harradan before the siege started. Although now, in the waning

154

light, he had to admit that that was probably a stupid idea; he wouldn't see a damn thing in a few more minutes anyway.

Juma and his men would provide some illumination as they would be carrying torches. As Juma had informed Forge just before they set out, the Harradan were expecting to meet him on the path. That way they would know the Ashkent men had been dealt with. Juma insisted that this deception must still take place; otherwise they would not be able to achieve the surprise they wanted. He also pointed out that the Harradan would have scouts out and it was vital that they send word back to the main force that all was well.

Juma and two of his men now sat in the path about thirty feet to the right of Forge. Next to the Captain lay Holis Lode. He had agreed to come on this sortie before he and his men left the fort for safer places. Along with him were Juggs, Fuzz and Sleeps. Because of the necessity to move fast, it was felt that Arald and certainly Old Hoarty would lag too far behind as pursuit followed. Neither man had appeared to be particularly put out by this and happily wished their younger companions the best of luck. The civilians weren't expected to get into the hand-to-hand fighting but rather to use their bows and crossbows to aid the initial launch of the attack.

'Remember, Captain. Stick to the road when you pull back. Wouldn't want anything nasty happening to you,' Lode whispered.

'Me neither. What about you guys. Where you heading to after this?' Forge asked.

'Well, me 'n' the boys reckon we'll just head north. Hole up for a while then make our way back to Noel's Gap.'

'But I thought you said it was destroyed?'

'It is. But I don't think the Shifter fur trade knows that. I don't think they would have known about the attack. We make them money. I think the Harradan did it off their own backs; maybe Duke Burns told 'em to,' he shrugged. 'Whatever. I reckon we can go back to fur trapping again; times should be good with less competition around. It'll drive the prices up.'

Forge laughed softly. 'Business is always business. Drives everything at the end of the day.'

'Got to make a living. I figure we've done almost enough to pay them back for what they did.'

'You have. Thanks to you we can even up the toll they took at your town; a few times over if I have anything to do about it. Whatever happens, thanks for helping us out. I'll say it now because in a little while things will get a bit hectic.'

He reached out to shake Holis's hand but the younger man didn't take it.

'I said almost enough, Captain,' Lode smiled. 'You was worried about that far bank.'

'Yeah. Those archers got protection. We won't be able to get any fire down on them.'

'Well, Old Hoarty came up with an idea. We'll clear out when you get across the bridge but we won't be far away.'

'No?'

'Nope, we got a ropeway up from the clearing. Got it tied off under the water. I expect that the hairy arses might have a look up there for a crossing but they won't find it. It's tied just where it starts getting too rough to cross.'

'How'd you get it up there.'

Holis tapped the side of his nose. 'Trade secret.'

Forge smiled.

'When they start firing,' Lode continued, 'they'll

probably be too busy to notice us. We'll try and soften the shower a bit. Then pull out. That's you on your own after that.'

'More than I could have asked for. Thank your mates for me.'

He stuck out his hand again and this time the trapper gripped it.

'Good luck, Captain.'

Forge nodded and they both settled back down to wait.

A little way down the line Ronin Locke was sweating. He could feel the beads on his forehead and uncomfortable drops running down the length of his back every few seconds. He felt hot and bothered and it had nothing to do with the camouflage on his face or the clothes he wore. He knew he was panicking and he knew why. Until now his experience of combat had been limited; even his injury on patrol had been so fast and unexpected that he had had no time to worry about it. Before this moment, in all of his time in the field, the concept of closing with another, to kill before he himself was killed, had always been an abstract concept; something to be imagined. Suddenly, for the first time, he was expected to fight up close and personal. In the dark there would be blades flashing out in all directions; there would be men wanting to kill him. All those childhood daydreams of being a gallant hero, where enemies were vanquished and wounds easily laughed off, seemed absurd now. This was for real and it scared the shit out of him

What made it worse was that he couldn't talk to anyone about it: he couldn't talk to his men, which would be showing weakness; the sergeants would consider him a fool; and the Captain? Well, he would just laugh in his face

157

and call him a coward. No, he would not get a sympathetic ear from any in the company. Instead each man was expected to do his duty and die like a good soldier. For that was soon to be their fate. They would prick the ire of the enemy and would then be crushed whilst hiding in their little fort. And what would it achieve? Nothing. Except Locke's own death. And as he lay there waiting in the gathering dark, crouched amidst the undergrowth, he felt singularly alone.

They didn't have to wait long. A few minutes later in the now-deepening gloom Corporal Jonas came jogging into view. There wasn't anybody who could have mistaken him in the darkness. He slowed down and started looking into the trees. Juma called out and indicated where Forge was lying. The scout came over and pushed his way into the undergrowth.

'They're about five minutes behind me. An advance party of twenty men. I couldn't see the rest.'

'OK. Let's hope Juma's bluffing skills are up to scratch.'

'He fooled us, boss.'

'Don't remind me. All right, pass the word. And get yourself a spot.'

Corporal Jonas nodded and moved off to warn the rest of the ambush party.

As the scout went past them, Juma and his companions lit the torches they had been carrying and then sat back down by the side of the road. As if they were in a very good mood, they chatted and laughed and hooted without a care in the world. The light of the torches pushed back the dark and shadows. Forge felt a brief moment of panic. It seemed like he must be standing out like a sore thumb and wished he'd made more of an efffort to camouflage himself. He took a deep breath through his nose and calmed himself down; they couldn't see him. The light would help to ruin the night vision of the Harradan party and he had confidence in his men not to give themselves away too early. In his right hand he gently held on to a ball of mud, roughly the size of a large apple. Portal had given it to him earlier in the evening after the brainstorming session for the defence of the crossing. The wizard had been asked if he could provide something to create a neat surprise for the ambush. The result had been this lump of muck. Forge had gazed at it doubtfully on taking it.

'What is this? A mud bomb?'

'Treat it gently, Captain. A hard concept for you I know. Do not drop it. When you are ready, throw it. I advise you and your men to close your eyes,' Portal had said in his usual arrogant style. 'But that is up to you,' he added.

The wizard had then walked off to work on the fire trench. Apparently he believed he could increase the flammability of the wood, thus making it catch and burn quicker. But it would take time. Judging on his lacklustre performance so far, Forge wouldn't be surprised if the wizard conjured up a mini bloody rain cloud instead.

A few moments later he heard the tramp of feet and the occasional soft clang of metal on metal. A few moments later he could make out dark shapes moving down the trail. Juma heard them too and called out. They stopped and a few seconds later a reply was barked out. Forge couldn't make out the language. It was rough and coarse. Juma laughed and said something in reply, beckoning them forward. He and his companions stood up. In one hand they each held their spears, held vertically. Juma appeared to have learnt a fair bit of their language as well at some point. Clever man. The enemy walked onwards cautiously and met up with Juma. More words were spoken and Juma laughed cheerfully. For a moment Forge panicked and thought that the Bantusai might betray them. But he quickly admonished himself for that.

In the light he could see the Harradan pretty well. Tall, well-built men with a tough, confident look about them. Most were bearded and had long hair. Real clansmen from the north these guys were. They were dressed in furs and leathers and carried their weapons with ease. Fighting these blokes was not going to be a pleasant experience. On a word from the group leader, one of the Harradan detached himself from the main group and headed back down the trail, no doubt to take word to the main column. The party on the trail were in discussion and it was clear that the leader wanted to go forward. Forge gathered this from his raised voice and insistent hand gestures. Juma, master bluffer that he was, remained jovial and was trying to convince the men to stay put and wait for the rest of the group. He then produced his ace in the hole by offering up the three flagons of ale that he had put to one side. The leader eagerly took one of the flagons and drank deeply. It certainly appeared to appeal to his thirst. This act seemed to convince the man that all was well. His men seemed to be more than happy with this development as they began to share out the drink between them. After a tense couple of minutes Forge began to hear the main body moving up. It was almost time.

A long line of figures were now plainly visible to Forge's left-hand side. As the lead men came level with him that was the signal. He rose swiftly and hurled the ball of mud on to the pathway in front of the warriors. As it flew he turned his head and closed his eyes, fully expecting to be speared for throwing a ball of dirt at a thousand angry clansmen. As the ball of mud struck the ground and spilt apart, a dazzling flash of light burst from the wet casing. It was bright enough for the light to penetrate Forge's eyelids, even though he had covered them with his hands just for good measure. A massed cry of consternation came from the path as the Harradan lead troops were temporarily blinded. The Bantusai in the trees next to him stood and let rip with a flight of arrows, supplemented by the fire from Jonas and Lode and his men. Shouts came up from the marching column. This distraction caused many in the scout party to turn their heads in confusion. As the leader turned back to Juma he was taken in the stomach by the other's spear. His two companions were caught equally unawares by the nearest Bantusai.

Simultaneously Forge's men crashed through the trees to engage the rest of the scout party. Forge, too, pushed his way on to the trail, sword in his right hand and a dagger in his left. He stood between the two groups of Harradan and turned to see the havoc to his left. From behind him came a shout. He turned to see a northman running towards him, having escaped the melee ahead. Forge saw a glinting shape raised above the head of his assailant and hastily put his sword up to parry the incoming axe blow. As he blocked the strike, which damn near jarred his arm off, he immediately slammed his dagger into the Harradan's stomach, the shock causing him to drop the axe. The momentum of the charge kept the northman moving and he cannoned into Forge. The two of them landed in a heap and Forge quickly pushed the other man off. He stood and forced his sword into the man's neck slicing through his windpipe. He quickly withdrew his sword and looked up.

The gap between the two groups would allow them to

161

finish off the Harradan scouts without having to engage the main force. It also meant a breathing space to allow them to hightail it off towards the bridge. Meanwhile the Bantusai were raining confusion with their arrows. In the darkness the Harradan were not sure from which direction the arrows were coming and it therefore delayed their mounting a foray into the trees. As more of them fell, the others began to pull back into the rest of the column, which was trying to advance and also to ascertain what was going on ahead. It was clear that an ambush was taking place and many were rushing to get into battle. All they succeeded in doing was running into their own men.

When the light ball had flashed and the ambushers had charged out of the trees the world had become a chaotic, screeching, howling place. Locke had made to move along with the other troops to engage the enemy. But in an instant of indecision a plan had formed in his mind, halting his movement. Instead, he hunkered down and lay still. As the fighting raged, Locke's mind raced. This was all madness, all of it. Why should he lay down his life in such a meaningless way? Instead, he could live. And now was his chance. He scrambled up and headed at full pace through the trees, across the path and past the struggling combatants. In the melee he doubted that anyone would have noticed him. He entered the treeline and pushed south for a minute, the sounds of battle receding. He then stopped to catch his breath. He experienced elation – he had escaped! All he had to do was head south for a while and then find a place to cross the river. He would then head back to his own lines, no doubt he would be picked up by friendly troops soon enough. Then all he would have to do is tell them that he was the soul survivor from the defence of the river. Tell them that Forge had commanded him to leave his post and carry the message of their destruction back to the Ashkent Army. The company was doomed anyway, help would never reach them in time and there would be no one to challenge his story. He smiled, glanced around him and then pushed on into the dense, dark undergrowth.

Forge watched as the gap grew between himself and the Harradan down the trail. He guessed they would soon recover and he ordered the withdrawal. He bent to pull out his dagger but found that the man had his hands about the blade and held it in a death grip. Looking up he saw his men had finished off the scouts and were already on their way home. Cursing under his breath he stood and turned to follow them. Shit, but he'd loved that bloody knife, had had it for years. He thundered towards the bridge. Behind and to either side of him he heard rather than saw Lode and his men following hard behind. A few moments later, he saw that he was being overtaken by a couple of them. Inwardly he chafed at that but was too busy breathing hard to articulate. The Bantusai regrouped ahead of him and fired one more volley as he ran past. They did not follow him, but pulled back into the trees on the southern side of the trail in order to lure the Harradan after them. Juma had told Forge that their ability to sing to the trees did not end with simple materials. Awaiting the pursuers was a maze of vines and branches that had been woven together by Bantusai magic. Forge would never see the results but Juma had said the trees would snare and strangle those that touched them. He emerged into the clearing followed by the sounds of shouting and screaming from the forest on both sides of the trail as the magic of the

Bantusai and the man traps of Old Hoarty and his mates did their gruesome work.

As Forge reached the crossing he had to slow down and wait as the bridge had been stripped to nothing more than a single line of planks and a guide rope, so it was now a bottleneck. As, one by one, figures crossed over, Forge glanced back at the trail entrance. Waiting there was Corporal Jonas crouched low with his bow drawn. Now he could see black figures running past him as the Bantusai angled back towards the clearing. Forge now took his turn and carefully walked as fast as he dared across the plank bridge. He hung on to the guide rope and was glad it was so well secured. He soon reached the other side, ran down the pier and stood there looking back.

A stream of Bantusai were now gaining the bank and were immediately turning left, heading for the southern end of the clearing. Forge tried to make out Corporal Jonas from the figures moving along the plank. He then spied a shape detach itself from the trees and run towards the crossing. Beside Forge, Juma jumped from the pier, clapped him on the back and ran off to join his men. Their job now was to watch the river to the south. Forge wandered if he would see them again. Corporal Jonas was now halfway across the water. From behind him the Captain could see lights and shouting figures coming from the trail entrance. Suddenly a bright bloom of light akin to the one created by Portal's mud ball flared out from a point above the trail. Forge cried out in alarm and shielded his eyes.

'What the hell was that?' he shouted.

He looked over to the five Ashkent soldiers who had been waiting patiently on this side of the bank. These were the only others of his command carrying bows. They, too, had been caught by the flash and were trying to recover their night sight.

'Covering fire!' Forge commanded.

The men began to loose shafts across the river. At best their aim was approximate; their eyes were no longer able to track movement in the dark. But it appeared to stall the advance for a few moments. Corporal Jonas leant down and heaved the plank into the river.

'Someone's being clever over there, boss,' he said as he stood up again and sawed through the guide rope.

'Someone's using our own tactics against us. Wasn't expecting that,' agreed Forge. That was magic, he thought to himself. That puts a new spin on things.

As Corporal Jonas finished cutting, the Harradan launched another charge into the clearing, their numbers too many to be halted by the five archers. He looked up at Forge. 'That's it.'

'Everyone back to the fort,' Forge ordered.

The seven men left the riverbank and headed for the safety of the walls. Behind them could be heard the frustrated cries of the Harradan. They reached the gateway and one by one ducked inside. Forge counted them through. As the last man crossed the threshold he followed them in and then ordered the entrance sealed shut. He made his way to the eastward-facing rampart. Portal joined him and rested a hand upon the stone.

'It would seem the ruse worked then, Captain.'

'Like a dream,' he replied. 'But I guess you saw what just happened.'

Portal nodded. 'They have a magic user with them, Captain. That much is obvious. And they clearly have some ability. I fear that my own will be no match for it.'

Forge glanced at the gaunt-faced wizard. Perhaps it was

just the lack of light but the man looked tired, exhausted in fact.

'You OK?'

Portal nodded. 'I find that my abilities have waned in the intervening years since I first studied magic. To invest power in objects is always physically draining. And for those with but little schooling it is all the harder.'

Forge picked up on the offhand admission by Portal as to the true, limited extent of his talents.

'I hear you have been at the fire trench for hours. Must have taken a lot out of you.'

Portal did not reply. 'And, as much as I hate to say it, your surprise package did the job. Well done!'

That got a reaction. Portal seemed genuinely taken aback by the Captain's praise. 'It would seem tonight is a night for congratulations. I heard your men talking about my flare. They were impressed. One even clapped me on the back when I had finished on the trench.'

Forge had to smile at that.

'That's the guys for you.' He jerked his head back towards the courtyard floor where men lounged on the ground, discussing the night's escapades. 'You gave them an edge. Means they have a better chance of getting through the fight. Do that and they'll love you for it.'

'Something I have little experience of,' said Portal. There was a bitter edge to his voice.

'Go get some sleep, wizard. We'll deal with their magic man as and when we have to. There'll be more work for you come the morning no doubt.'

Portal nodded to the Captain once more and made his way slowly towards the nearest ladder. Forge watched him until he vanished from sight, then swept his gaze back over his redoubt.

No light was burning within the courtyard. No point in drawing attention to themselves yet. He could now see a whole lot of lights and shapes milling around on the far side. He was tempted to order his men to send some more shafts over but decided against it. They had precious few as it was, no more than a score each. Tonight's engagement would already have eaten into that. Sergeant Mac came up to join him.

'Everyone accounted for?' asked Forge.

'Everyone 'cept the Lieutenant.'

Forge shot the First Sergeant a shocked look.

'Really?' he asked.

'Yup,' replied Sergeant Mac. 'I asked around; nobody's seen him. Not during the fight, not after.'

'Damn, I had forgotten about him. Now I think about it, the last time I saw him was when we took our positions for the ambush. I was even thinking about how he'd do just before we attacked.'

'Well, boss, looks like he didn't do good enough. Probably got himself speared before he knew what had hit him. Never did much like that lad,' Sergeant Mac stated.

Forge shook his head. 'Damn!' he uttered and then paused for a moment. 'Can't quite get myself upset over it though; never really took to the guy. Still, my responsibility though.'

Mac nodded and decided to change the subject. 'Doors are sealed shut, Sir. And Lode and his boys have taken off.'

'Right,' nodded Forge, his thoughts of Locke ended. 'Apparently, they're planning one more job on them across the river before they go.'

'Good lads.'

'Yeah, got balls all right.' Forge sighed. 'So that's it then. Less than one hundred men to hold off an invading army.'

'Yeah, but they got all the work to do now, haven't they?' stated Sergeant Mac simply.

'Then let's hope they balls it up every step of the way.'

Sergeant Mac did not reply. Together the men gazed out across the dark night.

Every few minutes for the next hour or so, a cry of surprise and pain would be heard drifting across the water. At that, the men of the fort would grin evilly at each other; another hapless northerner had found one of the surprise packages left for them.

For the Harradan, the night had not gone well. Thirty men lay dead and at least another seven would not see the dawn. Seven more had wounds that would leave them useless. Five of these had been caused by cowardly mantraps laid within the forest. Vorgat could guess who had placed those. He had not lost any of his own troops; that cost was borne by one of the other clan leaders. But he was not blind to the damage to morale that these incidents caused. Vorgat was not a stupid man and he had been born with a degree of pragmatism; a trait often lacking in his people. This streak, combined with his innate ambition, afforded a different view of many of the Harradan traditions. Foremost of these was the desire to be first in battle. It was considered an honour to be given the vanguard of any armed force. It meant that leader would have the chance to close with and kill more of the enemy than those that followed him, thus heaping honour on his name. Vorgat, as nominal leader of the combined clans, would let himself be seen as a fair-minded and generous individual, always allowing another of the clans to be first in the column. Many would then admire his political skill, even if the canny amongst them might see it for what it was. When the trap was sprung, the Bear Claw clan had been in the lead. Fortunate in a way because they were Kron's closest allies and now that clan had been badly weakened. As the rest of the Claws had charged forward, Vorgat had held his men back. Too much confusion could be created in the dark. By his side at that moment was Captain Lordswood, who had bridled at his inaction and had ordered his own men forward into the crush.

Once the excitement had died down, Lordswood had returned. Vorgat was waiting for him by a newly built camp fire. Around him his men were making camp for the night. Vorgat noted the man was sporting a gash over one eye.

'Damn you, Vorgat,' said the archer on his return. 'Why did you not fight?'

Vorgat regarded the man and then shrugged.

'Why did you try and fight an enemy you could not see?' said Vorgat. 'From what I have heard, Shifter, you lost a man. Spitted by a Bear Claw spear.'

'Well, perhaps if you had tried to establish some discipline in your troops ...'

'Perhaps. But we are Harradan. My people would rather cut you into little pieces than take some of your ... discipline.' He grinned evilly. 'But you are welcome to try.'

'If you were in my company ...'

'Do not try to threaten me, Shifter.' Vorgat's voice lowered dangerously. 'Remember your place.'

The Shifter officer backed off a step. 'I apologise, I am just ... eager to ensure our mission does not fail.'

'Then, perhaps, you might wish to follow my lead, Captain. My people are making camp. At first light I will send scouts forward. It would be foolish to lose more men to those traps. Do you not agree?'

169

The officer nodded his assent.

'Good. In the morning we will look to cross the river. Those that have been dogging our movements have found friends. We must learn their strength. Then we will know how to defeat them. Our captive might well hold the answers to that.'

'Then perhaps I might be allowed to question him?' asked Lordswood.

'No, Shifter. Leave that to me. Do not fear, I will tell you all that I rip from his lips,' said Vorgat smiling.

The officer nodded stiffly.

'Very well. Then I will look to my men and await your next move with interest.' He turned and strode off into the night.

In fact, Vorgat knew what he faced, the Duke had suggested as much. The woodsmen were just an extra itch. His witch had said as much. It was she who had responded to the ambush and had created the second flash of light at his bidding. Afterwards she had used her sight to spy out the nature of the men facing them. These were proper, professional fighting men; no doubt about that. And that meant they couldn't be Graves regulars; from what he had heard of *them*, they were not *that* good. Vorgat had concluded that the crossing was to be contested by the southern soldiers from across the sea. These he had heard of by reputation: hard-nosed and well versed in the ways of war, better than the Shifter troops who accompanied him.

These southerners were supposed to have been dealt with. He had been betrayed by the slaves sent to build the bridge. The Shifter plans had clearly been poorly laid. It did not matter to Vorgat. He would act swiftly; he had to if he was to maintain control of his loose alliance and win

170

the booty he had been promised. This venture was now a matter of personal pride; if it were to go wrong his standing amongst his own people would be fatally weakened. Already he knew that Battlebane would have started to whisper against him. None of them had expected to face an armed force at the river. The losses they had taken thus far had rattled the other clan leaders. He now had to ensure that any Harradan displeasure was directed against the southerners. That they were holding the river crossing was to his advantage. It meant they could be engaged in a straight fight. Their destruction would improve morale after the hit-and-run tactics they had endured up until now. Standing up, he left his fire and walked to where the captive was being held.

Locke's arms had been forced behind him and tied around the thick trunk of a tree at the edge of the Harradan camp. His legs, too, had been forced apart and secured by ropes. His body was torn and bruised, his face battered and he could barely see due to the blood that had almost dried his eyelids shut. His hair was slick with sweat and he was having trouble breathing. No doubt he had at least a couple of broken ribs. Every part of him ached.

They had found him blundering around in the woods a short time after the fighting had ceased. Locke had not reckoned on the forest being so dense and he had quickly lost his bearings. He had damn near stumbled on a search party of these brutes. They had set upon him in a fury; he had had no chance to put up a defence and he quickly succumbed to their blows, passing out in the process. He had come to and found himself tied thus. Though guarded, his captors had made no further moves towards him and he was thankful for the respite. Locke knew that

171

he was probably dead, though he hoped they wouldn't torture him; he couldn't cope with that. He'd rather tell them everything; it would make no difference to the fate of the company anyway.

He heard someone approaching. He forced his eyes open and blinked a few times, trying to get them to focus on the man before him, another of these wild-haired brutes. The Harradan regarded him for a few moments. Then his hand lashed out and slapped Locke across his left cheek. His head snapped round to the right and a mix of sweat and blood flew from his face. Locke gritted his teeth and looked back at the newcomer. This one was obviously a leader; you could just tell from the way he carried himself. If he was to survive, the decision would be in this man's hands. If he could try and earn some favour with the Harradan leader then there was a small chance. The faintest glimmer of hope formed within Locke.

'Speak, tell me what I face. Speak,' demanded Vorgat Stoneson. He punctuated it with another swift slap to Locke's other cheek. Taking that as his cue, Locke shook his head to clear it of the stars that he was seeing, then he took a breath and began to speak. He told Stoneson of the plan to deny the Harradan safe passage across the Rooke and the subsequent delaying action. He also told him of the numbers and make-up of the forces arrayed against the Harradan–Shifter alliance. All the while Vorgat Stoneson's face remained inscrutable; his eyes never left Locke's. He asked no questions until the younger man had finished.

'What of the slaves? Can they fight?' he asked.

Locke shook his head. 'They fight with spears and wear no armour. They were captured once before, so I doubt they can do much other than their fancy magic.'

'And the hunters? Those that have bled us for days?'

172

'I don't know,' replied Locke. 'I think that they have already left. They did not want to get involved in the fighting.'

Vorgat nodded his head and was quiet. He cast his eyes down and appeared lost in thought. Locke waited quietly. He had spoken honestly and left nothing out. Hopefully that would be enough.

Vorgat looked up and at Locke.

'You are a coward. You would vomit all your knowledge at the merest touch. You have no spirit.' He turned and stalked away.

In alarm Locke called after him.

'Wait. What are you going to do with me?'

'Me? Nothing,' replied Vorgat as drew level with the guard. 'Burn him,' he ordered.

Locke's composure finally gave way and he howled in despair. There would be no quick death for him.

As Vorgat returned to his fire, he reflected on the turn of events. So it was true; the Bantusai had indeed turned on them. He had not been entirely sure of their treachery due to the confusion of the ambush, but now they would die along with the soldiers they had allied themselves with. Everything came down to time. The longer they were detained here, the harder it would be for Vorgat to realise his aims. The other clans would become restless and the Shifter soldiers would lose heart. He would have to finish these southlanders off swiftly. To that end he already had the makings of a plan that would see them across the river and down the throats of their enemies. He went to summon the other clan leaders.

Chapter Twelve

The morning was an unexpectedly calm and almost peaceful one. The skies were blue and the sun was pleasantly warming. Some residual mist drifted off the water and over the green grass but soon dissipated. Birds sang in the trees and men could see a herd of deer wander amongst the ruins of the old town on the edge of the forest. Most of the residents of the fort were sleeping; only a few had been left on stag. These sentries had seen little activity for some time. The only sign that there had been any action the night before was a few arrows that could be seen sticking out of the ground on the eastern bank. Any bodies had since been removed. Sergeant Pike had, of course, got up a half an hour earlier, and was already busy chivvying his men along in the preparation of breakfast. A fire was burning merrily and a pot of porridge was on the go.

'It doesn't bloody matter if we make a noise now; they know we're here so we might as well die with full bellies,' he was heard to announce.

Nothing much happened during that first daylight hour. Forge had actually got a good night's sleep and felt pretty rested. It hadn't escaped his notice that even the weather had taken a turn for the better since they had headed north. He munched contentedly on a sweet roll and slurped on his steaming-hot mug of coffee. All in all, things seemed remarkably positive. His men were in good spirits and it was a beautiful day. This was helped by knowing that not one man had been left behind the night before. Well, that was not strictly true of course. Locke had not been accounted for; presumably he was dead. Forge did feel responsible for the loss – the young officer was one of his men – but the man had proved himself to be nothing but a liability and, to be honest, his loss had done nothing to dent the morale of the men. In the final reckoning, the night action had helped in reducing the odds a bit; put the enemy on the back foot. He wondered what the Harradan leaders would be thinking on the other side. I bet they're pissed off, he thought. Been walking for days, taking a load of casualties from some strays from Noel's Gap, think they've got rid of them, then they stride into a full-blown ambush. And to add insult to injury they are betrayed by the people supposed to be working for them! Then, of course, the best bit – a restored and fully manned fortification, but no bloody bridge. He figured they might already be thinking about jacking it in now and heading off home. As it was, the events of last night must have put their plans into something of a spin. And the longer they debated it the better. It was all time. Every bit was precious. Every minute they did not go south increased the chances of their mission failing.

In fact, nothing happened for the rest of the morning. Forge had to be honest, he was starting to think that maybe they had decided to sack it all and go home. As there was nothing to do but wait, most of his men were lounging about, sleeping or playing cards. There was only one man on sentry duty now, currently Corporal Jonas. He was stuck up in the 'crow's nest', as the boys had taken to calling the small construct on top of the third storey. There was little need to present easy targets for the Shifter archers, who must by now have positioned themselves in the woods on the eastern bank. In fact, the only men now on the ramparts were the five archers who had laid themselves out on the wooden walkway. Below in the courtyard most were underneath the walkways so as to be covered from any incoming fire. Engaged in the never-ending business of feeding a hungry force, only Sergeant Pike and some of his men moved about in the open.

It wasn't until after lunch that things started to happen. It was Private Smitty who first noticed it. Trees were swaying in the forest to the east. Swaying then disappearing. So that was their game. They were preparing something. Forge had climbed up to the third storey and stood gazing to the east, his hands resting on the ramparts. Sergeant Mac stood with him.

'What do you see, Smitty?'

'Fair bit of movement, boss. Reckon there's a whole bunch being cut down.'

Forge looked at Sergeant Mac. 'What do you think? Rafts?'

Sergeant Mac hawked and spat. 'Could be making a bridge.'

'Have to be a bloody big one.'

'Not really. We still got those supporting posts in. They don't need anything permanent.'

Forge slapped his hand down on the stone embrasure.

'Damn.' He stalked off, turned round and came back to the wall. 'This plan of ours has got more holes than a pin cushion. They can come at us from the south, they can come at us from straight across the river. Hell, if they wanted to they could put those rafts in further up north and float down.'

'We got both those flanks covered, boss,' pointed out Sergeant Mac.

176

'But not with many soldiers. Not enough anyway. The only thing we got going for us is that they don't know how many we are. If they did try the raft idea from the north in any numbers they could get people across.'

'But they don't know that. And if they do try, at least we can get people to hurl a few discouraging suggestions their way.'

Forge nodded at this but made no reply.

'And at the end of the day we have done as much as we can do,' Sergeant Mac continued doggedly. 'If nothing else we've already bought a day, and it didn't cost us 'cept some ball-breaking construction work, which, I might add, was your idea.'

Forge smiled. 'Sorry for being a slave-driver then. But I didn't see you getting your hands dirty.'

Sergeant Mac sniffed. 'Twenty-odd years in the Army. Man and boy. First Sergeant. My value is in my supervisory position. Years of experience.'

'Of telling other people what to do,' laughed Forge. 'Just like me.'

Sergeant Mac grinned back. 'Lazy sons of bitches these days, aren't we?'

'Well, we bloody deserve it!'

'See, just like I said.'

Forge laughed and clapped him on the back.

A mile to the south the Bantusai waited close to the river's edge. They had concealed themselves well and had watchers out over a span of a quarter of a mile. On his signal, the line would fold in on itself and his men would converge on the crossing point wherever it may be. Juma had judged this to be the nearest and easiest stretch of water in relation to the fort and therefore expected that

177

any attempt to cross would be here. From what he could hear from the other side his expectations were proving correct. Kely moved up silently to join him.

'It seems that they are trying to build rafts, Kai.'

'Yes, Kely. And by the way they chop at the trees they are attempting some form of stealth.'

Kely snorted. 'So only the birds and beasts within five miles will be startled by their racket.'

Juma smiled. 'Indeed, yet their leader is cautious. I believe he will send men across through the water to check this side. If so, we will allow them to cross before we strike. Make them feel they are safe.'

'As you say.'

There was a pregnant pause. Juma glanced over at the big Bantusai and smiled. 'You are thinking again, Kely. I can always tell. You have a look of pain in your face.'

Kely gave his characteristic shrug. 'It is just a strange place we find ourselves in. The forest is a strange one, yet it has its own life, its own bounty. And then I think of home.'

'Ah yes. I know, my friend,' responded Juma. 'You wonder what, in the name of our fathers, has caused us to be here, now, in such a place.'

'Yes, Kai. How did we come to be fighting alongside our captors, men we were to kill? Instead we wait to kill those who were to be our allies and whom we have seen but once in darkness. Men we do not know or understand.'

'Kely, I am your Kai. Yet I can give you no easy answer. We must do what we think is right, always try to be men of honour. That is what makes us who we are. Bantusai. Feared and respected. Forge is a good man; his men are rough souls but they have nobility about them. We are lucky, my friend, to be able to choose the manner in

178

which we leave this world. Perhaps for what we do now, for this white-skinned man, we will be repaid. Perhaps in the shedding of our blood, some of us may get home, and those that do will tell our people of how we died.' He reached out and clasped Kely's shoulder. 'And they will be proud.'

Kely nodded, grinned and slapped his Kai on the back. He turned to look at the far bank and was silent for a moment. 'Kai,' he said softly and indicated the river with a flick of his head. 'Men now enter the water.'

Juma followed Kely's gaze across the Rooke to the far side some twenty yards away. All along the far bank, Harradan, perhaps a score, shorn of armour and bare-chested, were entering the water. Some of them carried thin ropes, whilst others wore weapons strapped to their backs. Juma quickly motioned to his men to pull back into the trees. The signal was sent down the line of watchers and they quickly faded. Cautiously the Harradan swam across the river, the current causing them to reach the far bank some distance further to the south of their entry point. They quickly scrambled out of the water and those that were armed drew their weapons and gazed into the treeline. Seeing nothing they signalled back across the river. Those bearing the thin ropes took up the slack and pulled. The ends of the ropes were tied to thicker, heavier lengths that were dragged through the river and then tied off around nearby sturdy-looking trees. There were shortly five of the ropes in place. A further five were pulled across but not attached

On the far side, activity increased as more Harradan manhandled crudely made rafts through the trees and then into the water. Men scrambled aboard and quickly grabbed hold of the ropes to steady the craft; others joined

179

them carrying the arms and armour of those who had already crossed. The five ropes that had not been tied off were now tied to the raft themselves so that they could be hauled across by those on the far bank. Once fully laden – each raft carrying about ten men – the Harradan holding on to the ropes shouted to their fellows. Men on the west bank began to pull, whilst those on the rafts steadied the crossing by moving hand over hand along the thicker guide ropes.

The Bantusai struck when the rafts had reached the midway point. Twenty arrows flew out of the undergrowth and peppered the armed but not armoured Harradan. The Bantusai followed this up by a bellowing charge into the men manhandling the ropes. Within moments the Harradan clansmen on the west bank were all down. There was uproar from the far bank and something resembling panic as those on the rafts tried to pull themselves across unaided, knowing full well how exposed they were. A few arrows flew from the eastern side but did little to bother Juma and his men. As they began to shoot at those on the rafts, others got to work at cutting the ropes. The cries and shouts grew even louder as men were hit and pitched into the water, whilst those remaining put up their shields to cover the men pulling on the guide ropes. None of the rafts made it to the far side as one by one the ropes were swiftly cut and the wooden platforms started to drift unhindered down the river. The Harradan started to pull back towards the east bank whilst continuing to take harrying fire from the Bantusai. As its riders took hits, one of the rafts lost its lifeline and began to move downriver, its surviving Harradan jumping into the water in panic.

Juma laughed at the chaos before him, the northmen

would certainly think twice before attempting a crossing like that again. The other rafts were now emptying as the Harradan gave up on the ropes and leapt for the bank. Many began to flounder as their weapons and equipment pulled them under.

Kely joined Juma. 'Kai, another force is crossing to the south.'

Juma whipped his head around in alarm. 'What?'

'In similar numbers to these. Our farthest man caught a glimpse of movement and stayed to check.'

'Then his wisdom has saved us. Have they gained this side?'

'No doubt they will be fixing their ropes now. Perhaps they have heard their friends and move quickly,' said Kely.

'It is too late to go and close with them. They will be warned of our presence. Quickly! Tell the men to pull back. Perhaps we cannot fight them, but we can surely sting them, if only for a few minutes. We will hit and run. Go!'

Kely nodded and moved to gather the others. Juma bit his lip and swore. These northmen were not all as stupid as they looked. He turned and watched the Harradan scramble out of the water, helped by their fellows. Then he followed his men back into the woods.

A short time later the attack over the bridge began. The first wind of it came from a small, silent shower of arrows appearing from the undergrowth of the eastern bank. The lookout had no time to shout a warning. No less than ten well-aimed flights peppered his post. The first arrow took him in the chest, a second found its way to his throat. He lay slumped in the watchtower, his lifeblood flowing down the wooden struts. Nobody noticed immediately as the second wave, much larger than the first, fell upon the courtyard. It was fortunate that most of the men were positioned either low upon the eastern parapet or sheltering below it. The only hit scored was on a bucket of water that Sergeant Pike had been humping across the open space. It embedded itself firmly in the bucket with a thunk. The Quartermaster looked at it in surprise. 'Fuck!' he cried as he dumped the bucket and legged it towards the shelter of the walkway. 'Fuck, fuck, fuck!'

At the time Forge had been in the bottom floor of the tower. He ran up to the third level and keeping low moved to get a view of the river. Sergeant Mac and two others were already there, crouched behind the wooden wall portion of the tower. Most of the arrows appeared to be heading for the main courtyard, however. Down below he heard Sergeant Grippa telling everyone to hold their positions. The archers on the eastern wall had already been briefed not to return fire. There really wasn't much point.

Forge crouched next to his sergeant and looked out on to the fire bank. He could see figures over there, but they kept themselves away from the edge of the water, firing out from gaps in the trees. Sergeant Mac tilted his head and indicated the dead lookout.

'Corporal Lens.'

'Shit.'

'No chance of us hitting 'em from here, boss. Our boys below have only got short bows – no penetration.'

'Get Jonas up there; see if he can't use that bloody longbow of his.'

Sergeant Mac nodded and motioned to one of the others to go and fetch him.

The arrows continued to fall for another minute or so

and then stopped. Moments later Corporal Jonas emerged, humping his bow and two sheaves of arrows in his pack, his entire supply. He kept low as he moved to the tower. Behind him came the other soldier, who now bore a shield on his back; better protection against an arrow as he worked. Jonas gave his kit to the soldier and quickly climbed the ladder to the Crow's-Nest. Working his way into the small platform he got his hands around the legs of Corporal Lens and heaved him out. The body gave a dull thump as it hit the wooden floor of the tower.

'Over the side, boys,' said Sergeant Mac.

Whilst they always tried to bury their dead with dignity, it wouldn't help now to have a cadaver just lying around stinking the place up. The men of the company were nothing if not pragmatic. The two soldiers pulled him over to the northern side where the tower joined with the outer wall. They took off his weapons and then got a hold of either end and, with a quick count of three, stood up and hauled the body on to the stone parapet and then rolled him off, none too gracefully, to fall to the ground below. They quickly dropped down and scuttled back to the crouched sergeant and captain, just as Corporal Jonas cried out 'Incoming.' Another flight of arrows clattered on the floor, thumped on the parapet or mainly just overflew the tower. It was a purely opportunist shoot. A couple did strike the Crow's-Nest but Corporal Jonas had already ducked.

'Fuckers!' was his only slightly muffled response from behind his wooden railings. The next second he raised his head, squinted and then stood up. As he did so he pulled back on his bow and loosed an arrow. Forge barely saw its flight. Such was the strength needed to pull back on a longbow that the arrow flew with incredible power. The shafts could easily pierce armour at a fair distance. He saw it enter the trees but nothing else happened. He quickly ducked back into cover again. 'Get him?'

'Got him.'

'Good.'

A further ten minutes later Corporal Jonas called down to Forge.

'Better look at this.'

Forge looked up from the knife he had been sharpening, taken from the dead and dumped soldier. You didn't worry about the provenance of weapons in his job. He turned and raised his head over the side. Above the trees he could see streamers of smoke. Following their course down he could make out a number of dots of firelight. The afternoon was well advanced now and the eastern forest was beginning to darken. He guessed that it must be darker in there than he thought.

'Can you hit any with those markers?' he asked his scout.

'Reckon.' Corporal Jonas stood up, fired and then ducked again. There was no answering volley. 'Guess they are waiting for me to poke up again.'

Forge glanced out again. There seemed to be more dots of fire now, many more. The next thing he saw were little balls of flame take to the air and stream towards the fort.

'Shit.' He ducked, expecting to see the arrows thump around him. Bloody fire arrows. They were trying to set light to the fort then? That was hardly going to work. They had deliberately soaked all the new wooden additions to the fort the day before. He glanced up again and saw that none of the arrows had actually entered the fort. They had fallen in and around the fire trench!

'Those fuckers,' he announced to the world in general. 'Corporal Jonas!'

'Sir?'

'Fucking shoot the bastards.'

'Right.'

Forge then made a break for the stairs and leapt down them. Taking advantage of their divided attention, Jonas loosed another arrow into the trees. In response, several of the hidden archers switched fire and again struck the Crow's-Nest. Many hit and held in the wooden posts and two landed on top. They were still burning. Jonas ducked down and shouted to the soldiers beneath him.

'Better get a bucket!'

Forge burst out of the eastern rampart door and ran bent-double towards the south-facing wall. He joined Sergeant Mac, who was leaning casually against the rampart.

'Those bastards are trying to set light to our bloody trench,' Forge declared breathlessly.

'That's cheatin',' agreed Sergeant Mac sarcastically.

'Is it catching?'

'It will soon. They got a lot of rounds there and some are right on top of the kindling wood.'

'It will be faster than that, Sergeant,' said Portal, who had come to join them. 'See?' He gestured with his hand to one end of the trench. 'Already it takes hold. Remember I spent much of yesterday ensuring it would.' If anything, Forge thought, he looked even worse than last night. The man looked to have visibly aged.

As they watched, a series of sparks ignited along the trench and a gentle 'woomph' accompanied the eruption of flames all along the length of the earthwork.

'Bugger,' muttered Sergeant Mac.

'Another good job, Portal,' observed Forge.

'A pity,' the wizard conceded.

185

'What they trying to do? Smoke us out with our own fire?' asked Sergeant Pike, who was looking through a gap in the gate.

'Seems to me, that maybe they are trying to keep us in,' observed Sergeant Mac.

Forge thought about it for a moment and nodded. 'If that's so, and I think you're right – then they are giving themselves some cover. They're planning on coming across soon.'

'There it goes,' said Sergeant Mac, pointing to where one of the kindling piles was blazing merrily. It gave out a great deal of smoke as it did so. That was deliberate. Forge had got his men to collect pine branches and other smoke-giving plant-material. It was a more effective shield as long as the wind was right. However, the intention had been to fire it only once the enemy had crossed the river and was about to attack. 'Perfect cover from view,' he muttered. 'They aren't as stupid as they look. Kind of hoping they would have been. How do you reckon they hit on doing that?'

'Perhaps they had prior knowledge?' suggested Portal. 'We know they have a magic-user. In fact, I have spent much the night trying to contact them.'

Forge looked over in surprise. 'Really, you can do that?'

Portal shrugged. 'Unfortunately I am not adept at true communication. But I can at least reach out with my feelings, get a sense of the potential of the person.'

'And what did your feelings tell you about this bloke?' asked Sergeant Mac.

Portal shook his head. 'Not a man, Sergeant. A woman. You can tell the difference in the way the magic is used and accessed by someone. I would expect she is some kind of witch. A seer, a weaver of dreams and curses. They are quite common amongst the Harradan.'

186

'And how powerful is she?' asked Forge.

'I could not be sure. She keeps herself hidden, her thoughts well shielded. But I would say that she is at least the equal of me. I doubt that I could counter her or stop her watching us from afar. I can shield my thoughts but not those of others around me,' replied Portal.

Forge chewed his lip. 'Odd that, I don't think Holis Lode and his people would have been able to stay ahead of the Harradan if there had been magic used against them.'

'Is it worth trying to put the fire out?' asked Sergeant Mac.

'Nah, let it go,' replied Forge.

As they watched, the fire quickly started to spread. They barely noticed that the bow fire had slowly dwindled off. Corporal Jonas had. He had been watching, looking for another chance to shoot. For some reason, those that had been on the northernmost point of the line had quit firing before the others. He didn't think they had run out of arrows so soon. He did see a fair bit of movement in the trees but it was quick and he couldn't draw a bead on it. It seemed as if they were pulling back. But they were heading northward; some of them at any rate. He didn't know why and shrugged his shoulders. Maybe they'd pissed off a bear or something. At least it had stopped them for a bit.

Jonas turned to watch how the fire trench was progressing. There were now several spots where the fire had taken. He figured in about ten minutes the whole length of it should be burning merrily. He then moved his gaze to the far side of the bridge crossing. He couldn't quite make out what it was he was seeing. Several lines of trees seemed to be marching along the trail. He squinted and leaned further, ignoring the possible threat of arrows. As

187

he did so the trees burst out on to the crossing area. But they were not trees. They were mantlets, about seven foot in height. They were quickly put into position, one next to another in sequence. A perfect screen for the Harradan. He had to give someone over there some credit, the Shifter commander perhaps? Even at his angle he could only hope to drop arrows behind them, with no hope of aiming and little more of hitting anything. He shouted down but needn't have bothered. Through the gathering smoke the rest of the watchers had spotted the mobile shields too. The Harradan could now get right up to bridge without fear of violence from the fort. The fire trench would further obscure the view.

Forge watched helplessly. There was nothing he and his men could do to disrupt the crossing. They had cleverly used his own defences against him. Granted the trench should buy them some more time, but not much. Another shout drew him back from his private musings. He looked up at the tower and saw his men pointing south. Such was the hour and the smoke that it took him a few moments to be able to focus on what they were pointing at. Then he saw it. A group of dark figures had emerged from the south and were running full tilt across the clearing. The Bantusai. Shit, he had clean forgotten about them. They would have to get a move on to clear the trench. He turned to give the order to unseal the gate hatch. He didn't get a chance. Another cry went up and he turned to look at the bridge site again. His men were crying out from the tower.

'They're coming!'

He felt his heart sink.

Across the river, the Harradan were making their assault on the crossing. With the protection of the mantlets, gangs of men were bringing forward crude ramps, nothing more than logs tied together. They were easily wide enough to touch on to the vertical struts lying in the water. Gathered just at the edge of the trail, a whole mass of men waited to cross. The Bantusai were going to run straight into them as they crossed. They would be cut off. Sense suggested to Forge he should stay within the protection of the walls, but bugger that. He had made a promise and in so doing they had become *his* men. He was damned if he was going to give up on them.

He crouched down and half lowered, half leapt to the floor, shouting as he went.

'Sergeant Grippa, your squad with me now. Sergeant Mac, fire support when we need it. Unblock that damn door!'

Already men were working loose the sealed gate hatch. Sergeant Grippa and a flying squad of ten men formed up behind him. As soon as it was free Forge was through and leading his men across the open space between the fort and the fire trench. He picked a spot that seemed slightly less fierce than the rest of the burning defence. Thanks to the bund he cleared the trench and continued onwards towards the bridge. The Harradan had quickly lain the ramps over two-thirds of the span. He could see men go down as Corporal Jonas picked them off with his longbow. But numbers and momentum meant that the last ramp to this side was coming down no matter what.

Sergeant Mac and Portal watched as Forge led his men toward the river. The Sergeant turned his nose towards the fire trench. It was now well and truly ablaze. And the flames were damn high.

'Yes, Sergeant, stronger than a normal fire and longer lasting,' observed Portal.

'Going to be a nightmare to get back across then.'

189

Mac spat then glanced left. 'Sergeant Pike!'

'Yes?' responded Pike from further down the rampart.

'Better get some buckets of water and find something we can lay across that bloody fire. We need to make a path for the boys to get back in.'

'Right.'

'It'll take more than that to put those flames out, Sergeant,' Portal stated loudly as he gazed at the flames.

Sergeant Mac gave Portal a hard look. 'Magic?'

'Indeed.'

'Damn me but you're better than I gave you credit for. So can you deal with it?'

'If I try to extinguish it completely then there will be no relighting it. Besides, I might not be permitted to. Their witch might decide to take a hand.'

'Looks like we don't have much of a choice then.'

Portal remained silent for a few moments.

'I am not sure if I can ...'

Ahead of Forge the Bantusai were fifty yards away. The final ramp was laid and the first northerners commenced their crossing. Screaming a battle cry he charged at the Harradan. His men took up the cry and smashed into the leading ranks of warriors. They met where the ramp hit the pier. The speed and fury of the Ashkent attack took the Harradan by surprise. They stalled and were pushed back a few feet. Such was the width of the ramp that fighting was restricted. Indeed many Harradan found themselves being pushed over the side in the crush. Forge, who had slammed his sword like a spear into the gut of a bare-chested warrior, had little time to withdraw it before the press of bodies turned the fight into a scrum. Neither side could swing a weapon and it turned into a pushing and shoving match. Forge changed tactics and headbutted the nearest enemy whilst around him fists flailed.

Slowly and inexorably the press of men against his small group told and they were forced back off the pier. As that happened, it freed up movement and Forge found himself able to use his weapons again. He hacked at the neck of an assailant, burying the blade deep. A fountain of blood erupted as he tore it away. Turning half left, he smashed the nose of another with the hilt of his sword. He was dimly aware that the Harradan were gaining a foothold and his men were swamped. Suddenly he heard a screaming cry of voices and the Bantusai swept into the Harradan flank. All about him their ranks thinned as they were taken down by the spear-wielding tribesmen. He could hardly credit it but they had taken the fight away from him and his men, who stood about him taking a moment's respite. All he could see was a blur of bodies as the Bantusai used their weapons with skill, striking with a swiftness that made him dizzy. Another Harradan got past them and charged at Forge, who raised his weapon. Juma appeared by the man, tripped him with the blunt end of his spear and then forced it into his exposed back. He looked up and smiled. 'Are you well, Captain?'

Forge wiped some sweat from his brow and grinned. 'Just getting warmed up.'

'Sir!' cried one of his men.

Forge and Juma turned to see another force of Harradan emerging from the trees, exactly where the Bantusai themselves had exited the forest.

'More guests!' observed Juma.

'We need to pull back.'

Juma nodded and gripped Forge's shoulder. He fixed him with a hard stare.

'You remember your promise?'

'I do.'

'So do I.' He smiled at Forge clapped him on the back and laughed. He then shouted a string of commands to his men and pressed forward. 'Go, Captain. Go.'

Forge quickly ordered his men to pull back, expecting Juma to follow. Instead, the Bantusai increased their attack, driving the northmen further back across the bridge. At the front of his men was Juma, flanked by two other Bantusai. They had now pushed the enemy back and beyond their final ramp. Forge watched as the tribesmen fell back, leaving Juma and his two companions to continue the fight.

'What the hell are you doing?' he shouted.

Before he could act he watched in dismay as two Bantusai lifted the ramp and cast it into the Rooke. They then turned and ran for the fort. Forge stood and watched Juma fight his way along the bridge. It was an extreme act of bravery. Worthy of a noble, bloody fool.

Forge turned at the shout of his name. He looked to his right and saw that the Harradan from the trees were almost upon him. He turned and ran. As he made for the fire trench he saw that it was now completely ablaze and his men were gathered on the wrong side of it. Suddenly the flames began to part and a small channel formed. The soldiers began to stream through it and then quickly the last of the retreating Bantusai were through.

As Forge angled towards the gap he could see Portal, his arms outstretched holding the flames apart. Even at this distance he could hear shouts of pain from the wizard as he struggled to maintain the space. Behind he could hear and sense the pursuit gaining on him. Arrows began to flash past his head and he heard grunts and cries of pain as his people gave him cover from the fort. On the far side through the smoke he saw that they were firing from the parapet, which caused him some concern as the smoke was obscuring his view all too well; he hoped it was easier for them to see him.

Twenty yards from the trench he passed across a depression in the ground. His foot landed heavily at an angle and he felt his knee give way. He fell and cried out in pain and anger. He quickly stood up and tried to run again but his leg collapsed a second time. He swore in anger. He wasn't going out like this; getting stabbed in the back like a wounded animal. With a shout he pushed himself up, transferred his weight on to his right leg and spun round to face his pursuers. One Harradan was only yards away and as he drew near Forge swept his sword round and down in an arc that cut into the warrior's leg. It unbalanced Forge and he fell on to his right side. He got himself up on to his knee and skewered the fallen man in the chest. As he did so he looked and saw another charging at him with axe raised. An arrow thudded into the man's chest and he was thrown backwards still holding the axe. Large black arms were suddenly around him and he was hauled to his feet. He saw that his helper was Kely. The big man got an arm around him and together they stumbled towards the fire trench.

Around them arrows began to fall as the Shifter archers came back into the fight after their brief hiatus. The gap in the fire was now thinning dramatically. Portal was screaming in agony as the mental and physical drain of his magic tore him apart. Kely literally threw Forge across the trench and followed after. More of his men were on the other side with shields raised to ward off the arrows from across the water. These were more random in flight as the smoke from the fire now obscured the vision of the Shifter men. Except where Portal stood. As Kely rolled on to the ground in front of the gap two arrows punched into the wizard and he flew backwards. The two walls of flame slammed into each other. Ignoring the arrows, Forge crawled over to Portal. The man was breathing in shallow, ragged gasps. Blood was spreading out from the two wounds. Portal, skin deathly pale, turned his gaze to the soldier. He smiled, his teeth stained with blood.

'Best damn magic I've ever done ...'

His eyes rolled back and his breathing stopped. Forge gently closed the man's eyelids. He looked into the flames and then turned to stare back at the fort.

'OK, let's go. Push him into the fire.'

Kely and a soldier, flanked by shield bearers, quickly pushed Portal's corpse into the flames. Kely helped him up and they headed for the gateway whilst his men followed up behind. None of the Harradan attempted to cross the trench to follow them. Forge stumbled through the hatchway and was laid gently to the ground up against the wall of the fort. As the last soldier came through, the gate hatch was put back in place and a bar and buttresses put across it. He looked about him and saw the remaining Bantusai and a few of his own men, looking tired and grimy up against the eastern wall. Many had the blood of dead foes upon them. Several bore their own wounds; it looked worse for the Bantusai as they wore no armour to hide the cuts and bruises received in battle. Kely dropped his big frame next to his.

'Thanks,' said Forge.

Kely did not respond. He sat facing into the courtyard, his chest was heaving and covered in beads of sweat. His head was tilted forward and his eyes were closed.

' Juma ...?' Forge was about to ask.

'He fell. That is all,' said Kely. He turned and regarded Forge with a blank expression.

Forge knew well enough that at times like this there was nothing else to say. He turned his head and looked up at the smoke-filled sky.

Chapter Thirteen

An hour later and the fire trench, enhanced as it was with Portal's magic, was burning fiercely with no apparent sign of dying out. The light from it illuminated the entire area around the fort keeping the night-time darkness at bay. Both sides had retreated beyond bow range and settled down to watch the trench burn itself out. Forge guessed that wouldn't be for a while yet; Portal had really gone to town on it. From his position at the top of the tower, Forge could see pretty much all of the clearing and on to the far bank with ease. It had taken him a painful five minutes to mount the steps of the tower. He could now move under his own steam again but his leg was stiffening up. There would be no more running for him for a while. Down below Sergeant Pike had started dinner and men were greedily tucking into their meal. The Quartermaster wasn't too bothered about rationing at this stage and let the men have their fill.

Looking back, Forge watched the Harradan moving in the semi-darkness. They had been steadily consolidating their positions on the western bank. Further mantlet screens had been erected in a straight line across from the bridge and extended out by fifty yards. It was probable that they realised the Ashkent force had only a few bowmen and could trouble them little. Behind the safety of the screen the main force had moved across the ramps and had now set up a camp down by the southern edges of the cleared zone. They hadn't trusted the wagons to get across and had been humping all the supplies over the river. They were now leading the mules across one by one. They would probably be used as pack animals now.

The Harradan had lit campfires and their light added to the bright glow in the night sky. A camp of two thousand men was no small thing and they sprawled out all along its southern edge and crept around its western fringes too, taking care not to drift too near inwards and in range of Corporal Jonas and his bow. Not that their own fires were more than a marker for Jonas, but to shoot was a waste of arrows. Still there might be a shade less than two thousand men now. There had been a fair few bodies left on the western bank and by all accounts the crossing further south had lost them a few more. Sounded like the Bantusai had caused havoc. Good for them. The Bantusai had lost two men to arrows further south; it appeared that the second crossing had been supported by Shifter archers. They had lost another four in the fight at the bridge; one taken by an arrow on the retreat and the three who had held the Harradan off to allow the others to escape. Forge was surprised at how stoically they took their prince's death. He guessed it was just a cultural thing. He had liked Juma. Silly bugger.

Forge paused to consider his own losses. Sergeant Mac had come up earlier to give him the news. Three men had been lost in his charge down to the bridge. That included Sergeant Grippa. If he included young Locke, he had now lost ten of his command all told. Not good considering his plan had been devised to minimise losses. It would make holding the walls against a determined attack that much harder.

197

Sergeant Mac joined him, surveyed the scene for a moment and then spat.

'Funny old thing about Portal.'

'Just goes to show I guess,' responded Forge.

'Yeah, you know I think he might even have started to like us. Given time.'

'The man saved my life. Either he was actually reforming or just bloody stupid. Really could have done with him staying alive,' sighed Forge

'Kely is here, boss,' said Sergeant Mac.

Forged turned round to see Kely. He stood erect, held his spear in one hand and his bow and a clutch of arrows in the other.

'You the ... Kai, now?' Forge asked him.

'No, not Kai. But I ... leader?'

'OK. Well, here it is. I promised your Kai that I would make sure you'd get home. I can't do that. Chances are none of us are getting out of this. But whilst it's dark you and your people could still get out.' Kely listened impassively and just to make sure, Forge gestured to show what he meant; though he felt like a twat for doing it. 'Go over the north wall, pick a spot where the flames are low, and make a run for it. They might have watchers but I doubt they could stop all of you. I don't think they would waste their time trying to chase you.'

Kely failed to respond. Captain Forge looked at Sergeant Mac. Sergeant Mac looked at Captain Forge.

'Do you understand? You can go.'

Kely looked at him.

'We stay.'

He turned and walked down the steps. He spoke again as his head disappeared.

'We like Sergeant Pike's cooking. Very nice.'

198

Captain Forge looked at Sergeant Mac. Sergeant Mac looked at Captain Forge, who sighed tiredly.

'How's the leg?' asked Sergeant Mac.

'Hurts like a bastard.'

'Usual then.'

'Yeah.'

'Good, good,' said Sergeant Mac in an absent tone and then wandered off.

Forge was glad he had Sergeant Mac around.

Later that night Privates Smitty and Thom shared a pipe as they stood the watch on the north wall. Sat the watch was nearer to the truth. One or the other would occasionally look over the ramparts to see how the fire was going and then settle back down. They sat quite contentedly puffing away when a fist-sized stone landed on Smitty's lap.

'Fuck!' he spluttered. He rolled it off his legs like it might jump up and bite him. 'Fuck!' he added for extra emphasis.

'It's all right, mate,' said Thom laughing. 'I don't think they need to start hurling wee beasties at us yet.' He reached over and picked up the projectile. That was when he noticed that the stone was covered in a piece of cloth that might have been mistaken for white in another life. He unwrapped the cloth and squinted at it. Written on the piece of material was one word: 'ROPE'. They exchanged a look. Private Thom crawled forward and leaned over the walkway.

'Sarge!'

Ten minutes later a rope was lowered over the side between two embrasures. Thom and Smitty peered out to either side of the gap whilst the half-dozen archers lay behind the wall with their bows drawn. Down in the courtyard Sergeant Mac and Captain Forge waited. Five minutes after that, in the corner of the fire trench where the northern line met the eastern line right by the edge of the water, a figure scrambled across the flames and crawled up to the foot of the wall. It grabbed the proffered rope and was hauled up. The man fell on to the floor of the rampart. Holis Lode looked up and grinned at Forge.

'Fancy seeing you here,' he said brightly.

'You just can't leave us alone, can you?' smiled Forge.

'I'm like a bad smell,' replied Lode, propping himself up against the wall.

'What can we do for you?' asked Forge.

'Thought you'd might like to go on a little raiding party.'

'Always open to ideas. Come down and get a coffee.'

'A beer would be good.'

'We could do that, too.'

The two men and Sergeant Mac climbed down to the courtyard and Lode availed himself of the ale supply. He drank deep, wiped his mouth and then helped himself to some more.

'So what did you have in mind?' asked Forge as he sipped coffee.

'Well, as you can imagine they have got watchers in the woods to the north.'

'Indeed.'

'They change shifts about every two hours. So that means you got an hour give or take to go for a swim.'

'Go on.'

'The lads are back in the trees.' Lode looked back towards the north wall. 'We lost Arald a while back.'

'Sorry to hear that,' said Forge.

Lode nodded and took a swig of ale.

'Silly sod was getting too old anyways. As I was sayin',

200

the boys are back in the trees. We took care of the sentries. Only four of 'em. Archers actually. Which was handy.'

'Less to worry about,' agreed Sergeant Mac

'Yeah, what with the ones we sorted out earlier that is about half of 'em dead.'

'Good work,' said Sergeant Mac in approval.

'And we got those four's bows and arrows. We'll bring 'em over in a bit. Now, about that plan. Best as we can figure, they got nobody on sentry all the way over to the encampment proper. You could walk right up to 'em through the trees.'

'So you're thinking we might cause some trouble?' said Forge, a plan already forming in his mind.

Lode grinned again.

Ten minutes later the plan, ad hoc to be sure, was put into action. Lode and Corporal Jonas slipped back over the wall and disappeared into the night. A few moments later a mixed force of Ashkent and Bantusai, some twenty in number, went over the wall one at a time. Leading them was Kely. They had been picked for their speed rather than fighting prowess and the Ashkent men had shed all their armour. Only weapons were carried. Forge watched them go. A part of him wished to be going with them; it didn't feel right. But the older and far more sensible part of him pointed out that, in his present condition and advancing years, he should stop being so stupid. The force were now making their way around the perimeter of the forest and would make their move in twenty minutes' time. He just had to sit back and wait to see how things panned out. So he settled back against the wall and threw bits of stone at an imaginary target. Ten seconds later he got up and started pacing.

Corporal Jonas had cussed and cursed when he heard his part in Lode's plan. It wasn't that it was a bad plan. It was just that it involved him getting piss wet through and bastard cold to boot. The two men had gone back into the woods, met briefly with Lode's crew and had then slipped into the river. They carried only knives for protection and were clothed only in their undergarments. As expected, the water was freezing. Corporal Jonas mouthed an oath.

Lode looked over and smiled through gritted teeth. 'You're lucky, this is the second time I've had to do this today.'

'Lucky my arse. If I was lucky I wouldn't be in the middle of all this shit,' Corporal Jonas replied.

They pushed out for the centre of the river and allowed the current to take them downriver aided by a gentle breaststroke so as not to draw attention. As the crude bridge came into view, they both steered themselves to the posts near the eastern side. Lode took the nearest and Corporal Jonas the one that stood behind to it. Lode looked above him and then to either side. There seemed to be nobody on the bridge and no one left on the eastern bank. He turned to Cororal Jonas who indicated that there were two men standing on the western side of the rampway. As he looked, Lode could see that their backs were turned and they were deep in conversation. Hardly a surprise. Who would expect any silly fool to come down the river? Nodding to Corporal Jonas they set to work on the rampway. Using their knives they began to saw at the ropes that held the wooden poles together.

As they cut, Lode began to feel the cold eat into his bones. He felt himself begin to shiver in the water. His fingers were getting bloody painful. Once all the rope he could reach was cut he manoeuvred to face the next post along. Kicking out with his feet at a ninety-degree angle to the post to account for the current, he reached out and made a grab for it. The river got hold of him but he got an arm round and hugged himself to the wood. Corporal Jonas was already working on the next downriver post. They repeated the process and took off for the third in line. Lode was really suffering now. He barely had the strength to hold his arm up to slice the rope above him. Many times he had to stop, get a better grip and start again. Each time he got weaker and weaker. The diversion should be happening any time soon. Now would be better.

As he cut the final strand he lost his grip on the post and was swept off by the river. A hand reached out and grabbed him. Corporal Jonas pulled him back towards his own post and Lode quickly got a grip around it. The two men then spent a few tense moments shivering in the water. Then a cry went up from a distance away and this was followed by a whole chorus of shouts and cries as the camp erupted into chaos. On the far side, Kely and his men were launching their diversion. Quickly the two men pushed out for the western bank. This close to it they could stand up and gain some purchase against the current. Corporal Jonas made a splitting motion with his fingers and he went to the left and Lode to the right of the western pier. As they emerged from the water the two sentries had moved off a little and were looking out towards the source of the noise. Many men were up and about carrying torches and heading towards the fight.

Further along the line of mantlets, Lode saw more guards. If their attention had not been diverted elsewhere they might have seen the two of them creeping up on the pair at the bridge, so clearly were they illuminated by the two torches that burned on either side of the pier. As it was, only the two sentries presented an immediate problem. Lode wasn't sure if he had enough energy left to tackle his target. Walking slowly behind the man, he held his knife ready. Making no noise on the soft, well-trodden grass, he got to within a foot of his prey. Out of necessity they were still wearing boots, but fortunately the soft and now sodden leather made no squelching sounds. Looking from the corner of his eye, Jonas was ready to strike. Reaching out quickly Lode got his arm around the mouth of the Harradan. He firmly drew his blade across the man's throat and kicked him under the knee to bring him down. As he did so he jammed his knife into the neck of the dying northerner. He then dragged the man back towards the river and out of sight. Checking to his left Corporal Jonas had already disposed of his body. Jonas nodded to him and they mounted the pier and started to loosen the first ramp. Their luck held and they caused the ramp to split apart. Tree trunks fell into the river and dragged in their neighbours. The Harradan would now have to make a new ramp if they wished to cross the river again.

Behind them the shouts from the camp were dying down. It was time to go. Lode worked his way round the nearest rampart and made for the fort. Behind him, Jonas stopped for a moment, picked up the two torches and placed them on to the nearest mantlet. He turned to go but something suddenly stopped him in his tracks. Ahead of him stood a dark figure, cloaked and formless, though clearly small in build. The hood of the cloak was pulled well over the head, keeping the face hidden. The figure was silent and motionless and Lode felt himself being scrutinised. He was confused – why didn't they raise the alarm? Well, he didn't have time to worry about it and readied himself for a charge.

'You should leave. Get away from here,' said a soft, feminine voice.

Again Lode was shocked into inactivity. He had not expected a female and certainly wasn't comfortable about knifing one. But there was something about that voice ...

He raised his hands in the air and walked slowly towards the woman. 'I mean you no harm, woman, just let me pass,' he said. From the corner of his eye he spotted Corporal Jonas who was now edging quietly back towards him.

'I know you don't, Holis. You never have,' said the woman. She drew back her hood, letting it fall behind her.

Lode felt his heart skip a beat. 'Lissa!' he whispered. 'I never dared hope ...'

Lissa smiled sadly. 'I know what you would say. But you have no time. You must know whom you face. You cannot win here. Only die. Please go now whilst you have the chance. I can help to shield you from pursuit, just as I have these past days.'

Lode felt his anger grow. 'Then if Vorgat is here, perhaps it is time to settle the score.'

'Do not!' pleaded Lissa. 'You could not get to him, and if you did he would cut you to pieces. Let it be enough that you know I still live. It gives me a small joy to know the man you have grown into.'

Lode reached out and placed his hand on her cheek. 'And I would be no kind of man if I ran now. I'll make my stand here. Not just for you but for all the friends that I have lost. If I can't kill that bastard, at least I can hurt him. Come on, come with me.'

Lissa reached up and gently removed his hand. She smiled but her eyes were rimmed with tears. 'I cannot, Vorgat is ... He ... I cannot.' Lissa stopped, looked away

205

and shook her head. She turned back to look at Lode, but her eyes had grown cold. 'You go back to your doom, Holis. I will pray for you and tend your body when it is over.'

Lode felt his throat tighten up. He swallowed and nodded his head. He looked over to Corporal Jonas who was crouched behind a mantlet watching the exchange. With a short glance at Lissa he moved away from her and ran over to join his companion.

'Friend of yours?' asked Corporal Jonas.

'You could say that,' he replied. He turned and looked back. Lissa had not moved and continued to watch him. 'Let's go.'

They ran along the riverbank towards the far treeline. Moving back into the undergrowth they picked up their weapons and dressed. Old Hoarty joined them and told them the trappers were keeping a lookout for the Harradan coming north. Apparently there were a lot of lights moving round the far edge of the clearing.

Just as they finished dressing, the diversion force came steaming through the trees from the west. Without stopping they raced across the fire trench, which was now little more than embers, and used three ropes to climb up the outer wall. Kely came last, breathing heavily.

'Many come,' he whispered hoarsely to Lode before making for the wall.

Forge looked westward and saw Harradan torches in the trees only fifty yards away now. Looking back at the trees ahead of him he saw Jonas, Lode and the others running across the trench. They began to pass up the captured bows and arrows to the men above.

'Come on, come on!' he shouted.

The Harradan were at the treeline. A few moments later arrows began to strike the walls. Forge's men returned fire. Sleeps was shot in the back as he reached the top of the wall and fell back down to the ground below. He was hit a second time in the head as he tried to struggle up. He did not move again. On the wall Juggs screamed in despair and made to climb back down the rope. Lode and Fuzz quickly pulled her back and away from the edge. The Harradan did not follow but continued to send arrows across the divide. Looking back to the south, Forge could see that one of the mantlets was on fire and men were rushing to pull away the adjoining mantlet.

Now that everyone who was coming had climbed to safety, Forge slumped down behind the parapet. Corporal Jonas crab-walked over to him.

'All done, boss,' he said.

'Well, nice to now we get some things right,' remarked Forge.

'Didn't like that bloody river though.'

'Sorry, Corporal. I'll bear that in mind next time I order a daft mission to demolish a bridge.'

'Oh and you might like to know we had an unexpected meeting,' said Corporal Jonas, nonchalantly picking at his finger nails.

'Really?'

'Yeah, seems our young war genius knows someone on the other side. A woman. Got most of the conversation. Reckon she might be their witch woman and that the two of 'em might have some romantic history going on.'

Forge exhaled loudly. 'You know what Corporal? What with all that's happened over the last few days, it really doesn't surprise me.'

In the eastern sky, dark-red and orange threads were

streaking through the blue–black of night. Down below, Juggs wept and the remaining men of Noel's Gap sat a silent vigil around her.

'Well, dawn's here. So that means they'll be coming soon,' he said. This was the start of the second day of the siege. He did not think there would be another.

A fountain of blood shot out from Kron Battlebane's severed neck. He fell to his knees and clawed at his throat. Seconds later he pitched forward, the blood from the wound seeping into the ground. Vorgat wiped the blood from his sword on his arm, then sheathed it. He spat on the corpse, then spun round and walked back to his clan's camp. He noted with satisfaction that none of the remaining members of Kron's clan or the Bear Claws attempted to stop him. His leadership would now be unquestioned.

Soon after the surprise attack on the western end of the encampment began and word had reached him of the sabotage of the crossing, Vorgat knew he would have to act. It certainly had been no surprise to him when the attack had happened. He had correctly guessed the thinking of his foe and had expected more acts of daring from them. Once the attack had begun he had passed word to his lieutenants not to engage in the pursuit of the southerners. He had then walked over to the ambush site. As predicted, he was confronted by Kron and a handful of his men. The rest were still in the forest. He had deliberately placed the two most fractious clans on the western side of the encampment. They had not questioned this and did not think themselves vulnerable. Kron had probably welcomed the chance to start consolidating his own plans against Vorgat. Instead, his supporters had yet again suffered losses and were only now returning from their pursuit within the forest. As predicted, too, Kron had challenged the continued attack on the fort and had questioned Vorgat's decision to lead this campaign south. At which point Vorgat had drawn his sword.

An hour later he faced the remaining clan chiefs and Lordswood. Not so strangely, the leader of the Bear Claws had been found with his throat cut within the forest.

'Battlebane did not agree with my continued leadership of this campaign. Do any of you disagree?'

'What if we do, Vorgat?' asked the Broken Tooth leader. 'Would you kill us and all of our men? I think three would be harder for you than one.'

'Perhaps,' agreed Vorgat. 'But your men are tired and mine are still fresh. You do not have the numbers, I think, to challenge me.'

'So what do you propose?'

'That we do what we always planned to.' He looked at the tired- and drawn-looking Shifter captain. 'Have you been given orders to give up?'

Lordswood shook his head wearily. 'I have been given no such orders. But I do not see how we can hope to achieve our mission ...'

Vorgat held his hand up. 'Do not worry, Captain. I will see to it. Now gather your strength. We will launch the attack.'

The clan chiefs nodded their heads and departed. The Shifter captain, shoulders sloped dejectedly, walked away He, like they, now realised he was a slave to Vorgat's plan. The clan chief smiled as he watched them go. He felt, rather than heard, the witch behind him.

'I thought you had put wards upon our camp witch.'

'I had, Lord, but they were upon us too quickly. There is

209

something about those tribesmen. They have a way about them ...'

'And the river, did you not think to watch that?' Vorgat interrupted.

Lissa hesitated. 'I did not think ...'

Vorgat did not allow her to finish her sentence. He whipped around and delivered a powerful backhand blow to her face. Lissa cried out in pain and fell to the floor.

'You're job is not to think, bitch; it is to obey my wishes!' thundered Vorgat.

Lissa spat blood from her mouth and kept her head bent in supplication. It had been some time since Vorgat had struck her, but she remembered not to induce him to more violence. Those distant days had been hard lessons.

'Are you sure their wizard is dead?' he asked, his voice returning to its low growl.

'Yes, Lord. I felt his last life breath.'

'And these tribesmen – have they magic to stop us?'

'No, Lord, theirs is a singular power. It will not stop us.'

'Then tomorrow we shall finish this. Do not fail me again, witch. You will use your sight and make sure that no further surprises happen without my foreknowledge. Only that way will I believe that it's still useful keeping you alive.' He turned and strode away from the cowering witch. As he left her vision, Lissa began to weep.

As he walked through his clan's encampment Vorgat brooded. It was obvious to him now that this venture to the south was a doomed plan. They had wasted much time on this skirmish. More importantly, the spirit and energy of the other clans and the Shifter troops had been badly mauled. Their ability to fight further battles to the south was affected. But he would see the southerners crushed. He would kill the Shifter officer and his men.

Then he would give the clans a choice. Swear fealty to him or die. He would return to the north and he would become the high chieftain of all the clans; there was no one to stop him.

Chapter Fourteen

The attack came three hours later. The fire trench was now nothing more than an inconvenient obstacle. As Forge had guessed, the assault came from two fronts. The mantlets were pushed up to the trench line from the south, whilst from the north the remaining Shifter archers took up positions in the treeline. Behind them could be heard, if not seen, a large body of men. There appeared to be a great deal of cheering and chanting going on from the Harradan. Clearly the bastards were in good spirits before the fight. Forge himself was standing on the southern wall to the right of the gate. As he watched the mantlets move up he glanced around the fort and took in his dispositions.

On the northern walls, he had stationed Kely, a small handful of Ashkent troops and the surviving Bantusai. Their arrows were more useful over short distances anyway. And thanks to the tower they had less wall frontage to defend. Both doorways into the tower from that northern wall would be kept open for as long as possible. On the top of the tower he had placed Holis and his three surviving companions. As civilians he still felt an obligation to at least to try and protect them, even if it was only to keep them safe for a little while longer. Besides, regardless of the mayhem they had caused for the Harradan, they were not really fighting men. Their talents lay in shooting. Stationed up there they could draw a bead on both sides of the fort and when their arrows and crossbow bolts ran out they could dump rocks as good as the next man.

He was tempted to put Corporal Jonas up there too, but decided against it. He was too good a knife man to leave out of the defence of the walls. He had split his own archers, now ten in number thanks to the extra bows, on either side of the southern wall. A further ten men stood to on either side to engage the enemy. Down below Sergeant Mac had a flying squad of six men to plug any gaps. The remaining Ashkent troops were placed upon the eastern and western walls. Whilst the walls on these sides were longer and the manpower worryingly thin upon them, Forge expected less pressure there, at least in the initial stages. Forge glanced down at Sergeant Mac. The man looked implacable as he stood by the front of the gate chewing a plug of tobacco. He looked back up and shifted his weight. He rubbed his aching leg. That was really going to be useful in the coming fight. Not that he had ever been a graceful fighter, but he had always relied upon a certain momentum to get his hits in. He guessed he'd just have to rely now on brute arm strength.

The assault was announced by a flurry of arrows against the north wall. A few drifted into the courtyard and one landed not one foot away from Forge. The soldier next to him grinned and Forge gave him his best scowl back. A shout from the north wall told him that men were now moving against it; the Bantusai were up and firing. He quickly turned his attention back to his own front. The mantlets were right up against the fire trench.

'Ready to pour it on, lads,' he ordered. His men stood and drew their bows. A cry came from the Harradan and the mantlets were pushed on to the trench. Forge hadn't quite expected that. A handy ramp for them. With a collective roar the Harradan charged across.

'Fire!' Forge shouted. His men began to loose shaft after shaft at the charging enemy. At such a close range it was hard not to miss and many men tumbled and fell. Those that followed simply pushed them to one side or ran across the bodies in their haste to get to the wall. Behind the first wave came men bearing crude ladders, nothing more than small tree trunks with horizontal branches tied to either side. The ladders were quickly brought to the base of the wall and pushed into place. Forge counted at least a score on the southern wall alone. The Harradan men began to climb the ladders whilst his own people tried to push them away. Immediately in front of Forge a head appeared over the top of the wall and he thrust his sword into its face. The long day's killing had begun.

On top of the tower Lode fired an arrow into a Shifter archer who had emerged from behind a tree and had been taking aim. He was getting quite a tally of these guys. Whilst Juggs and Fuzz were busy firing into the melee below, he and Old Hoarty had decided to keep the pressure on the archers in the trees. Having fired, he ducked down behind the screen of stone and heaved back on his crossbow. Old Hoarty stood beside him, his own weapon resting on the stone wall. The solid surface kept it steady and Old Hoarty lined up another shot. Whilst the archers below kept up a greater rate of fire, the two trappers had greater accuracy and could aim and fire before a bowman could get a good-enough bead on them. Old Hoarty fired and swore. He quickly ducked and sat next to Lode.

'Missed. Reckon them bastards are getting wise to us. Moved back into the bushes 'fore I could hit 'im.'

214

'Sure you didn't...' Lode paused and grunted with effort as he put the bowstring into place. '... just *miss?*'

'Less of the lip, young feller.'

Lode laughed and turned and stood up to fire again. As he scanned for targets he saw that the Shifter troops had moved position and had fallen back along the treeline to the west. It gave them more cover but they could still put fire into the fort. Instead he tilted his weapon and fired into the press of figures below. The attack on the side was being held. A whole mass of Harradan had come crashing through the woods and had swept right over the fire trench with arrow fire following them in. The Bantusai had sent off several volleys before battle was joined at the walls. A large number of Harradan were left in the fifty yards of no-man's-land between the wood and the wall. The fighting was fierce but the speed of the tribesmen meant they could hold their length of wall easily. But their numbers were being whittled down by the constant nagging of enemy fire and Lode wondered how much longer they could hold.

'Hoarty, might as well start picking off climbers. We can't do much more against their archers.'

'Righto.'

As he sat back down to reload he saw that he was down to his last three bolts. Old Hoarty had about half a dozen.

He wondered where Lissa was, whether she might be watching him even now. It gave him an odd feeling in his stomach. All the old wounds had been opened and yet, seeing her, seeing what she had become, had caused a strange feeling of detachment. It felt that maybe the woman he had known was dead. The Captain had approached him about the meeting and Lode had given him a potted story of his life. Forge had scratched his chin and looked up at the sky and then asked, 'Don't s'pose she wants to switch sides?' Lode shrugged in response. 'Ah, well. Worth a try.' The Captain then reached over, patted him on the shoulder and said, 'Good job last night. Gutsy.' He had then wandered off, leaving Lode feeling bemused.

'Hey, Holis. Watch this!' said Fuzz.

Looking up he saw Juggs and Fuzz, who had both run out of arrows, heave a large stone onto the mass of Harradan to the left of the tower.

'That's for Sleeps, you bastards!' Juggs called down and then laughed manically to herself as he went to take another rock off the pile. Lode figured he would be humping those stones himself in a minute or two.

Sergeant Pike was killed on the western wall. An arrow lodged in his throat. Sergeant Mac ran to where the body had collapsed. There was a look of surprise in the Quartermaster's face. Sergeant Mac had always figured the man would die of a stroke. He was always far too fond of his own greasy cooking. Looking around, he tried to gauge the tide of the battle. As it stood, the Harradan were still pressing on the north and south walls and had committed less to the sides. They were holding their own. The longer the northerners were held back from gaining a foothold, the harder it became for them. As the dead gathered at the foot of the walls, they encumbered those waiting to climb. Almost as if in recognition of this, a horn sounded. It came from the south.

Forge took a moment to pull his sword from the body of a Harradan and then forced the dead man off the rampart. He looked up at the sound of the horn. The Harradan were pulling back to the encampment to the south; no doubt a chance for them to regroup before renewing the assault. At least it gave him a chance to rest up for a few moments. He leaned against the wall and watched the enemy withdraw. Sergeant Mac joined him and passed over a waterskin. Forge nodded his thanks and took several long gulps. He turned and looked towards the tower. A figure, which looked like Old Hoarty, waved at him. Forge snorted.

'So how're we holding up, Sergeant?' he asked his companion.

Sergeant Mac scratched his nose for a few moments and then nodded his head appreciatively. 'Not too bad. Loads of bodies.'

'Our losses?'

'Oh, a dozen or so.'

'That all?' Forge was surprised.

'Yeah. Good job we had the Bantusai. They really get into the spirit of the thing.'

'So, reckon they'll try for the walls again or concentrate?'

'Ah, well, what with our manpower situation, reckon they can do pretty much what they like.'

'True,' agreed Forge.

'Still, boss,' Sergeant Mac slapped his captain on the back. 'We did what we set out to do. Way I see it, those boys out there are here purely to finish the job on us. They won't be heading south.'

Forge looked at his old friend and smiled. 'Going down fighting and saving the day by doing it,' he grunted ruefully. 'Never thought of ourselves as heroes, Mac.'

'Sergeant Mac smiled back. 'We ain't, Sir. We're professionals.'

Another horn call drew their attention to outside the walls.

Forge's heart sank at the sight. Rolling forwards was a

hastily constructed ram. It was nothing more than a large tree trunk that had been crudely sharpened at its end. It was being pushed forward on wheels and had been tied on to an axle. No doubt one of the enemy's own supply wagons had been dismantled for this. Easy enough to do with their manpower. They must have moved it during the night because he was damned if any of his men had noticed it and they sure as hell didn't get any other wagon parts across after Lode and Jonas had cut up their bridge. A whole gang of Harradan were manoeuvring it over the fire trench across yet another ramp they had thrown across it. Forge had hoped they might get a respite; that the Harradan might pause before renewing the attack. No chance of that now. He had to hand it to whoever was leading this mob. For all the blocks and delays Forge had thrown against him this guy knew how to conduct a siege. And he feared it might be coming to an end very soon.

'Sir,' said Sergeant Mac.

'Yes, Sarge?'

'See you later,' Sergeant Mac held out his hand and Forge gripped it tightly. The grizzled soldier nodded, let go and headed for the courtyard. Forge watched him go with an odd feeling in his stomach. He shook his head. Now wasn't the time. He watched the ram cross the fire trench.

'Shoot those bastards!' he ordered his surviving archers who weren't already engaged. The ram had cleared the trench and was now beginning to pick up speed as it charged towards the gate. A few arrows flew towards it, hitting a couple of its crew. There were plenty more to take their place.

Down below Sergeant Mac also watched the ram heading towards him. For all that this gate was sturdily built he feared it wouldn't stand up to much punishment. He stood his small squad a few yards from the gate.

'Right, lads. Steady. When it hits, hold your position. Wait for it to break through. When it does don't wait for them. We charge straight in. Catch them off balance and kill as many as you can.'

His men nodded and stood their ground. They looked tense and anxious. Sergeant Mac was not surprised and he didn't blame them. It was a hard thing knowing that soon you were going to die. But they didn't run. That was what counted. That's why they were soldiers.

The ram smashed against the gate with a heavy thud. The wooden structure shuddered and creaked but did not give. Sergeant Mac shouted up at Captain Forge.

'Sir. Time to pull back.'

'I know!' he shouted back. But he didn't give the order. If they withdrew now, that would be it. They would be back in that tower. It suddenly seemed more like a death trap. Below him the ram was being pulled back for another run. There were no more arrows left to fire at it. It appeared that the assault on the south wall had lost its momentum. Both sides were waiting for the inevitable outcome. The ram picked up speed again and with a roar the Harradan threw all their strength into the last few yards of the charge.

'Sir, now!' shouted Sergeant Mac.

Forge dragged himself out of his indecision. He couldn't wait any longer.

'Pull back. Everyone back to the tower!'

As he shouted the ram smashed into the gate again. This time the wooden barricade did not hold. With a loud crack and a hail of splinters the ram and its carriage continued its path through and into the courtyard. With a battle cry

Sergeant Mac and his men charged into the Harradan who were clustered at the gaping hole left by the passage of the ram. Many had continued pushing it from the rear and they found themselves in the centre of the courtyard. Before they could cause mischief Lode and his friends burst out of the tower entrance and engaged them. Old Hoarty swung his crossbow, which connected with the face of a Harradan. Lode threw a knife into the throat of another. In the melee Fuzz was killed by an axe to his back. All around the ramparts Forge's men tried to disengage from the fighting. Those at the front with him leapt from the walkway and down into the courtyard. Some got caught in the fighting at the gate whilst others ran straight for the tower. Forge launched himself on to the back of a Harradan below him. He knocked the man to the floor, grabbed him by his hair and then butted his head into the ground. Pushing himself up, he parried a sword stroke to his right, following it up with a left hook to the face of his assailant. As the man took the blow and turned to his side Forge got two hands to his sword and swung it around and up. The man's head snapped back as the weapon connected and he fell to the ground. Forge saw he had space and started to hobble to the wagon barricade by the tower door. To his left and right on the ramparts he could see that the Harradan had gained the walls and his men were slowly getting pushed back along them. On the west wall they were already cut off from reaching the tower on their level by a fierce fight on the northern section.

'Jump down. Form a line on me. Get the fucking tower doors shut!' he ordered.

Some of the men on the western wall jumped down and ran to Forge. Others were cut down as they tried to do so. He could see his defences were collapsing quickly. They had to control their fall back or they would lose it completely.

On the north wall, the western tower door was shut and barred whilst a lone Bantusai held off a determined assault along the walkway. He skewered the first man with his spear, withdrew it and whipped its end round to smash into the helmet of the next. A Harradan spear then took him in the stomach. The eastern side was faring better as there was less pressure by the Harradan. Privates Smitty and Thom slowly backed down the rampart keeping the attackers at bay. Smitty swung his large broadsword, knocking aside any Harradan that charged down the walkway. Behind him Thom battered any of them that tried to climb over the wall.

Thom looked behind him and saw they were the last on the wall and the doorway was open. Kely beckoned them forwards. He turned and slapped Smitty on the shoulder.

'C'mon, mate. Time to go.'

As he did so a Harradan leapt on to the walkway behind Thom. Kely shouted and as Thom turned the Harradan buried his shortsword deep into him. Smitty then swung round. Seeing his friend collapsing on to his knees, he screamed and hacked savagely at the Harradan. As the northman fell to the ground, Smitty knelt beside his friend. Thom was already dead. He screamed in agony, picked up his sword and smashed it into another northman who was following behind the first.

'Come on then, you bastards. Come on!' he screamed as tears rolled down his face.

He almost killed Kely as the big black man pulled him back towards the doorway.

'Your friend is dead. You are not,' said the Bantusai firmly.

Smitty struggled at first. His grief and anger were overwhelming him but the Bantusai continued to drag him back. He gave in and followed Kely through the doorway.

Together they closed and barred the hatch.

In the courtyard Forge and a few others withdrew back to the tower. They reached the wagons, where above them men already stood. One by one they slipped into the gap between the tower and the barricade. Forge got through and mounted the fighting step. It was then that he saw Sergeant Mac and three others were still engaged at the gateway. They were slowly getting pushed back and were being overlapped as the Harradan spread out and were joined by others. Forge watched helplessly as Sergeant Mac shouted at them to withdraw. But it was too late. Already the Harradan were behind them and their escape route was blocked. One by one he watched his men fall until only Sergeant Mac and one other remained. His senses screamed at him to charge out and help his friend but he couldn't. He had to stay and take charge, just like the First Sergeant would do in his place. Sergeant Mac's companion was felled, in response he turned and thrust his sword into the man's killer. As he did so he was swept to the ground by the rush of Harradan. Forge could not see Sergeant Mac but witnessed the rise and fall of half a dozen blades as they hacked down.

'No!' Forge howled in despair.

The rush of Harradan reached the wagon barricade. The Ashkent soldiers stabbed down at the northerners as they tried to get round. The Harradan could not get through the gap as the first two who tried fell to the defending swords. They then took to trying to pull the wagons down, whilst others with spears tried to pierce the defenders if they strayed too far over the top of their barricade. There was almost no shouting as men stabbed and hacked. The sound

222

of steel on steel and the battering of wood was all that could be heard. The men were too intent and too weary, all their energy went into surviving. Try as they might the Harradan could not get enough hands on the wagons to pull them over without getting stabbed for their trouble. Forge lost himself for a time. All he could think of was his friend. Laying out in the courtyard. Hacked to pieces. And so, in turn, he hacked and battered and bloodied any that came near his place on the barricade. He didn't care what was happening around him. He didn't care that he was supposed to be giving orders. He just sweated and heaved and continued to stab and slice. He did not immediately notice the sound of the horn or that the Harridan were withdrawing. He slowly registered the withdrawal only when his sword kept stabbing at thin air. He then looked up and wiped the sweat from his eyes. The Harradan pulled back to the gateway and then went through it. He watched them go. He then realised that he was breathing hard. He felt the damp, sweaty clothes and armour he wore. He also felt how damn tired he was. Looking about him he saw that the barricade had held. On the ground before it were a pile of bodies. Some still moved and others were crawling, trying to drag themselves back out of the fort. He tried to pick out the spot where Sergeant Mac had fallen but in the midst of the carnage, he could not distinguish between the Ashkent uniforms and the Harradan tartan. He then, finally, looked to his men. He counted five still standing: two down below by the gap and three with him up on the step. A further three were dead on the floor. Five, tired, sweating men who were breathing hard and gazing out at the battlefield just as he had done. He touched the nearest soldier who turned sharply, a wild look in his eyes.

'Sir?'

223

'All right, lad. Take it easy. Let me know when they come back.'

'Yes, Sir.' The soldier nodded, took a deep breath and turned his gaze back to the gates.

Forge stepped down. Passing the two who had defended the gap he noted that one was now propped up against the wall of the tower. The other crouched by him holding a water bottle. The first man was clutching his stomach, blood seeping between his fingers; a slow, fatal wound. The man would not survive. The soldier looked up at Forge. His eyes said it all: a grim resignation. The man knew. Forge knelt, clasped the hand of the soldier and locked gazes. The soldier tilted his head slightly in acknowledgement. Forge gave his hand a tight squeeze, reached out and gripped the man's shoulder. He then stood and walked into the tower. Inside he found two more wounded soldiers. One was still standing, a rag tied to his arm. The other lay in a corner, a bandage wrapped round his head. He nodded to both of them and walked stiffly up the stairs, his leg still paining him. On the next level he found Kely sitting with three Bantusai and Private Smitty. He indicated for Kely to follow him. He stood and the two climbed to the top of the tower. There he found Corporal Jonas, the trappers and two more of his men. The soldiers were busy working loose some of the stones of the parapet.

'Just getting some more ammo, Sir,' said Corporal Jonas.

'Looks like you are the only non-com left, Jonas.'

'Looks that way,' the Corporal replied.

Forge gazed absently at the scene around him. The sun was warm, and smoke still drifted up from parts of the fire trench. He could see birds flying in the distance.

He looked down at the river and followed it down to

where the bridge had been. The skeleton of it still stood there; much of the rampway that Lode and Jonas had worked on had not collapsed into the river. But enough had gone to make it impossible to get across in its present state. The Harradan had obviously not bothered to repair it during the night.

'Got any arrows left?'

'One.'

'One?'

'My lucky arrow.'

'Why's it lucky?'

'Don't know. I've never fired it. And I'm not dead yet.'

'OK.'

He looked over at the trappers. It had only just occurred to him that there were only three of them now.

'I see you're still here, old-timer,' he said.

Old Hoarty grunted and grinned his one-toothed smile. 'Life in the old dog yet.'

Forge smiled back and turned his gaze back towards the southern end of the clearing. Lode stood up and joined Forge.

'What now?' the younger man asked.

Forge looked at the fur trapper who had given up on a chance of life to stay and fight, then at Corporal Jonas and at Kely, who stood a little way behind them. The de facto leadership of what was left of his little coalition.

He gestured for them to follow his gaze. Forming up were the Harradan. A whole line of them stood just on the far side of the fire trench. He could see a few figures down by the encampment of the night before but the main force was gathered before the fort.

'How many do you reckon we killed then?' asked Forge.

'Many,' remarked Kely.

225

'Three, four hundred maybe?' said Corporal Jonas.

'Not bad,' said Lode.

'Yeah, not bad,' agreed Forge. 'A thousand more would have been nice.'

'Wouldn't have hurt,' said Lode. 'Saw something interesting though. Just before they pulled back I saw a whole bunch of 'em break off and head south.'

Forge raised an eyebrow. 'Reckon we actually caused a split in their command structure.'

'Well, we ain't seen 'em come back yet, Captain,' said Lode.

Corporal Jonas squinted and looked to the south. 'Reckon he could be right. That mass of men looks a lot smaller than it was.'

'So, maybe we might have halved their numbers,' Forge mused.

'Which means they ain't strong enough to march south, boss.'

'Looks that way,' Forge agreed. He turned and smiled at Lode. 'Looks like you were right, lad. I think we just stopped the invasion.'

'Nice work, Holis,' said Old Hoarty. 'Now what?'

'Well, I would have suggested we pull out and go hide somewhere till they go away. But ...' Forge gestured to the scene in front of him. '... I think it might be a bit too late for that.'

'Least we fucked 'em up.' said Lode.

Forge grunted. 'Oh we did that. Corporal Jonas?'

'Boss?'

'Go and let the boys know. Tell them we did what we had to do. We stopped 'em. Cold comfort but at least it'll have been worthwhile.' Forge wondered if he actually believed that.

226

Vorgat was furious. During the last assault an entire clan had broken off and headed south. Three hundred men! No doubt they planned to swim the river and head back north. Damn their bastard, cowardly hides. He had called off the attack to try and restore order, lest the other two remaining clans joined the flight. If they hadn't cut and run he would have taken that damn tower. It was ready to fall. The implication was not lost on him. If those fleeing got back to their own lands before him, they would spread the word about Vorgat's actions. The remaining clans would not trust him or his intentions. On his return he would no doubt find his own people put to the sword and their lands razed to the ground. Not to mention a force of men ready to challenge him. He had no time. It must end now. All deception was over. He immediately confronted the two other clan chiefs. His own men still outnumbered theirs combined and they quickly swore fealty to save their own skins. It was clear he was in no mood for politics. The Shifter officer now approached him. The man wore a sad, resigned smile.

'Vorgat Stoneson. Our game is done. No doubt you plan to kill me and my remaining men?' asked Lordswood.

'No doubt.'

'Well, I cannot stop that. But if we are all to die, perhaps you might permit us to do so in action?'

Vorgat was surprised. Was this fool finally showing some backbone?

'I have a score to settle with the southerners. I would see it through to the end. Whatever you decide to do after that ...' The officer shrugged and sighed deeply. '... Is up to you. It makes no difference to me.'

'Very well then, go and prepare your men for the attack.'

The officer inclined his head in thanks and departed. Vorgat unsheathed his sword. He would take the head of the enemy leader himself.

Forge watched as down below a group of men ran forward of the main force. As they entered the courtyard they became recognizable as the last of the Shifter archers, about a dozen in total. They spilt and climbed on to the walkways.

'Sir!' shouted the soldier from below.

'Get back inside,' Forge shouted down. 'And close the door after you.'

He watched as the men quickly withdrew into the tower. The soldier with the stomach wound did not go with them.

'No point in trying to hold that now. As soon as they put their heads up they'd get shot.'

'Want me to use my lucky arrow?' asked Corporal Jonas.

'Might as well.'

'I guess your relief isn't coming then,' said Lode. It wasn't a question.

'Guess not.'

Once the archers were in place the Harradan moved forward. A large body of them moved into the courtyard and ran at the barricade. The first man to reach it was struck down by Corporal Jonas's lucky arrow. The watchers on the tower then ducked as the archers fired a few speculative shots at them. They didn't really need to see what was going on anyway. They could hear the wagons being pushed over and dragged away. A quick look by Forge confirmed that they were dismantling the battering ram. The slope on which the tower was built meant that the ram wouldn't reach it on the wagon.

'Right, gents,' he announced. 'I'm downstairs if you need me.'

He stood up, oblivious to any missile fire and walked down the steps. Kely followed after him. On the second level Forge stopped and spoke to the men gathered there.

'I expect they will try and force through these doors eventually. Hold them as long as you can then get upstairs to the top.' He looked at Private Smitty then at Kely. 'Good luck.'

He then continued down to the bottom floor and stood in front of his men. He looked at the walking wounded soldier and gestured at his sitting companion. 'You get him up to the top floor. Fresh air will do you good.'

The standing soldier bent down and helped the other up. The pair then struggled up the stairs. Forge watched them go, then turned to the four remaining men. 'As for the rest of you. They're going to try and break through the doorway. That'll slow the bastards down and give us the advantage. We'll keep 'em from getting in just like at the barricade, OK?'

His men nodded grimly and readied their weapons, whilst outside they heard voices and movement. A few moments later, they could hear the sound of many feet coming towards them. From up above they heard a warning shout. Not that it mattered, as a moment later the door shuddered from the impact of several hundred pounds of wood hitting it at speed. Again and again the ram hit the doorway, the angle making the barrier harder to breach. On the fifth attempt it finally gave way. The log was pulled back and the Harradan tried to force their way through. Forge and his men went to meet them.

The first few to approach the entrance were quickly dispatched, thanks to the tight space and blades of the

Ashkent soldiers. As the press of men grew, Forge and his men started to give ground. Spears were thrust through the doorway and were deflected by shields and blades. It was a frantic dance and the sound of metal and wood merged with the grunts and cursing of men as both sides sought a way through the confused mess. One of the troops reeled away screaming with a spear point thrust into his belly. A Harradan, beard matted with blood, charged inside batting away the swords of the Ashkent men and threw himself barehanded at Forge. The two of them fell to the floor with Forge's own blade thrust up into the groin of the squealing northman. He quickly rolled away and got to his feet. Another Harradan ran at him with a hand axe. Forge stepped in close under the swing and rammed his sword home. He followed it up with a swift headbutt before pulling his sword free.

He heard the sound of stones being hurled from above and Jonas shouting for people to duck. No doubt to avoid the archers ranged along the wall. Forge was breathing hard but he had some respite to survey the scene. The attack was faltering. Where once the door hatch had blocked the entrance, now the bodies of the dead Harradan provided a new choke point. It was becoming too difficult and dangerous to mount an effective charge. His three remaining men were ragged and bloodied too and were using the lull chance to rest against the walls. Forge was thankful that they hadn't just grabbed a small mantlet as protection and used their numbers to force their way in. It's what he would have done. As Forge and the others looked on, the bodies were hauled back out of the entrance by their comrades. Outside there were more voices and movement. Forge stole a quick look but saw only a crowd of Harradan gathered waiting for something. He quickly pulled back as an arrow shot past his head.

'Shit! Right, find something to block this doorway with. Quickly, whilst we've got a chance,' he ordered. His men ran to manoeuvre an empty barrel into the entrance.

Lode poked his head down the hatchway.

'They're going to try and smoke us out!' he shouted.

At that, a large bundle of brush was thrown into the tower before his men had put the barrel in place. The brush bundle had been lit deep within its centre and was starting to smoke heavily. It was followed by another, then a third. One of the soldiers tried to intercept this one and push it back outside. He was rewarded by an arrow in his leg.

'Pull him back,' Forge ordered angrily. The other two pulled the wounded man away. As the smoke began to build up in the chamber his eyes began to sting. 'All of you. Back up the stairs.'

His men retreated up to the next level. They were greeted by the start of the assault on the two entrances.

'They're coming through up here,' Lode shouted down to Forge.

'Then fucking kill 'em,' he shouted back.

A crash and further shouting told him they had broken through. The lower room was now dark and filled with the choking smoke. Forge's vision was now severely hampered and tears were flowing. He retreated to the stairs, gripping his sword in both hands. He saw shapes moving through the doorway. He risked a glance upwards but could see nothing as the smoke had already spread up the stairs. He then turned back towards the Harradan who were advancing through the murk. A wave of hopelessness and defeat spread through him. There was nothing more he could do. All the men who followed him, his friends, were dead or dying. In that moment of his despair a rage burst forth. A blind anger at all that had led him and his company to this point. He cursed the Duke and cursed himself even more so. Because he could have cut and run, could have pulled back, but instead he had condemned them all.

With a howl of anger he launched himself at the Harradan. He charged at the first figure, using his sword as a lance thrusting it clean through the torso. He tried to pull it back but it held fast in the body. He released it and the man sunk to his knees. Forge picked up a discarded short sword and parried a blade coming at his head from above; he then brought the sword round and hacked at the legs of his attacker, who fell back out of range. Forge pushed himself up and swotted away a sword aimed at his midriff. If they hit him he didn't feel it. He slashed and hacked and stabbed at the figures he could barely see. If he killed them he didn't care; there were always more coming through the entrance, forms made dark by the smoke or his own rage. He never heard the horns sound. He never noticed that after a time the figures stopped coming, that the fires had burnt themselves out. He certainly didn't notice one final figure come through the doorway, a hulking brute of a man with murder on his mind and a sword swinging to strike him. Nor did he witness a smaller man come down the stairs and launch himself at the other, burying a knife deep into the Harradan's back.

Chapter Fifteen

The 3rd Company of the 7th Mounted Infantry took the Harradan encampment by surprise. The few who had not joined in the final assault, mostly the sick and the lame, barely had time to register the shock of a hundred horsemen emerging from the trees coming at them full tilt. Those that couldn't get out of the way were cut down as the 3rd Company thundered through the position and headed towards the fort. Whilst not a cavalry unit, the Ashkent force had decided that the sound of their mounts and the shock of their appearance would easily make up for their restricted skill at arms whilst riding at speed. It did the trick. Faced with this new threat from the rear, Harradan warriors quickly formed a new battle line along the edge of the fire trench. Half their numbers were inside the fort perimeter and had yet to realise the threat. Even though they still outnumbered the relief force by at least five to one, they were tired and dispirited and, like their leaders, had rapidly come to the conclusion that the whole venture had been a pointless waste of time. They had little experience facing a large and disciplined cavalry force and did not possess sufficient numbers of spears or pole arms to defend themselves with. As the screaming cavalry galloped towards them, many broke and ran for the river. But, of course, there was no longer any means of crossing. Many panicked and threw themselves into the water. A number of warriors drowned in the crush or were swept away by the current. Others made a break for the fort or the woods. Most didn't get very far. The Ashkent charge swept through them, cutting them down as their backs were turned.

There were still a large number of Harradan troops in the fort and their leaders gathered them together to make a defence at the shattered gates. Whilst part of the cavalry force continued the pursuit of the fleeing northmen, the majority swiftly dismounted, formed their battle line and closed with the Harradan. To their rear, the attack on the tower had stalled. Bursting from the rampart doorways, the surviving defenders closed with the Harradan so that the attackers now found themselves assaulted from two fronts. A short and bloody fight ensued as the Ashkent relief troops maintained a tight formation that steadily carved its way through the press of warriors. Once the 3rd Company had pushed to just within the gateway, the Harradan defence finally broke and, realising the killing ground they now found themselves in, those that remained scrambled up on to the ramparts and launched themselves over the walls. Within the courtyard not one northman was left standing. A few reached the safety of the northern woods but they had a long and hard road to get home. The only other survivors where a half-dozen soldiers from Shifter. Once it was clear the battle was lost, Lordswood bid his men lower their weapons. Then they waited on the parapet to be captured.

Major Dav Jenkins found his friend sitting on the steps leading out from the tower. He sheathed his sword, dismounted and removed his helmet. His face was streaked with sweat and grime and he felt knackered. He had forgotten what it was like to be in battle, which

234

surprised him as he had spent a large part of his adult life doing it. Funny how a staff job had become so comfortable. He'd also forgotten how many bloody aches and strains came from riding a horse at full pelt over dozens of miles. On their ride up, they had encountered a fleeing force of Harradan that had obviously cut and run from the fighting earlier. They were busily trying to organise a river crossing. Now that the battle had been won here, he had sent half his troops to help them on their way. He eased himself next to Forge and promptly poured half his water bottle over his head with a contented sigh. Forge watched him perform all of these actions and smiled.

'How you doing, old-timer?' he asked.

Dav Jenkins looked him up and down. 'Feel like shit, but I still look a damned sight better than you.'

Forge laughed. 'Didn't think you were coming.'

'Honestly. No faith in your old pal.'

The day after Forge had met with him at headquarters, Dav had recalled the 3rd Company back to the regiment. They had been on border duty further south and had seen little action for some time. He deemed that things were pretty quiet and their loss could be spared from that sector by speeding the arrival of a newly created Graves Defence Force unit. He knew that Forge would never have come to him if things had not been desperate. In itself this was unusual for Forge. Perhaps if he hadn't come in person Dav might not have done anything about it. But a personal plea from his old friend was something he just could not ignore. He had also decided that he would travel with the replacement troops himself, thinking how it would be good to get away from the admin bullshit that came with his job. Some nice little excursion it turned out to be!

'To be honest, I didn't think you'd make it. Hells, I only sent Corporal Kyle a few days ago,' said Forge.

'No way we would have done,' responded the Major.

He smiled at Forge's questioning look and told him of the events concerning their arrival.

'It seems that Duke Burns wasn't expecting our paying a visit to him. When he heard we were coming he jumped ship. He and his personal guard buggered off east towards Shifter. When we rode into his camp we found it virtually empty. Just a few of the local soldiers left sitting around with their thumbs up their arses.'

'No change there then,' remarked Forge.

'Apparently not. What we got from them wasn't too pleasing either. Seems that the Duke had sent a lot of his men back to their homes. It looked to me that he had been planning something and a bunch of Ashkent infantry riding into view didn't seem to fit into it. Found out from the local lads about where you had gone off to. I put a few things together and that got me even more worried. So instead of heading after Burns I decided to head north.'

'Good decision.'

'Especially when who comes riding along on a half-dead horse but Corporal Kyle. So now that I had the full picture I sent word back to regiment and we hightailed it up here as fast as we could. We met a woman not so far from here, seems she was a Harradan who decided to switch sides. Told us what the state of things was, said that their rear was wide open. So a nice flanking manoeuvre presented itself. Looks like you and your boys just messed up something that could have really caused the shit to stink.'

'Yeah,' said Forge. Dav could hear the weariness behind that simple word. The slump in Forge's shoulders said it all.

'I'm sorry about Sergeant Mac, Jon. He was a good man.'

'Yeah. They all were.'

Forge pushed himself to his feet. The anger had worn off and now his body just ached terribly. Especially his damn knee. He felt old.

'Lost our horses.'

'Yes, we know. Found some of them back on the trail. We are bringing them back. Got yours.'

'Good. Don't fancy walking home.'

The Major nodded behind him. 'Spoke to a Shifter captain who was attached to the Harradan. Says the big warchief was fixing to cut you up personally. Charged into the tower just before we had them under control. We found him with his own sword embedded in his skull. Nice touch.'

At that Forge turned and looked up at the tower.

'Can't remember that … Burial detail?'

'Already at it. Thought we'd use that fire trench of yours.'

'Right.'

With that he turned his back on the tower and in pain walked across the courtyard and out into the open to help bury his dead.

Two hours later they were ready to ride.

The troops were already riding out on the trail at the southern edge of the clearing. The enemy Harradan had been left where they lay. Even now a flock of scavenger birds were making a very decent meal out of the pickings. A line of swords were thrust into the ground along the line of the refilled fire trench. Each sword represented a fallen Ashkent soldier. There was no other way of distinguishing

237

each grave. Every fallen man was as precious as the next. It was a tradition of the mounted infantry. Private Smitty was at the back of the line. He turned his horse and tipped a salute to the dead. 'See you later, brother,' he said softly. He lent down and gently slapped the side of his mare's neck and rejoined the troop. The fort, looking almost like it had when Forge had first looked upon it, stood silent and empty. The bridge site would soon get overgrown and worn down by the river. The remains of the battle would mix and become part of that older, long-gone settlement that once existed here. Forge doubted that anyone else would come here. When they did, all they would find was a place of death. A place where long ago a battle had been fought. And they probably wouldn't even know why.

On the side of the trail stood Lode, Old Hoarty, Juggs and, beside Lode, the woman Lissa. Each had been given two horses.

'Sorry you didn't get a reward or nothing,' said Forge.

'That's all right. We got what we came here for,' replied Lode.

'Vengeance?'

'Yeah, something like that. But somehow it doesn't make me feel any better.'

'Killing never does.'

'You know, up until a week ago I had never raised my hand to another man in my life.'

'Really?' Forge was surprised at that.

'Only ever hunted animals. Guess I started thinking of the Harradan as animals; they weren't my people anymore. Made it easier every time I shot one. Just as if I was shooting a buck or some such,' shrugged Lode.

'What they did to our town, they deserved no better,' said Juggs.

238

'That's right, lad,' said Old Hoarty softly and not unkindly. 'We never asked for trouble. They brought it.'

Lode shrugged. 'We killed a lot, didn't we?'

Forge nodded.

'We got all of them.'

'Doesn't seem real now. Except, of course, whenever I think of my friends back there.' He nodded at the line of graves. Sleeps and Fuzz, who had died with an arrow in his throat, were buried there. Arald was somewhere back on the eastern side of the Rooke. 'Good of you to bury them with your guys.'

Forge said nothing. The Bantusai had also been buried with the Ashkent troops. Each with a spear planted in the soil where he lay. The four surviving men would go with the Ashkent forces and be given safe passage home aboard the troop ships. Portal had also been given a place; it felt only right. The man had given his life for him and the company. If for nothing else in his life, the almost-wizard had earned a decent burial for that.

'Well, take care,' he said to them and clasped Lode's hand. The younger man seemed to have aged. He'd always had a fire in his eyes but now he'd got ice too, the Captain thought to himself. No one kills without it leaving a mark. Not if they had any humanity in them at any rate. He nodded to the others and tipped a half-salute to Lissa and said, 'Always nice to see something good come out of this.' Then he mounted his horse.

'Hey, Hoarty. Send us a new pelt when you bag a good one,' he called as he rode down the trail.

'All wrapped up in a nice bow for yer!' laughed Old Hoarty

Forge raised his hand in goodbye and then trotted down the path after the rest of the troops.

239

Lode turned and looked at his companions.

'Well, Holis. Ain't much of the season left is there?' said Juggs.

'What we doing, youngster? Got a plan?' said Old Hoarty.

Funny how even now, after it was over, Lode still found himself being treated like the leader. What did they do now? He couldn't help but feel that it still wasn't over. It didn't seem like it was. He shrugged and looked at Lissa. She reached over and grasped his hand.

'Don't know,' he said.

It took the Ashkent riders five days to get back to Regiment headquarters. On the way they passed through the old camp near Duke Burns' lands. It was empty now. Anything that had been worth stealing had already been taken. Only bare patches of earth, trampled grass and fire-burnt cooking pits showed where the troops had stayed. There was still the circular ditch and bund of the original Ashkent encampment. They did find two Ashkent riders who had come up from the south. They brought word that McKracken had alerted all the allied troops on the front and had mobilised a strike force to counter the Harradan if it was required. However, further news suggested that this was no longer necessary. It seemed that, with the flight of Burns, Shifter had finally sued for peace. It had stood down all of its border forces and returned them to their barracks. Having seen the Ashkent troops preparing to receive their assault, the Shifter generals had figured their final throw of the dice had probably failed. Good news for the Shifter prisoners, who would now be sent home on arrival at the camp. Effectively the war was over. As long as Shifter behaved, the Ashkent Expeditionary Force could look to going home.

It was cold comfort to Forge. Thinking over the turn of events, he could see that the trigger for the end had been the simple arrival of Jenkins and his troops at Burns' camp. The Duke had cut and run and in so doing had caused a chain reaction. In fact, working it through, Forge and his men need never have held that damned fucking bridge and fort. They could have pulled back, joined up with the rest of the regiment and then kicked the Harradan's arses in one fell swoop. He would have laughed at the stupid pointlessness of the whole thing if he hadn't been so damned tired.

His first night back at Regiment Forge couldn't sleep. Earlier he had gone to the HQ and reported to the boss. He found General McKracken himself waiting for him. There were congratulations and sympathetic noises. Everyone knew the score and most knew Forge well enough to know that he really didn't care. He had left and gone to look after his men. He had started the war with over a hundred men and had received a number more in replacements. He now had ten. He had his two scouts, Jonas and Kyle (who had led the 3rd Company to them), and eight other private soldiers. Five of them were wounded and of those, three would not be seeing active service any time soon. The company would survive, but it had taken a grievous wound. In losing so many of its old hands, such as Sergeants Pike, Grippa and, of course, Mac, it had lost its soul. And for each one of them he would bear the mental scars for the rest of his life.

As he walked back through the regimental camp to where his men were bivouacked, he stopped off at the storehouse and livery stables and made a few arrangements. He then continued on. He found the four surviving

Bantusai clustered round a fire. Sitting with them were Private Smitty and some of the other soldiers. He stopped and stood by the fire. Kely stood up to join him.

'I've made some arrangements for you lot. The Commanding Officer is feeling pretty well disposed to me at the moment and has granted you a wagon, supplies and an escort to the port. From there you can catch one of our supply ships back across the Gulf. Here is a letter written by McKracken.' He handed Kely a rolled parchment that had a wax seal bearing the symbol of a bird of prey. 'Give this to the Warden of the Port. This letter grants you privileges, safe passage and the financial means to get you home. With the warm thanks of the Expeditionary Army of Ashkent.'

Kely gave Forge one of his big bright smiles.

'Thank you, Captain. You are a good man.'

'I am sorry I couldn't get you all home.'

'So are we.' Kely's voice became sombre and reflective. 'But our Kai believed you and followed you. We follow our Kai. He would not have stayed if he did not trust you. That shows you are a man of honour.'

'A dubious one at best,' he smiled, 'but I take your point. And Juma was a good man also.'

'He died a good death,' said Kely proudly.

'If there is such a thing,' replied Forge.

He then shook each of the Bantusai's hands and took his leave.

He had lain on his cot for an hour, staring into the shadows above him. He felt empty inside. But that wasn't strictly true. What he really felt was that there was unfinished business. He couldn't leave it like this. All that death. Just because of one man. Forge had always been practical. His thinking firmly rooted in the harsh, hard

242

realities of life. He had come to terms with losing people early in his career. But that was in war, in battles that had to be won. He guessed in this respect he had been lucky. It was a luxury to have led such an uncomplicated life, not having to deal with the uncomfortable concept that the deaths of his men were not worth the result. He snorted. Shit, who am I kidding? he thought. We all knew what we were doing when we signed up. He had just got used to always being on the winning side and taking orders from halfway competent generals. What grated was that he had been tricked. Used by a man who wasn't even from Ashkent. That bastard should never have been allowed to fuck with his boys. From the day they were sent north, the company's fate was sealed. However, it was not McKracken's fault; it wasn't *his* fault either. He would have held that fort anyway, even if the Duke hadn't been part of the treachery. He would have held it because it was the right thing to do. It was for the soldiers of Ashkent that he did it. But not so that an overweight, slimy little shitbag could make a play for power over the bodies of his dead men. He rolled off his bed, strapped his sword belt back on and stalked off into the night. After five days on horseback his leg felt a lot better.

Dav Jenkins looked up from his cot as Forge pushed through the tent flap and sat himself down on a chest near the entrance. A single candle burned by a bedside table next him. He hadn't been sleeping much either. He could only vaguely make out Forge sitting in the soft light. Shadows played across the features of his friend. His face was set like stone. A grim visage.

'Wondered when you would drop by, Jon.'

'It isn't over.'

'I know,' said Jenkins. 'Burns.'

'Where is he?'

Dav sighed. He had been expecting this.

'I could order you not to go.'

Forge stared hard at his friend. Dav threw his hands up.

'All right. Last reports were that he and about fifty men crossed the border into Shifter, spent a week there waiting to see what happened. He wasn't stopped. Apparently he has some friends over there who have offered him protection. Even though he fucked things royally, seems that Shifter thinks he might still be useful. And he has some financial interests going on. I had one of the Force magic men do some scrying for me. He's heading cross-country. Leisurely pace. About three days east of here. Following the old trail to the City Port of Salm on the River Corn. Hang on ...' He reached under his cot and pulled out a roll of parchment. He threw it over to Forge, who caught it in his right hand. 'Got this map. Marked his position. Thought it might come in handy.'

Forge couldn't help but feel touched. It was nice to know he hadn't lost all his friends.

'Thanks. I'll see you in a week or so.'

'Whatever.'

'Don't pull out without me.'

'Unlikely.'

Forge stood to go but Dav stopped him.

'Oh, one more thing. Shifter still have a few border patrols. Try to avoid them. A dead Burns is one thing. You leading a one-man invasion of Shifter is another,' warned Jenkins.

'I'll try and remember that,' said Forge.

Dav nodded impatiently and ushered him out. He then lay back down on his cot and blew out the candle.

Chapter Sixteen

Noon the following day, Captain Jon Forge crossed over into Shifter. He had raided the commissary in the pre-dawn hours and had taken a few days' provisions. He had been of a mind to take a pack mule but figured that speed was more important. Besides, he didn't really think he'd be coming back. As he had ridden through the border zone he had gone past some Ashkent pickets. They had raised their hands in greeting and wished him happy hunting. Obviously Dav had spread the word.

For the next two days he travelled at a steady pace, heading slightly north and east. He had soon picked up on the old Salm trail and it was clear that it had been used by a body of horses recently. The tracks and spoor were but days old. He began to parallel the trail, sticking to whatever cover might be present. The land before him began to turn rougher and steadily climbed. On all sides he could see hills and peaks in the distance. On two occasions he had passed Shifter patrols. One had been heading along the trail to the west and the other on the far side of the track on high ground following a ridgeline. Both times, he had been lucky; he had been shielded by the copses of trees that lay scattered along the path. The first group had been but yards away from his hiding position. He had studied them carefully. These were regular cavalry. Their mounts look reasonably well tended, if a little shabby. Their riders were grim-faced and alert for trouble. Likewise, they appeared to have been in the field for some time. Armour had lost its lustre, uniforms were muddied and their weapons were in various states of over- or under-use. Shifter had, no doubt, become very fearful of its own security after its disastrous involvement with Graves. Forge couldn't imagine they had many units left that hadn't been beaten up by his guys. No doubt this unit had learned the hard way. Who knows, give them a few years with the right experience, they might even make a decent fight of it.

At night, Forge would snatch a few hours sleep. He did not build a fire and ate his rations cold. When it was light enough to follow the trail again he would rouse himself and continue the pursuit. It was odd that, as the days passed, the rage he had felt within him had dissipated. What was left was a sense of resignation. He was going to extract some kind of justice, some settling of scores. But he was not blinded by rage. Hate gave him no extra strength or resources. He was just doing what he had to do. There was nothing else, only his personal sense of duty. He was a soldier and all that mattered was those who soldiered with you. They became your family. He had always believed in the soldier's code. That you did what you were told to do; never took it personally. Life and death were just part of the job. All you could do was look after your own and hope that your sword arm was stronger than the man you were fighting against. The battle they had fought around the redoubt had been different. The rules had changed. Burns had used him and his family. Burns had to pay. Any man in Forge's position would have done the same. Sergeant Mac would have. Well, he probably would have done it with a company of hard-nosed infantry at his back. He had always been the sensible one.

246

It was noon on the third day when he finally caught up with Burns' party. It was the spoor that gave it away first, still warm upon grass that was freshly imprinted from the hooves of many horses. There were also ruts from a number of wagons, no doubt Burns' worldly goods. Topping a rise he spotted them, a few miles away, skylined on the next substantial high ground. Although he didn't rate Graves troops much, added to the fact they were well into Shifter territory, they still might have outriders looking for pursuit. No point in advertising the fact that he was one man. Forge slowed his pace. There was no point in hurrying. He knew where they were, he just had to wait for nightfall and then he'd go in. As it was, Burns' group set camp a couple of hours later. Clearly, they were more relaxed than he had thought. As he had reached the top of yet another gentle, wooded slope, the trees quickly thinned and led downhill into a dale. A stream flowed westward from a modest range of hills and aspiring mountains. It continued its course in a gentle meander. Forge figured it might even join up with the Rooke. The Graves men were bustling about setting up camp some half a mile away by what appeared to be a ford. He quickly steered his horse from the path and walked back downhill and into the trees.

Dismounting, he tied the reins to a low-hanging branch and struck back up the slope. Making his way through the trees he moved to a covered spot just over the brow that afforded him a view of the dale. Looking at the land ahead of him, he saw that it sloped down towards the open area of the valley. He guessed that there was some four hundred yards of open ground to reach the river. More than a minute's gallop for a tired horse. On the other side the trail began a steep climb through woods that began only two hundred yards from the stream. Forge did some quick calculations. If he tried to approach from the north bank he would have more cover but would then have to cross the stream on foot. He could not expect to charge out of the trees on horseback and then get the beast across a body of water that he had no knowledge of. That would slow him down and would be a bad place to get caught in the open. Whilst he realised this was definitely a suicide mission, he did at least want a small chance of reaching Burns before he was cut down. Getting skewered with a dozen arrows whilst trying to gee up an old nag was no way for a soldier to go. His approach from either east or west would mean a longer distance moving in the open. He could, of course, just shadow them for a while; wait for an opportunity to present itself. But that meant going deeper into enemy territory and a greater risk of being discovered. No, he had had enough of this pursuit as it was. As his old blue-blood captain had once announced, 'When in doubt, straight up the middle with bags of smoke!' Well, he didn't have anyone to provide smoke. He would have to get as close as he could, then charge. Ah well, it'll shock 'em if nothing else, he mused. Turning round he made his way back to wait for nightfall.

He awoke with a start, shrouded in darkness. A gentle breeze stirred the canopy of branches overhead and he caught a glimpse of stars. He was surprised that he had fallen into such a deep slumber; he'd expected just to snooze. His last thoughts had been about his friend Sergeant Mac and the men who had died with him. He had not dreamt; he had slept too deeply. He had not realised how dog-tired he was. He turned his head to his right where his horse was dozing but still standing. Well, it would make saddling easier, he thought. He was not entirely sure of the time but it felt that night was well progressed. Good enough. Forge stood, breathed deep and began buckling his weapon belt. Once that was done, he saw to his mount. He fed it some oats from his near-empty feed bag and took time to smooth and calm the beast. Chances were she would be as dead as he would be soon. He then mounted and steered the mare up and over the hill. As he went down the other side he could see flames through the trees.

'Shit, too damn close,' he muttered his breath. He had expected pickets but some clever bastard had pushed an outer cordon to the edge of the trees. The firelight penetrated well into the foliage and scuppered any chance of him being able to creep up to within striking distance of them. Knowing his luck they probably had crossbows. Forge quickly rethought his plan. The guards would expect trouble to come in a large group, not one man. So instead of charging hell for leather he would have to get as close as possible, spin them a yarn, then literally cut and run. He shook his head, spat and headed back to the trail. He then began his casual ride towards the dale. As soon as he was on the top of the slope he stopped for a second, deliberately skylining himself before heading down. That way there was a good chance they would see him coming. He certainly saw them. Two figures, indistinct but clearly outlined by the firelight between them. At the far side of the dale he saw a similar watchfire. Within the camp there was one central fire, and a couple of smaller points of light, probably torches, posted to either side of a good-sized tent. Thank you for pointing yourself out, Burns, thought Forge.

He was halfway to the picket fire. The figures moved

forward and stood in front of the light. This puzzled Forge. By standing on the far side of the fire they had ruined their night vision and helped to screen him to any watchers from the camp. He'd be able to ride up to within a few feet of them before they got a sight of the dagger in his right hand. Too bad for them. Good for him. As he drew closer and the two guards were easier to discern, something started to nag at Forge. It was something about the way they stood; it seemed … familiar. They didn't hold themselves like soldiers; they seemed positively relaxed. Now he thought about it, he couldn't even see drawn weapons or sword belts. But he did see two cradled crossbows.

'Evenin', Captain. Didn't think you'd ever wake up,' said Old Hoarty cheerfully. Next too him Juggs gave a toothy grin and waved. Forge was speechless for a few moments whilst his mouth tried to form words.

'Oh, don't ask the obvious "But How, Where, When did you?" questions, Jon,' said Holis Lode's voice from behind him. 'Just rest assured you had five expert trackers on your trail. You weren't hard to follow.'

Forge turned and saw Lode at the edge of the trees, arms folded, smiling at him. Behind him stood Lissa sporting a rueful grin. Forge had never seen her smile so much. It suited her.

'Bloody left a path a blind and lame dog could've followed,' added Corporal Jonas, who was leaning against a tree next to Lode. Beside him was Corporal Kyle who had a bow resting against his knee.

'Right I'll get the boys.' Corporal Kyle stood and pushed back into the undergrowth.

'What are you bastards doing here?' was the best Forge could muster.

'C'mon, boss,' said Corporal Jonas. 'We ain't stupid, it

250

was obvious what you were going to do. Me and Kyle and the rest of the boys checked in with the Major. He reckoned you might need some company. So we headed off after you. And wouldn't you know, guess who should we run into?' Jonas inclined his head towards Lode who shrugged his shoulders.

'Old Hoarty and Juggs decided that we still had unfinished business with that bastard over there. So we thought we might seek our fortunes in Shifter,' he said. 'Lissa helped to make the guards a little more inattentive than usual, a bit sleepy if you get my meaning.'

'And those pups in the camp pushed these guys so far out it was no bother to get rid of 'em without anyone noticin',' added Old Hoarty.

'I should have bloody expected this,' said Forge, scratching his beard. 'Getting addled in my old age. You know we might not make it out of this. We might get caught by Shifter troops and start the whole bloody conflict up again.'

'Their mistake if they do,' said Corporal Jonas.

Through the treeline a group of horses were now gathering. As Forge watched, he could pick out the riders. Damn, it was all of them, all the survivors. All of his men, the last of the First. Kind of poetic that, he mused. The group included the Bantusai. Kely reined in before him and nodded.

'Didn't know you boys could ride,' said Forge.

'We cannot,' replied Kely. 'My arse hurts like a bastard. So ' He quickly dismounted and pulled his spear from the saddle. '... We will run.' His three companions followed suit and commenced a brisk jog toward the camp. I see his language skills have improved, probably Jonas's fault, thought Forge.

'Shit, that feller has got a head start. I bet him two crowns that he couldn't get there before me on horseback,' moaned Private Smitty from the back of the horsemen.

Old Hoarty punched Juggs in the shoulder. 'C'mon, I ain't gettin' me old bones shook to death in a cavalry charge. Let's wander over there and do some damage with these.' He patted his crossbow and winked at Forge. They both turned and followed after the Bantusai at a gentler pace.

'Best we get there before them, Captain,' said Holis.

'We're ready, Sir,' said Corporal Jonas, now mounted, his longbow held with an arrow notched.

Forge gazed over his men feeling overwhelmed. He felt pride and, more than that, he felt belonging. He realised that he had felt truly alone and that that was the cause of the emptiness he had gnawing at his stomach. For the first time since the death of his First Sergeant he smiled with pleasure.

'Right, let's get that bastard.'

He turned his horse, kicked the flanks and began a steady gallop. To either side of him, his men formed a line abreast. Halfway there they overtook the Bantusai. From the end of the line Private Smitty let out a whoop of joy. This caused a general bellow of shouts from the other riders. Forge lent his own voice to the howl, and he began to laugh. Ahead he saw figures running in all directions within the camp. Oh, aren't they in for a bad night, he thought.

The noise and uproar awoke Duke Burns. He emerged from his tent blinking and trying to focus. He stood open-mouthed as around him chaos reigned. Men were waking up and trying to arm themselves. Someone was shouting orders to form a battle line. A soldier broke ranks and ran for the stream, then two more followed. He watched in horror as a line of horsemen smashed into the camp and commenced the slaughter of his shocked men. He stared, rooted to the spot as a dirty, bearded warrior charged at him. It seemed to Burns that time took on a dreamlike quality. Everything seemed to slow down and he was able to discern the man's features as he drew closer. The face was grim, the eyes flashed in triumph. He wasn't sure but even in the darkness he swore he knew the man. Then recognition and horror swiftly followed. He even registered the flash of a blade as it swept towards his neck.

REDOUBT

Alexander S. Janaway

Book Guild Publishing
Sussex, England

First published in Great Britain in 2008 by
The Book Guild Ltd
Pavilion View
19 New Road
Brighton, BN1 1UF

Typesetting in Meridien by
Nat-Type, Cheshire

Printed in Great Britain by
CPI Antony Rowe

A catalogue record for this book is available from
The British Library.

ISBN 978 1 84624 282 3